The Man On the Bridge

The Man On the Bridge

Stephen Benatar

FOREWORD BY GILLIAN CAREY

CAPUCHIN CLASSICS
LONDON

The Man On the Bridge

This edition published by Capuchin Classics 2012

2 4 6 8 0 9 7 5 3 1

Capuchin Classics
128 Kensington Church Street, London W8 4BH
Telephone: +44 (0)20 7221 7166
Fax: +44 (0)20 7792 9288
E-mail: info@capuchin-classics.co.uk
www.capuchin-classics.co.uk

Châtelaine of Capuchin Classics : Emma Howard

ISBN: 978-1-907429-35-4

Printed and bound by CPI Group (UK) Ltd, Croydon CR0 4YY.

For Eileen, Adam, Prue, Piers and Thea –
but mainly for Eileen.

Also in memory of my surrogate mum,
Daphne Odin-Pearce.

Contents

Foreword

'I hear you want to be a writer,' remarks Marnie, an established woman novelist to the nineteen-year-old narrator of *The Man on the Bridge*. 'What sort of thing do you hope to write?'

'At the moment I am working on a love story.'

'Between men?'

I was surprised. It hadn't occurred to me that there could be homosexual love stories.

This exchange tells us a good deal about the narrator and the period of the story he tells. Even in 1981, when *The Man on the Bridge* was first published, the *Guardian* referred to its material as 'tricky', and that was twenty-three years after the events in the novel. So, although he is in a homosexual relationship, the fact that adolescent, provincial John Wilmot should be surprised that there could be homosexual love stories, is not entirely surprising. Though there was pressure for reform following the publication of the Wolfenden Report in 1957, homosexual acts were still punishable by imprisonment. Decriminalisation did not come until 1967, two years after the abolition of the death penalty for murder. The two issues are implicitly linked early in the novel by the precise fixing of the date of the action to 1958, six years after the execution of the nineteen year old Derek Bentley - 'nearly a mental defective'- for a killing done by a friend of his. For the narrator, John Wilmot, the Bentley case was a vague memory – he was at school at the time. For Oliver Cambourne, a successful, fashionable, thirty-nine year old painter, it was an appalling injustice, to be laid beside the oppression of homosexuals as examples of the inhumanity of the institutions of state. They are the subjects of the two paintings by Oliver most fully described to us. A third is of his country house, the focus of his private life.

The background of the late fifties is recalled by Stephen Benatar with vivid and discriminating accuracy, and by his narrator with the self-consciousness, would-be sophistication and self-absorption of 'callow adolescence'. Almost the same age as John Wilmot in 1958, Benatar remembers what it was like to be eighteen, particularly then. When John is first taken to a restaurant he calls it 'small and unpretentious. We had avocado, coq au vin, lemon meringue pie and Stilton.' It is a menu absolutely of its time. Second World War rationing had finally ended three years previously and the well-to-do were enjoying more exotic foods. But my guess would be that John is tasting avocado for the first time. When his widowed mother and his great aunt come to his tiny flat in Gloucester Place for lunch on his birthday he gives them 'a lot of their favourite things' which he doesn't specify and 'a quantity of smoked salmon' supplied by wealthy Oliver. His mother wants to contribute to the cost of this expensive meal otherwise 'You'll be living on bread-and-scrape till Christmas.' Who now uses or even knows that phrase – or that UD stands for United Dairies, their stores a local standby?

One year after Harold Macmillan's 'never had it so good' speech it was a time of increasing prosperity or at least the hope of it. A whole series of American musicals helped chase away the gloom of post war austerity and divert attention from the underlying fears of the cold war and the atomic bomb. While John is terrified of a possible nuclear future, Oliver is haunted by his experience of the horrors of the last war. As in later novels Benatar locates his characters in the music of the period and in their individual musical tastes. So it is that, starry-eyed after a performance of *My Fair Lady* at Drury Lane, John Wilmot first sees Oliver Cambourne: 'He stood out from the crowd because of his height and impressive appearance... he looked bored'. He still looks bored the next day when he appears in the bookshop where John works. Smitten with his 'air of patrician wealth' the teenager is only too happy to be mentored by this Pygmalion, entering his world of culture, sophistication and privilege. On his first visit to Merriot Park he meets Oliver's steely mother and his distant cousins, the exceedingly rich Sheldons, and their adopted daughter Elizabeth. On the first morning at the house he revels in the fact that a maid brings him tea in bed: 'I said to myself: This is me drinking Earl Grey (I think) in bed at Oliver Cambourne's home on the eighth of November 1958; today can never be repeated; I intend to savour every minute.' Then he springs out of bed as 'head-of-house heroes are always supposed to', sings in the shower and presents himself 'for the world's inspection, in the dining room, shortly after nine.' The brief paragraph exemplifies Benatar's insight into mood and character, his humour, his irony, his appreciation of staginess. We can sympathise with John, knowing he is being ironical about himself, but the passage also prepares us for his future egotism. Though the novel has a clear architectural structure it is character that propels the action.

Benatar charts the ebb and flow of human relationships with great skill; he shows their potential for tenderness and for cruelty, both deliberate and unwitting. He is alert to prevarications big and small. Many adolescents do not wish to be entirely open about their first love affairs so we understand when John tells us that 'naturally' he pulls down his sleeve to hide from his mother the Rolex watch Oliver has given him. The use of that word is an example of the sophistication of Benatar's writing. It occurs many times, mostly unobtrusively, but tellingly. It calls on the reader to make judgements about John's behaviour – sometimes socially polite, sometimes a 'performance', sometimes merely weak, sometimes downright duplicitous. Increasingly we mind about his evasions, his lies, as, more and more, he hurts the people who love him and whom, at bottom, he most cares about. There comes a point in the novel when one wants to shout 'How could he? How could he?' But we see how he could. Not that other characters are blameless. Extravagant patronage can be thoughtless too; generosity, even with good intentions, can be manipulative. When John tells us that Elizabeth smiled 'beguilingly' he is describing an effect on him that makes her seem almost pretty. With hindsight the reader may interpret it differently, seeing an intention to be beguiling. But the reader may be wrong, and is anyway likely to feel that, when he tells Oliver that 'she is easy to get away from', he is doing her an injustice and may not be telling the exact truth. Even his motives for this prevarication may be mixed. Is he ingratiating himself with Oliver? Or is he sensitive to Oliver's possible jealousy, even protective of him? Or is it an instinctive part of his nature to be emollient? Benatar constantly keeps the reader guessing. Triangular relationships and scenes help shape the novel and exemplify different kinds of love. This is partly a coming-of-age novel but it also casts a sympathetic and discerning eye on middle-aged fears and the deprivations of old age. One of the final acts of love in the story is Aunt Clara's self-sacrificing recognition of her frailty. Hers is the final, innocent, duplicity in the novel: 'Do you think you could manage a doughnut – without mentioning it to your mother?'

Part 1, almost exactly half of the novel, is mainly concerned with the developing relationship between John and Oliver, while Parts 2 and 3 deal with the repercussions of the relationship. The mood darkens as John, like Oliver, experiences depression, and is forced to re-examine his actions and attitudes. Religious and philosophica issues which have been touched on, often lightly, in earlier conversations re-emerge with greater urgency. In the context of guilt, remorse and disintegrating relationships

Benatar's eye for detail can be memorably moving. 'I picked up a fragment of brandy snap, transferred it to my mouth' seems like dust and ashes.

At the end of the novel the reader must decide how far John Wilmot, (namesake of the 17th century Earl of Rochester, poet, sceptic, satirist, and death-bed penitent) is redeemed. From the outset he has been a sharp-eyed observer. Much remains hesitant, provisional. What we can be sure of is that he has learnt enough self-knowledge, discipline and imaginative insight to write his second book – the one we have just read.

Gillian Carey

Part One

1

I had never heard of him until the previous evening. I'd been inching forward patiently with the rest of the audience leaving Drury Lane when a woman in front of me had said to her companion:

'Isn't that Oliver Cambourne over there? The tall one with the black hair and the good profile.'

The man was some distance to our left. Roughly level with us. He stood out in the crowd not merely because of his height and impressive appearance but because amidst all the chatter and exuberance he looked bored.

'I went to his exhibition last month,' the woman continued. 'I don't always care for his paintings but some of them are interesting.'

And now he stood here in the shop.

He still looked bored. Yet for fully a minute I couldn't stop watching him. He had glamour. This may partly have derived from what I'd overheard; but his elegance and his air of patrician wealth were also commanding. I straightened my tie and walked over.

'May I help you, sir?'

'I doubt it.'

At first it seemed he wasn't even going to look up. But when he did I was still at his side. His eyes showed a flicker of interest.

I said: 'Excuse me but you're Oliver Cambourne, aren't you? The artist.'

'I believe I am.'

'May I say how much I admired your exhibition?'

'Thank you. You may say it as often as you like. And to as many as you like.'

'Actually, it's a small world. I saw you at the theatre last night.'

'Is that so?' He gazed at me quizzically for a moment. 'Then what did you think of it – *My Fair Lady*?'

'Magical,' I said.

'Really? To me it seemed tedious.'

I was astonished: that anyone, however jaded, could possibly hold such an opinion. For a second I was tempted to qualify my praise yet instinct warned me not to. 'But, sir, didn't you think the costumes and the settings must have been amongst the best we've ever had?'

'And what if I did? Are costumes and settings, then, the things which matter most?'

'Or that the songs all grew so fluidly out of the action – without any strain or lapses of taste? And that little or nothing appeared to have been left out?'

There was a pause.

'God save us all!' said Oliver Cambourne.

But he looked amused.

I carried on in the show's defence for at least a couple of minutes. I should certainly have done so longer – he was doing nothing to discourage me – if Miss Partridge hadn't returned just then from an unusually late lunch. The White Queen, First Lady of the Shop, my self-appointed benefactress. 'Good afternoon, Mr Cambourne. I'm sorry I wasn't here when you arrived.'

'Good afternoon, Miss Partridge. I daresay I shall never quite forgive you. You know that I need you *continuously* at my disposal.'

'Such a sense of fun!' said Miss Partridge.

But the one or two creases she put around her mouth didn't exactly set him in the same category as Jacques Tati. (Or perhaps, with her, they did.) One hand mechanically touched her rigid bleached coiffure – as though there could ever have been a single filament daring to go walkabout – and she remarked with some of the asperity she generally reserved only for the other assistants:

'All right, Mr Wilmot. Thank you. I'll take care of Mr Cambourne now.'

Yet she misjudged. Mr Cambourne demurred.

'No, Miss Partridge. I fear I might be thought a Philistine if I allowed you to effect my escape. Mr Wilmot is trying to educate me in the history of the American musical.'

The White Queen smiled tightly again.

'Mr Wilmot is sometimes a little too ready to educate anybody in anything. He holds his own. very forthright opinions.'

'Oh, but in this case I find them invigorating. You and I, Miss Partridge, are not simply old friends, we're old fogies. And I consider it's pleasant, occasionally, to let the fresh winds of youth blow over us.'

He looked in his thirties – maybe his mid-to-late thirties – and at least fifteen years her junior, but this coupling of themselves was clearly not to her taste.

'As you wish,' she said. 'I'll leave you then to Mr Wilmot. However, should you require any advice that's possibly less invigorating – although *marginally* more experienced – please don't hesitate to call.'

She withdrew, with yet another smile suggestive of ulcers, then went to stand by the cash desk, near her particular crony Mrs Gee.

'Oh dear,' observed Oliver Cambourne, quietly. 'I'm afraid I didn't handle *that* too well.'

'I thought you were extremely tactful.'

'Did you now?' He glanced down at a book on the table in front of us. 'I don't believe I've seen you here before.'

'I only started some ten weeks ago – and to begin with I was up in the stockroom.'

'Are you planning to make a career of it?'

'No, not at all.'

'I find that reassuring.'

'In the evenings I'm writing a novel.'

'Are you indeed? Free of strain and lapses of taste – where little or nothing appears to have been left out?'

'I'd swear you've had a peek at it.'

'Yes... Well, now you'd better help me choose a few novels not quite so comprehensive nor, I feel sure, nearly so interesting.'

He explained they'd be small gifts to sundry strangers who in some way had been supportive; either to him or to his mother.

'And I'm convinced,' he said, 'you're going to be resourceful.'

I, too, was convinced of it. I suggested a score of titles – kept going to the shelves for older publications – trying to stick to the ones I knew but expressing equally pithy judgments about those I didn't (which was fraudulent but fulfilling; it was just as well he'd stipulated fiction), every so often admitting, for the sake of credibility, that I hadn't actually read one. Three or four times, without meaning to, I looked up to encounter Miss Partridge's unremitting glare and knew that the last fifteen minutes had cost me her patronage. I didn't care. The signals she kept emitting seemed every bit as noticeable as RKO's. Even in the space of a few seconds I saw two of the other assistants glance from her to me and back again. I saw the shop manager, on his way to the music department, look curiously in our direction.

I felt that all we lacked was the lad with the clapperboard.

In the end, Oliver Cambourne bought six copies of a recently published book entitled 'Daisy and Sybella'. I hadn't even mentioned it.

He wanted them to go on his account. It was a Chelsea Embankment address.

'Do you deliver?'

He must have known we didn't.

And the book was relatively short – even a *dozen* copies wouldn't have been that heavy.

'But I could drop them round if you like.' I had aimed to keep my voice fully as casual as his.

'Very well then. If you're sure. This evening?' We agreed on seven o'clock.

Then he nodded and walked briskly across to Miss Partridge. She didn't appear too welcoming. After that he left the shop. He stood on the kerb for about a minute before an empty cab drew up. When he had driven off I turned and sent Miss Partridge a tentative smile.

But she ignored it.

2

I arrived at the Embankment late, partly because I took too long in my bath and partly because ten minutes after leaving my flat I had to return to it – I'd forgotten to bring the books! This was annoying but it was also mildly amusing. 'Keep the fellow in suspense,' I declared, whilst waiting for the taxi I had now decided I would need to take. 'Operation Insouciance!'

The block where Cambourne lived was a modern one. Having identified myself over the intercom to a male voice which wasn't his, I walked across a vestibule thickly carpeted in aquamarine – passed a tank full of weird darting fish and willowy vegetation – stepped into the lift and pressed the button for the top floor.

A manservant in a black jacket and finely striped trousers awaited me. 'Good evening, sir.'

A person of slight build and medium height, perhaps fifty, perhaps thirty-five, he had a noticeably unlined face, a thin coating of slicked-down dark hair, with a parting (dead straight) at its middle, and the sort of fingernails that – when he held out his hands to take first the parcel, then my raincoat – nearly made me wince, to see how brutally their half-moons must have been tortured into place.

'Mr Cambourne is expecting you.' He handed back the books.

The flat was a fittingly luxurious part of the great luxurious whole. Yet surprisingly it made me think *ascetic.* Acres of clean uncluttered space, oatmeal carpeting, white walls: in the sitting room, the rich blue of floor-length velvet curtains and the dramatic use of colour in all of Cambourne's paintings. . . I assumed that they were his. A low fire burnt in the grate; warm pools of lamplight further prevented the room from seeming cold.

'Good evening, Mr Wilmot.' Oliver Cambourne rose from an armchair to the right of the fireplace. 'I trust you had no trouble getting here?'

'None at all. I came by cab.'

He held out his hand and I shook it. 'Thank you for bringing these.' He placed the books on the mantelpiece. 'Now. . .what will you have to drink?'

I chose sherry, despite noticing it was whisky in his own glass. I was well aware my palate required an education but didn't think this was the time to start giving it. Supposing I were to take some absentminded sip. . .and he were to witness my grimace of surprise?

'Sweet or dry or something in between?'

'Dry, please.' In fact I preferred it sweet.

'James. A dry sherry for Mr Wilmot.'

For some reason the servant made me uneasy. As he deftly set a small table next to my chair – on the opposite side of the fireplace to Cambourne's – then placed my drink on it, I felt doubly glad I hadn't yielded, in front of *him,* to what I realized would have been a solecism.

He addressed his master. 'Will that be everything, sir, for the time being?'

The man departed, closing the door with care. I immediately relaxed. I said: 'I love this room.'

'Thank you.'

'I imagine that by day it looks out across the river?'

'Yes, by night, as well. Especially when the curtains aren't drawn.'

I thought I could have expressed myself a little better but never mind. *Operation Insouciance*!

'You'd miss it if you went away.'

'What? The river? No, I'd probably take it with me.'

'Wouldn't that become expensive?'

'You mean – my having to bribe the Port Authorities?'

'That, too, but I was thinking more of your having to bribe Pickford's.'

Then I left my chair and went to look at his paintings – conveniently, they were signed. Like the woman at Drury Lane, I wasn't sure whether I liked them or not but there was one in particular which intrigued me. I asked about it.

'Oh, that? The scene on the rooftop? Well, the boy to your left,' he said, 'the one who's being held by the policeman as a shield against gunfire. . .that's Derek Bentley. Do you know of him?'

'Vaguely. Wasn't there a shooting? Some ten or twelve years back?'

'Six,' he said. 'It was 1952.'

'I was still at school in 1952.'

'He was a nineteen-year-old illiterate – nearly a mental defective – who was executed for a killing done by a friend of his. The friend was too young to be hanged and it was said that Bentley had encouraged him. There was a reprieve petition signed by thousands.'

Oliver Cambourne gave a laugh, whose bitterness surprised me.

'But for some reason it pleased the Lord to harden the heart of the Home Secretary.'

Cambourne came to stand beside me.

'That fog enveloping him,' he said, 'isn't meant to be a representation of the weather, but rather of his state of mind. . .'

We stayed gazing at the picture for maybe a further minute; and I thought about this essentially innocent young man being led towards the gallows.

'Did you know,' he said, 'that throughout this decade, here in Britain, we've been hanging somebody under twenty-five roughly every two months?'

I stared at him. 'No. Is that true?'

'Roughly every two months.'

But then he gave a shrug. And almost at once his manner lightened.

'The question is – is the Law right? Come and sit down again and tell me if you, personally, are capable of reform.'

'Fortunately I have no need of it.'

'Ah. I wonder if Miss Partridge would agree?'

'Well, she would have done, until this afternoon.'

'Yes, I am sorry.' He got up, took my glass and poured me a second sherry. I stretched my legs towards the fire, crossing them at the ankles. We were quiet for a while. 'Well, this is the life,' I said. 'Epicurus would approve!'

'Oh, yes? Why?'

I was disconcerted. 'Wasn't he the one who said that pleasure was the thing we should all aim for?'

'No. That's only what he's been reported as saying. In truth he was an abstemious fellow who taught that peace of mind is the highest sort of happiness – and that therefore one should invariably strive after virtue.' He smiled. 'I'm not quite sure where that leaves us. Are you?'

I resolved to treat this as rhetorical. I looked into my glass and meditated on another form of the same question. *Where do we go from here*?

'Oh. . .incidentally. How much was your taxi?'

So there, already, was my answer. This was where we went from here. I must have proved a disappointment: dismissal after the second sherry.

I was aware of sounding terse.

'No, that isn't necessary. I could have come by tube.' (Begin as you mean to go on, I had told myself airily – somewhat discounting the fact of my lateness, and that it *had* been my intention to use public transport.)

'But I'm very glad you came by taxi.'

'Well, in that case, it was eight-and-six.'

'Including tip?' Still sitting, he rummaged for the coins in his trouser pocket.

'No. Ten bob with tip.' I stood up, accepted the four half-crowns, slipped them into my own trouser pocket, half-turned towards the door. 'Do you know where James would have put my raincoat?'

'Surely you're not thinking of leaving?'

'Well, I don't want to take up your time. I've brought the books. And doubtless there are things you'd like to be getting on with.'

'But do you *wish* to leave?'

'As I say, I was thinking more about you.'

'Have you eaten?' he asked.

'No, but...'

'Well, nor have I – and there's a nice little place around the corner. Why, we haven't even begun yet to talk about your future. Another drink?'

Instead of answering the question, I repeated the statement. 'To talk about my future...?'

'You think that presumptuous?'

'No.'

'I don't feel it is, either – not really – because...'

'Because... what?'

But he had evidently changed his mind.

'I wish I'd thought of asking you to bring your novel. I'd like to have looked at some of it.'

'I've only written fifty-one pages – too much of my time, recently, has been spent on wallpapering!'

Then I smiled, as I went back to my seat.

'Yet on the other hand my writing's not large and the pages *are* foolscap.'

'Is it good, though?'

'Who knows? All I can say is, when I'm working on it, time speeds up like a champion sprinter. I go to bed late, often can't sleep, have to get up to do some more; then suddenly it's four or five in the morning! Therefore, if sheer excitement can be seen as any sort of a guide. . .'

'Fair enough. Forget about letting me read it – me, or anyone. The thing is for *you* to think it's good. . .and also, obviously, to have the chance to get on with it. What do they pay you at the shop?'

I told him.

'Not princely. You could make a lot more if you were modelling.'

'What sort of modelling?'

'Every sort. Advertising. Fashion. Art school. (No, on second thoughts, perhaps not the last: the money would be too basic.) But no reason why you shouldn't do relatively well in either of the first two. Not if you played your cards right.'

'I intend to play my cards right.'

'Yes. I can believe it.'

He regarded me, reflectively.

'I've various contacts I could put your way.'

'Thank you.'

'And as a matter of fact. . .I myself happen to be looking for a model.'

I grinned. 'Would the pay be any good?'

He didn't answer that. 'How old are you?'

'I'll be nineteen in December.' I added, 'The same age as Derek Bentley. . .' I must have had him on my mind: that awful journey to the waiting hangman.

'You're very young,' he said. 'To be honest I'd thought that you were older.'

'Will it make a difference?'

'To what?'

'Those contacts you mentioned.'

'I can't see why.' He'd been about to swallow the last of his whisky but before the glass had fully reached his mouth he stopped. He asked abruptly:

'You don't still live with your parents, do you?'

'No. My father's dead. And my mother decided to stay on in Folkestone.'

He relaxed; returned to that final swallow. 'Well, now, enough of this weighty talk. I expect you're hungry. I know I am.'

The restaurant he'd spoken of was small and unpretentious. We had avocado, coq au vin, lemon meringue pie and Stilton. Two types of wine. It was all excellent and Cambourne made an entertaining host. He spoke knowledgeably on varied topics, including Pasternak giving up the Nobel award, the race riots in Nottingham and Notting Hill, the conference in Geneva on the ending of nuclear tests – and also a Guy Fawkes party which, under duress, he had been present at the night before. I found his conversation stimulating, even if, quite often, I hadn't very much to say and at other times would have worried that I was thereby exposing my ignorance. This evening, however, that didn't seem to matter. I thought it might be the influence of the sherry and the wine.

It was half-past-ten when we left the restaurant. 'Come back to the flat,' Cambourne said. 'A couple of points we still need to discuss.'

Once there, he offered me a liqueur.

'I imagine you have to give – what? – a week's notice.'

'Yes.'

'And you'll do that tomorrow, naturally?'

'Yes,' I said again, although I mildly resented the phrasing of his question. I wasn't even sure that it had been a question.

'Good. Then the week after next we'll make a start on the picture.'

'How long will it take?'

'Impossible to say.' Cambourne appeared to be assessing the play of light on his Benedictine. 'Now, please, would you like to remove your clothes?'

'Here?'

'Why not here? I never finally engage a model without taking a look at her first. Or him.'

'I'm going to feel very stupid.' But then it occurred to me I must be sounding coy. 'I'm sorry. Yes, of course.'

I undressed quickly – but not, I hoped, in some mere graceless scramble. I aimed for both dignity and nonchalance. I got down to my Y-fronts.

'Those too,' he said. He asked me to assume half a dozen uncomplicated poses; but seemed scarcely to be watching.

There came a knock on the door.

James entered.

'Will there be anything else, sir? If not I'd like to go to bed.'

'No, nothing. Thank you, James.'

'Then good night, sir.' He turned his eyes to me. 'Good night, sir.'

'Good night,' I muttered. *And may you be murdered in your sleep*!

After the servant had gone Cambourne continued thoughtful.

'All right, then. That'll do. You can get dressed.'

As I did so, I realized I was sweating. I hoped Cambourne hadn't noticed. He sat flicking a finger against the rim of his glass.

'Is the shop open on Saturdays?' he asked.

I was puzzled. 'Only in the morning. Even then, it's pretty dead. Not much trade in Wigmore Street on Saturdays.'

'But that still means, of course, you won't be free.'

'Well, no. Actually it doesn't. We alternate.'

'I see.' He looked across at me; I was more or less dressed by now. 'I have a place in the country,' he said. 'Near Guildford. This weekend a few friends will be coming down and I wondered if you'd care to join us.'

3

He had suggested we should meet the following evening at six – outside Somerset House in Lancaster Place – literally, a cricket ball's throw from Waterloo Bridge. Apparently he had some earlier appointment near St Paul's.

('Waterloo Bridge'. . .the film that had reunited Vivien Leigh with Robert Taylor. And she was no longer the brazen, egotistical schemer of two years before – oh, not at all! – the complete opposite.)

I spotted his car at once: a white Jaguar. I'd been half afraid James might be standing beside it, spotlessly trim in peaked cap, livery and gloves, waiting to hold the door open and even place a rug across my knees; but only Cambourne was there and he sat in the driver's seat.

'Sling your case in behind,' he recommended, after our initial greeting. 'I can see you believe in travelling light.'

'Tu te moques de moi?'

'Seulement un peu.' He moved out gently into the stream of Friday evening traffic.

'Anyway, it's the smallest suitcase I've got. Contains nothing but a pair of socks.'

A raw mist hung over the river. It felt good to be cocooned in our own little world of comfort and security. 'Do you speak much French?' he inquired.

'Enough to get by.'

'Enough to get by where?'

'I spent a holiday in Paris the summer before last.'

'I'd say you need about as much French to get by in Paris during the summer as you do to get by in Swiss Cottage.'

I watched a lighted train rattle over Hungerford Bridge. 'Swiss Cottage during the summer or during the winter?' I asked.

'Why?'

'I like to get my facts straight. There are people who make such awfully wild assertions.' I said it lightly but felt nettled by his cavalier dismissal of four weeks in which I had spoken hardly one word of English. I paused. 'You can try me if you like.'

His look was gently derisive. 'Oh, no. If I were you I really wouldn't risk it.'

'Scared?' I demanded.

'What?'

'As-tu peur?'

'De quoi?'

'Que mon francais est peut-être meilleur que le tien.'

'Do you *aim* to be thus provoking?'

'Oh, I can get much more provoking than this. I think you're trying to fob me off.'

He sighed. 'D'accord.' He considered a moment and then he began – very conversationally. He gave the impression his mind was as much on his driving as it was on what he might be saying. 'Est-ce que l'idée t'est jamais venue de plaindre Icare? Moi, c'est ce qui vient de m'arriver. Qu'est-ce qui a bien pu le pousser à tant s'approcher du soleil à ton avis? Il ne savait donc pas qu'il tomberait sur un bec? Dédale avait bien dû le prévenir pourtant. Alors, il se croyait plus malin que tout le monde? Il jouait les crâneurs?. . .'

I was already lost and this was only about half of it. Long before he'd finished I felt frustrated, foolish – almost victimized. I hadn't understood, even, that he was talking about Icarus.

'Did you really have to speak so fast?'

'I wasn't aware of speaking fast.'

'And did you *need* to use such a quantity of slang?'

'Again, I'd say it was colloquial rather than slangy. But would it help if I wrote it down?'

'It might help more if you gave me the French for patronizing. And smug.'

He did so. 'Actually I'm sure you do speak fairly reasonable French. One day it could be excellent. And you have a good accent, too. That's something to feel pleased about.'

Praise indeed. And I didn't want him to believe me huffy. 'Seriously, however, if you *could* write it down I'd be grateful.'

'But the problem is – shall I be able to remember?'

I nearly said, 'There you are, then! Called your bluff!' But on this occasion I exercised restraint. 'The bits you can, perhaps?'

We reached Merriot Park about an hour later. As we scrunched up the curving drive, the headlamps swept over lawn, trees and gravel. But I'd forgotten how dark it grew in the country and I couldn't make out much of the house itself. I saw enough, though, to realize there'd been a picture of it in Cambourne's flat. I had a hazy recollection of a long low building with a wing at either end and a clock tower in the centre. The building was painted in light beige and there were lots of dazzlingly white-framed windows.

'I saw your picture of this last night,' I said. I was about to get out of the car.

'And you may also have noticed it at the exhibition?'

'Yes. Certainly.'

The front door was opened before we reached it.

'Hello, Tranch,' said Cambourne. 'How's the sciatica this week?'

Tranch was possibly twice the age of James and I wondered if that accounted for the use of surname. He was thin and a bit stooped. Cambourne introduced me.

'Poor Tranch gets back trouble so he mustn't attempt to lift weights. But I reckon he could manage a pair of socks – even in a steamer trunk.' He himself had no luggage and Tranch insisted on carrying mine.

'Do you want to freshen up first or will you come to meet my mother?'

'I'll come to meet your mother.' Then I suddenly thought of something. 'Oh – do you change for dinner?'

'Well, no. . .not tonight, at any rate.' He, like me, was wearing slacks, with an open-necked shirt and sweater.

'Mrs Cambourne is in the library, sir. With Mr and Mrs and Miss Sheldon.'

'Most of our guests won't be arriving until tomorrow,' Cambourne told me, as we crossed the hall. 'These Sheldons are distant cousins – Americans. I've never met them. They're doing this cute little island of ours and tracing their genealogy. They've traced it all the way back to us. God damn them.'

But he said it without rancour.

Surprisingly, I didn't take to Mrs Cambourne. Yes, I'd felt a little nervous beforehand – naturally – but because I liked the son I had expected to like the mother.

And she greeted me charmingly.

Yet the charm seemed synthetic. She reminded me of some fellow guest – at a far larger party than this – who was looking over your shoulder to see if anyone more interesting had just arrived.

I knew that during this past summer she had turned seventy. Once, she must have been pretty – in a way, still was. Slim, elegant, she wore a long black dress adorned by a diamond brooch. Her hair was softly waved but of a pure and dramatic white. A gold-topped cane leant against the side of her chair.

There were aperitifs before dinner and while the Sheldons and I were making bland conversation I wondered what Cambourne would have told his mother about me, when – presumably – he had telephoned.

At table I was seated to her left. Following a minute or so of small talk, she made a remark which was slightly less conventional. 'After dinner I intend to speak to you.'

'Does that mean that during dinner you don't?'

'Amusing monkey! It means that during dinner my insufferable son will be present.'

I said to Cambourne: 'I didn't know you had a brother.'

There was polite laughter from the Sheldons. I was sitting next to Miss and opposite Mister. *Mrs* Sheldon was almost our hostess's antithesis. She was plump and friendly and seemed keenly interested in everything she heard – although she herself didn't actually say much.

Neither did her husband: a stocky, genial man with thinning sandy hair and freckles.

Their daughter was the most forthcoming. Plain but with a good figure, Elizabeth Sheldon would be twenty-one the following April. It was Mrs Cambourne who had asked her age.

Mrs Cambourne had little hesitancy about asking anybody anything.

'May I inquire what school you went to, Mr Wilmot?'

I saw Cambourne look at her sharply and it appeared as if he were about to say something. I concluded from this that Mrs Cambourne had a hobbyhorse and I was right. She didn't even wait for me to answer; yet for nearly half an hour – through most of the duck course – the talk was of public schools. Cambourne apparently hadn't been to one but had studied at home under tutors until he went to Oxford in 1937; and Mrs Cambourne now seemed bent on justifying a decision which – although it must have been difficult to make, obviously – had nevertheless been put into practice well over a quarter of a century ago.

'Maman,' protested Cambourne, 'don't you think all this could be a little boring for our visitors?'

'On the contrary, Oliver,' said Theodore Sheldon immediately. 'It's fascinating. These are the sorts of insights into the British way of life we were especially hoping for. Isn't that so, Mona?'

Elizabeth Sheldon had to be told what fagging meant.

'Fagging is the system by which older boys are allowed to make younger ones run errands,' explained Mrs Cambourne. 'Shine their shoes, make their beds, clean out their rooms – all that kind of thing.'

'It's like having servants,' I said.

I wondered if that was maybe going too far. But I felt irritated.

'With the essential difference,' put in Cambourne equably, 'that most servants receive a decent wage, good living accommodation, days off, et cetera; and don't have to fit their shoe-cleaning, bed-making and various other chores into an already, no doubt, crowded enough scholastic programme. Therefore, I imagine, they find it less tiring. Added to which, servants apply for their jobs and are pleased to get them. Otherwise' – he gave me a sweet smile – 'the parallel remains exact.'

'And usually there is only a *small* amount of bullying,' added his mother, in the same light tone. 'Tell me, Mr Wilmot, were you ever bullied?'

'No, I can't say that I was, Mrs Cambourne.'

'Perhaps your size protected you?'

'Perhaps it did.' There was a short but pregnant silence. 'And, no, I don't think I ever became a bully, either.'

'But how did you feel about all that emphasis on games?' She seemed to hint at some sinister connection.

This both amused me and shored up my determination.

'In fact I very much enjoyed games. And those who didn't. . . well, they generally managed to find some way around them. So where muscles weren't exercised, at least ingenuity was.'

Or, to put it just a little differently, madam – all was for the best in the best of all possible worlds.

'Yes, I can believe you were good at games, Mr Wilmot. And I suppose you basked in a lot of hero worship? They made you a prefect, of course?'

'Though not on my first day.'

'And did you become school captain?'

'Yes, I did.' That wasn't true; but in such a context I found it irresistible.

She smiled. 'I have often heard – I wonder how far you might agree with this – that public school life is dominated by the social struggle. To achieve popularity, I am told, position and power become the overriding factors. In the pursuit of success, boys are prepared to curry favour not only wherever but however necessary.'

Although she had faintly yet unmistakably emphasized the first syllable of the penultimate word, she gazed at me innocently – and expectantly.

I hesitated.

'Well, even if you're right, Mrs Cambourne, maybe you'll admit that it's not such a bad thing, after all? Public school then becomes a microcosm of the world at large. A good preparation for adult life.'

At this, her son butted in. 'My God! Someday he's going to be as cynical as I am.'

'Oh yes, Oliver, *you* can laugh, but with all due respect to Mr Wilmot I think it remarkably sad. Is this the attitude of young people in general? Elizabeth, my dear, what do you feel about it?'

'I feel. . .it's honest,' answered Miss Sheldon, after a pause.

'Oh, I don't think any of us could dispute that. Honest it certainly is. But all the same – isn't it a shade regrettable?'

'Well, I'm not sure, Mrs Cambourne, what it is you're referring to. If you mean that it's regrettable the situation should be like that – why, yes, I suppose it is. But if you also mean it's regrettable Mr Wilmot should be able to recognize it's like that – well, *there* I can't agree with you.'

I was impressed. Not only had I acquired an ally but acquired one who was articulate in the teeth of opposition.

'Borne down on every side,' cried Mrs Cambourne, gaily. 'But tell us, Oliver, whom do you consider right?'

When Cambourne replied, it was practically a drawl. 'I suggest you and Mr Wilmot should each have your bottom smacked and be given fifty lines.'

'Oh, what a *fine* teacher you would make!' laughed Mrs Sheldon, clapping her hands. 'Oliver, do you think you might enjoy it – being a teacher?'

Cambourne gave a shudder. 'That very thought could turn me bilious!'

His mother gazed at him despairingly.

'No, but please do tell us, darling! You know how I dislike any argument to be left hanging.'

I reflected that, to set against this, she certainly didn't mind a bit of woolly thinking. What was it, precisely, that her son was being asked to pronounce on?

He shrugged. 'Well, all I can say is, my love, you've always had both feet planted firmly in Utopia. It's one of your most endearing characteristics.'

It took me a moment to work out that he had actually come down on my side – on mine and Miss Sheldon's.

'Oh, and by the way,' he went on. 'Seeing things, Maman, as they should be, rather than as they are, you too might have enjoyed *My Fair Lady*.' He glanced in my direction. 'For those, however, who pride themselves on viewing the world more realistically I'm afraid I can't find any such excuse.'

This was preposterous – as he very well knew. Yet I refused to be drawn in: for one mealtime I'd had enough. And since the Sheldons had seen the show on its Broadway opening night,

I was for the moment more interested in listening to them (especially Elizabeth) than to either of our hosts. But while the naming of attendant celebrities was in progress I happened to glimpse an unguarded exchange of looks between Cambourne and his mother. It was as if he were apologizing for having had to adjudicate against her. Regret and forgiveness were meted out in that same instant, and something else that went beyond the requirements of either apology or absolution.

In one way, I was sorry to have witnessed it. It made me feel an interloper.

4

We rose from the table at ten-ish and returned to the library for our coffee, because that's where the best fire was. With the coffee, Cambourne, Sheldon and I had glasses of Cognac. Cambourne happened to mention that Armagnac was subtly different, then said he'd buy a bottle tomorrow, to enable me to judge for myself. He spoke of this in a particularly languid tone – possibly to hide the fact he was being kind. I wondered if Pygmalion, too, had sometimes sounded languid.

Half an hour later Mrs Cambourne stood up and wished the Sheldons goodnight.

'Mr Wilmot, you haven't forgotten our little chat? I'll send Janet down as soon as I'm ready. Oliver, I'm sure our guests won't mind my stealing you away for a couple of minutes. I'd appreciate your arm upon the stairs.'

I pictured Cambourne's arm upon the stairs.

'What a truly remarkable woman!' said Mr Sheldon, the very moment the door had closed behind them – maybe even a second or two before it had. 'John, did you ever see anything quite like it?'

'No,' I said. 'I never did.' But it felt as if something a little more were required. I followed his lead. 'Remarkable,' I declared.

At first we spoke only about the Cambournes and their home. Eventually I asked Mr Sheldon what his line of business was.

'Oh,' he said casually, 'I produce hinges and staples. In Boston, Massachusetts.'

'Ah. . .useful,' I murmured.

He nodded, with the kind of manfully suppressed pride which might have been more in keeping with admitting that you ran Twentieth Century Fox.

'Yes, I don't want to sound immodest, John, but the Sheldon Company's just about the biggest in its field on the East Coast. Has just about the finest reputation, too.'

'Oh, I see.' No wonder they could attend first nights on Broadway, then. (They'd also been present at the 'West Side Story' opening: 'That's the most, John. Believe us – that one really is the most!') Hinges and staples began to sound a bit more glamorous.

But Tranch came in at that point, with a small basket of logs. He inquired if I had seen my room yet or whether I would like him to show it to me. By the time I got back, Cambourne had returned as well.

'I'm afraid I'm an abysmal host,' he apologized to the Sheldons. 'Could I possibly ask you to entertain yourselves for yet a further few minutes. . .?'

He gave them various magazines and put on a record of Gilbert and Sullivan – then, taking some writing paper out of an escritoire, pulled his chair up close to mine and started to jot down the French he'd spoken in the car. He really was a little like Pygmalion. . .and that was fine: whatever he could teach me I would be happy to learn.

'As you can see,' he began, 'it was all a lot of nonsense. I was talking off the top of my head.'

The part I found most interesting came towards the end.

'. . .the feeling one's made so many mistakes that the only way of living with them is deciding not to mind making others. . .'

Nor did he limit it to writing down the French together with its careful translation. He went to so much trouble explaining every idiom that I was quickly reminded of what Mrs Sheldon had asked him at dinner. Despite his professed horror I thought he'd probably have made the sort of schoolmaster many of his pupils developed crushes on and therefore tried their hardest to impress.

We took far longer, however, than he must have anticipated. We had barely finished when Mrs Cambourne's personal maid came to fetch me; and Mrs Cambourne had left us at least forty minutes earlier. As I silently followed the bustling Janet up the stairs – the small, Scottish, flaxen-haired Janet, not a great deal younger than her mistress – I didn't know which emotion was uppermost: curiosity or apprehension. Even hostility? But once through the doorway my first feeling was one of surprise.

Surprise, I mean, at the evidence of femininity I found. Mrs Cambourne's bedroom was fairly similar to my mother's, except that it was larger and grander and there was a real fire burning in the grate. I'd have imagined my hostess to be more in favour of fresh air; less in favour of frills. She was sitting up in bed with a mound of peach-coloured pillows piled high against the headboard and a lacy white shawl draped around her shoulders. She wore a button-necked, pink flannel nightgown; and somehow seemed much softer than before.

She said, 'Ah, Mr Wilmot. . .,' and she gave a signal for Janet to withdraw.

Then she indicated a low satinwood seat conveniently placed for conversation.

'It's stronger than it looks. But if you'd prefer one of those striped armchairs, please feel free to bring it over.'

'No, this is fine.'

The civilities. . . I noticed her gold-topped cane propped against the bedside table – it added a touch of severity to the homeliness of books, pills, water, lamp. There was a shiny red apple sitting on top of 'Mary Barton'.

'It's good of you to humour an old lady. Thank you for coming.'

I smiled. 'But I could scarcely have refused.'

'Ah! So you see me as a martinet?'

Although I didn't deny this she may have thought I had. 'Oh, but I am! Disgracefully so! Especially as Merriot Park isn't even mine. I'm only here on sufferance.'

'No, I can't believe that.'

She chuckled. 'And of course you're perfectly right not to. Oliver and I mean the world to one another. I think you probably noticed?'

'Yes. I did.'

Either my words or my expression must have carried conviction. 'There! You're obviously perceptive.' There was scarcely a pause. 'You're also very beautiful.'

Annoyingly, I felt myself begin to blush.

But I gazed down at my shoes and enjoyed, in spite of my embarrassment, the way they shone in the soft pinkish light; enjoyed the sensation of being beautiful, with long legs and well-shaped ankles and shoes that shone in the soft pinkish light.

'Yet I have to say I always find them difficult to like.'

'Whom?'

'Beautiful people.'

'Though with some exceptions, clearly! Your son is very good-looking.'

I had intended to say *beautiful* but found I couldn't quite manage it.

'And if I may remark on it, Mrs Cambourne, you too. . .'

This wasn't insincere. Earlier, my assessment might have been grudging. Possibly it was the sort of face which improved on acquaintance. Possibly, it was the sort of face which a black dress didn't complement.

She gave a smile – albeit a grim one. 'Might that be how I came by my mistrust?'

'I don't know. Might it?'

'For in the main, you see, I think beautiful people are spoilt, And ruthless. And don't mind whom they hurt.'

'I mind very much whom I hurt.'

'That may be true. But excuse me – it's pathetically easy to say. And only time will tell.'

She pulled her shawl more closely about her.

'Let me,' she suggested, 'be a little more specific.'

I would have thought she was already doing all right in that department.

'To you my son may seem like someone who knows about life. He isn't. He's a baby. Time and again people have tried to exploit him; time and again he's allowed them to. For all his outer sophistication he remains naive. For all his claims to cynicism he remains trusting. For all his pretence of world-weariness. . . well, do I need to go on? No matter how he would deny this – and even as a smokescreen accuse others of the crime, myself included – at heart he's a romantic. He still imagines there are those who won't be swayed by the money which his paintings earn, or by the fortune which his father left him. Well, perhaps there are but my own faith in the possibility is not strong. All I *am* certain of' – and here she leant forward and fixed me with a regard so emphatic it was hard to maintain eye contact – 'all I *am* certain of is that I am not prepared to stand by and watch him suffer again. I am not! I hope you understand.'

I shook my head.

She'd made it too explicit.

I wasn't about to meet *her* frankness with a comparable one of my own.

'No, I'm afraid I don't. What has any of this to do with me?'

'Do you love my son?'

(Who says the English are reserved?)

'Love him?'

'Yes, Mr Wilmot. Are you in love with my son?'

I thought of standing on my dignity – I mean, of standing more upon my dignity. ('Mrs Cambourne, what *are* you suggesting? And why do you suppose my being a guest here allows you to behave in this manner? Shouldn't the very opposite apply?') I might have enjoyed that. But what good would it have done?

I said eventually: 'Apart from the fact I didn't meet him until yesterday. . .'

'Yes?'

'. . .well, apart from that, I don't believe that I've ever been in love in my life.'

And because I sometimes worried about this – wondering whether it might not be indicative of some rare, perhaps incurable, disorder – I now added a rider.

'At least I hope not. Otherwise all the poets and screenwriters have been woefully exaggerating.'

For a moment it appeared she had actually been sidetracked.

'*Never* been in love?' she repeated.

'No.'

'How extraordinary! At your age I had fallen in and out of love more times than I remember.'

I said nothing. I wasn't sure that 'Lucky you!' would have been exactly right.

'Mind you,' she went on. 'That now makes it easier to request a favour.'

Uh-huh, I thought. *Here* we go!

'And I would admire you enormously for granting it. I assure you, Mr Wilmot, you would rise high in my esteem.'

She plainly regarded this as a greater prize than I did. For – hardly to be wondered at – I had guessed exactly what was coming. And the irony of it made me laugh.

Literally.

I said: 'So if I promise to step out of your son's life forever I shall then become the sort of person worthy to remain in it?' Did this smack of something Groucho Marx had said?

In any case it made no difference. Mine or Groucho's, she clearly didn't appreciate such humour. Her manner grew cold.

'Yes, that's precisely what I'd like: that you should indeed step out of my son's life forever.' She didn't seem much interested in the sort of person I'd become.

Then the steely quality receded – she must have realized that it wouldn't serve her purpose. She leant forward again.

'Don't you see? You could leave here in the morning – first *thing* in the morning – well before Oliver was down! Thomas would drive you to the station!'

Her eagerness was pitiable.

'And that would be the end of it! We could invent some story. . .'

'Oh, Mrs Cambourne. . .'

'Yes?' Her energy was unabated.

I spread my hands. 'This is ridiculous!'

The light disappeared from her eyes. It didn't go fast – rather, it faded, as though the implication of that word couldn't instantly be assimilated.

And the difference in her tone was awful.

'I protect my son, Mr Wilmot, I do everything in my power to protect him! I'm sorry if that seems to you ridiculous.'

She added: 'However, I wouldn't think of insulting you by offering you a bribe. . .'

'No? Why not? Why stop at that?' I had risen to my feet by this time; it would have been virtually impossible to stay seated. 'Hasn't everything you've said during these past ten minutes been an insult?'

And I derived something darkly entertaining from the change in her expression.

'All right then, Mr Wilmot. All right. What figure might you have in mind?'

'Oh, I don't know,' I answered casually. 'Perhaps two thousand?'

She considered the proposition. Finally she nodded. She smiled thinly. 'Beauty obviously comes dear this year.'

'Beauty allied to much loveliness of nature.'

'But I'm not going to haggle with you. Naturally I shall want a line or two in writing to the effect that you've accepted this money and for what you have accepted it.'

'Of course.'

'Not that I should dream of ever showing it to Oliver. Other than in extremis.'

'But you would *have* to show it to him!'

I felt almost dismayed by the fact she hadn't thought this through.

'Otherwise, he'd come looking for me, wouldn't he? If only to seek out some explanation.'

'Would he? Yes, I suppose he would.'

'And he knows where I work.'

'But I would never have chosen to hurt him so. I would never have chosen it.'

'How could you not have? What kind of story did you think we could invent? Supposing I'd said, 'Yes, Mrs Cambourne, I *will* grant your favour!' – even then you'd have needed a note, even then you'd have needed me to take money. I would never have confessed to something so abominable if I hadn't actually done it.'

'I wouldn't have expected you to.'

'No, perhaps not, but. . .'

'Anyway.' She gestured tiredly towards a chest of drawers on the other side of the room. 'You'll find writing materials in the top left-hand drawer. You'll also find a chequebook.'

'Ah, yes! But that's another thing. How can I be sure that you won't stop the cheque?' It suddenly dawned on me that, in some thoroughly perverse fashion, I was actually having fun.

But then I remembered something.

I remembered the look that I had seen at dinner.

And it was a timely reminder: a sure indication of the love felt for this woman by the man who had invited me here; the man who was not only offering me hospitality, showing concern over my future and even an interest in my writing, but who had so recently – and, most convincing of all, as a guide to his integrity – been doing everything he could to improve my French.

So I turned to face her before she had replied to my question. (She might not have believed it *merited* any reply.)

'Oh, Mrs Cambourne,' I said again, wearily.

'Yes? What is it?'

'I really do apologize.'

'I suppose these things can't be helped.' She spoke in a voice every bit as weary as my own, yet it struck me as a generous observation. 'But please don't get sentimental. For better for worse we're all as we are. We can only hope that little by little we shall improve.'

'No,' I said, 'you don't understand. What I'm apologizing for is this whole nonsensical charade. I feel ashamed – but at the same time think you more or less deserved it.'

It again took her several seconds to adjust. I didn't wait for her to comment.

'And I'm glad Merriot Park doesn't belong to you and that therefore you haven't the right to turn me out of it. But I'm sorry if we're going to be enemies. I'm sorry if the next two days are going to be awkward for us.'

I didn't know, quite, how to bring this to an end.

'But do you think our talk might, in some small way, have cleared the air? Obviously, I won't say anything to Oliver. And I promise you I'll always do my utmost not to hurt him.'

She looked older. She was gazing down at her hands, which lay clasped before her on the eiderdown. Absurdly, I now noticed the scattering of liver spots.

'I'll bid you goodnight, then. Would you like me to send up Janet?'

She still didn't answer.

I left the room and went down to the library; opened its door but didn't advance far beyond the threshold. Cambourne and the Sheldons were playing cards. I expressed the hope they were enjoying their game. 'Don't let me spoil your concentration. I've only come to say goodnight.'

Cambourne said: 'We've nearly finished. Wouldn't you like a drink?'

'No, thanks. I'm feeling tired. It must be all that good food and country air!'

I sensed his disappointment, yet knew he'd be anxious to hear what had been spoken of upstairs – and I wanted to work out how I was going to present it. (Doctor it!) 'Where would I find Janet, in case your mother needs her?'

'Don't worry. There's a bell push by her bed.'

'Ah, yes, of course.' I smiled at the Sheldons. 'Good night.' I smiled at Cambourne. 'And thank you, Oliver, for everything.'

I realized this was the first time I had called him by his first name. It felt strange. 'You've been very kind to me. I appreciate it.'

He replied lazily and with none of the robust good wishes I'd received from the Sheldons. 'Oh, je t'en prie, mon vieux.'

'See you in the morning,' I laughed.

In the second before saying it I had become aware of something else. That very ordinary phrase was one which – tonight – would give me a peculiar satisfaction.

5

I got up some seven and a half hours later feeling thoroughly refreshed and even elated. A maid had brought me tea and biscuits. Though normally I didn't enjoy that kind of attention, for the present I revelled in it. I said to myself: This is me drinking

Earl Grey (I think) in bed at Oliver Cambourne's home on the eighth of November 1958; today can never be repeated; I intend to savour every minute.

So I drank the tea and then sprang out of bed, like healthy, wholesome, head-of-the-house heroes are always supposed to. I performed fifty-four slow press-ups; touched my toes twenty times; did some deep-knee bends, cycling and handstands; more sit-ups than I had ever yet managed – which I saw as a glorious omen – then spent ten minutes under a blissfully powerful shower. And all the time I felt obscurely that I was getting my own back on Mrs Cambourne. In the shower I sang 'D'ye ken John Peel?', 'The Eton Boating Song' and 'Over the Sea to Skye', and finished off by gritting my teeth and turning on the cold jet full force – soon to be rewarded by feeling both morally and physically invigorated, as I wielded a large and luxurious towel. I shaved, splashed on cologne, gave my hair its regular three-minute brush, got dressed in slacks and a tartan shirt – and eventually presented myself as fit for the world's inspection, in the dining room, shortly after nine.

The world turned out to be represented solely by Elizabeth Sheldon. She had finished her own breakfast and had been about to leave, but she sat down again and encouraged me to explore the half-dozen covered dishes keeping warm on the sideboard. I took a succulent-looking kipper.

'Before I forget,' I said, 'thank you for helping me out last night.'

'Good gracious, no call to thank me – I happened to agree with what you were saying! In any case, it didn't appear you needed much helping out, either from me or anyone.'

'But it's always nice to have moral support.'

'Cousin Sarah certainly enjoys an argument.'

'Yes, she does.'

That was all we said but then we started to laugh. There was no knowing what scandalous abuses we might not have committed if Mrs Sheldon hadn't at that moment come into the dining room.

'Good morning, John. You both seem to be having a good joke!'

But we didn't explain it to her and she didn't insist. She had come to collect her daughter for a walk in the woods – her husband was already waiting in the drive, in the sunshine – and assured me I'd be most welcome to join them. But I said that Mr Cam. . .that Oliver had spoken of taking me into Guildford during the morning to buy some Armagnac, and I asked for a rain check. This caused Elizabeth to say it wasn't kind of me to poke fun. I told her I wasn't poking fun at all – that I was only trying to make them feel at home. Whereupon Mrs Sheldon said she had guessed from the start I had a lovely nature – and I felt like suggesting she should run off posthaste to inform Mrs Cambourne about this. . .and maybe one or two others. And on that happy note we parted.

In fact we didn't go into Guildford. Cambourne didn't make his appearance until well after eleven and some of his guests were expected before lunch. I spent most of the morning in the library, reading about Christopher Wren and his plans for the rebuilding of London – and finding this totally absorbing; when Oliver at last came down he found me a volume of paintings by Canaletto, which added still further to my enjoyment. To my relief he didn't ask what Mrs Cambourne had wanted to say to me. (I'd been afraid of sounding arch: 'Oh, your mother made me promise not to tell. You wouldn't wish me to renege?') Tranch brought us coffee in the library and sitting there before the crackling fire, even on a crisp autumnal morning when it must have been good to be out in the woods, I still had the feeling I was probably in the right place.

The first guests arrived while we were looking at these books: a husband and wife in their early forties who were both interior decorators – it was they who had done up the London flat.

And Sylvia Renshaw had worked in Hollywood immediately after the war. At lunch she had some scurrilous tales to tell about the stars, probably quite untrue but certainly amusing. I was somewhat surprised Mrs Cambourne didn't shudder at her every utterance; but Mrs Cambourne seemed as entertained by her as the rest of us did.

No. Most likely *I* was the only one Mrs Cambourne wasn't entertained by.

Not that our encounters were as awkward as I'd anticipated; mercifully we were never alone, and we needed to exchange little more than the barest courtesies. Nevertheless I was aware she was watching me – not so much at table perhaps as in the library or the drawing room – and I was glad when a party of us went strolling about the grounds for an hour or so before tea. And what grounds! Cambourne said to me, 'Just wait until you come here in the summer!', which was a kindly and reassuring remark whether or not he actually meant it, but even in November I considered the place well-nigh perfect, a paradise, with its walks and its vistas, its blending of formality and wilderness. On our return we passed a swimming pool tucked away behind an orchard. Also, a tennis court. He asked me if I played. 'We'll have a match in the morning, then.'

'Before or after church?'

He answered with a straight face.

'My mother will no doubt be going at half-past-ten should you care to accompany her.'

'Are you two talking of having a game?' cried Sylvia Renshaw, catching up. 'Splendid! When? I can't wait to see you in your shorts.'

She gave her usual exaggerated laugh.

'You can't either, can you, Rachel?'

Rachel Millwood was another of the guests I particularly liked, an older woman who owned a gallery off Bond Street, was a capital light pianist and – following our ramble – read all our fortunes in the teacups. (I should soon be travelling in foreign parts! A great windfall lay ahead of me! Eventually I'd write a book which would turn out to be a real bestseller!) When I forcibly objected, she withdrew that 'eventually'; said she didn't know how on earth it had slipped in. Oliver called her Sybil and claimed he was disappointed all her prophecies weren't in verse but she told him she had enough of a problem getting them out in prose, thank you very much, and that she now asked no more than to be a source of poetic inspiration to others. And considering there were twelve of us drinking tea, excluding Mrs Millwood herself, and that she had found something a little different to say about each of us, she hadn't done so badly (as Elizabeth was the first to point out) even in prose.

Indeed, when we sat down to dinner, Mrs Cambourne apologized for this little oversight, as she called it, our being thirteen, and hoped that none of us was superstitious. She certainly didn't say so but I suddenly realized, from the way her glance – perhaps involuntarily – flicked over to me, that the oversight wasn't due to any careless planning on her own part. It was caused by an unexpected and last-minute invitation on her son's.

The spectre at the feast, I thought.

But nobody seemed to mind. It gave rise to a half-hearted discussion on walking under ladders, tossing spilt salt over your left shoulder – and reading fortunes in tealeaves. From there the talk somehow progressed to what was happening in Cyprus. But then Oliver made a plea for no politics during meals and I wondered (presumptuously?) if this was partly because he feared I might feel at a disadvantage. For a while we spoke on a subject I'd heard debated in the sixth form – a hoary old chestnut which yet retained its interest: had human nature changed in the past couple of thousand years? Oliver maintained it hadn't; if there were still gladiatorial games or burnings at the stake – if there were still guillotinings or hangings in the public square – people would flock as they always had, bringing their children and their sandwiches. I asked if he would. He said not. I suggested that he was being a little holier-than-thou, in that case, attributing to the populace at large a thirst for cruelty which neither he nor anyone present admitted to sharing. He thanked me and replied that I had absolutely proven his point. For he now discovered he had changed his mind and would with the greatest of pleasure come to witness my own execution.

The phrase 'born to be hanged' then led straight into an argument on fatalism; and the unanimous conclusion was that if there was no God how could there be predestination, whereas if there *was* a God he would be more like the Devil if any man was truly born to be hanged. ('Except for that tiresome fellow over there,' repeated Oliver. 'We could all understand that.' Only his mother didn't appear to be amused.)

But after dinner we stopped being quite so intellectual. A bridge table was formed in the drawing room, while another group played canasta and Mrs Millwood sat at the Bechstein Grand for over an hour, running expertly through Gershwin and Porter and Kern. For much of that time I was happy just to lean against the piano and request some of my favourite numbers – 'in the best tradition of all those admiringly draped Technicolor cuties,' called out Sylvia Renshaw – an observation which perhaps I could have done without, but which I acknowledged with a merry smile and a wave, like the unfailingly good sport I clearly was. Yet it was also during this period that Elizabeth, to whom I hadn't spoken on her own since breakfast, asked me if I'd enjoyed my trip into Guildford. When I told her we hadn't been, she immediately answered I should have to go round to the Savoy one evening and learn about Armagnac there, with my after-dinner coffee. That's where the Sheldons were staying while in London. They had a suite. I asked when they'd moved in. On hearing her reply I emitted a soft whistle.

'Two weeks at the Savoy already and another five or six before you set out on your little jaunt round Europe! You must be stinkingly rich!'

'Up to now, then, had you imagined we were paupers?' She smiled, beguilingly.

'What, purely because I'd seen you busking a couple of times in Leicester Square? Remind me: wasn't it one Sunday afternoon in that passageway next to the Warner, then the following weekend outside the Empire?'

'I can tell you like the movies!'

'Oh, yes, and I even like the buskers! I can picture you all so vividly. You were the strong man bursting out of heavy chains; your mother was the one who made a doll's house from paper; and – well, let me see now –'

'No, no,' she interrupted, 'you've got it wrong! The house-builder was Daddy. Mother was the strong man. *I* was doing the tap dance.'

'Anyway, there's only one thing I really care about. Was that invitation on the level? Armagnac with my after-dinner coffee?'

'Yes, of course! Are you suggesting we Americans are insincere? And it even includes the dinner which precedes the after-dinner coffee. How about that?'

A strange thing happened at around this point. By the time that we separated I was no longer thinking her plain. I remembered how I'd wondered if Mrs Cambourne's face were the kind to alter under variable conditions. There could be some enchantment on the house. Attractive women became beauties; plain ones grew almost pretty. Elizabeth Sheldon had grace and delicacy and charm – intelligence, a sense of humour. Such things all bordered on prettiness.

Therefore, it *wasn't* just the money. And, anyway, I had assuredly realized last night how wealthy they were. QED. *Not* guilty!

Having taken my leave of Elizabeth, I didn't go to wish anybody else goodnight, nor issue a general proclamation.

I didn't want to make a big thing out of it and maybe break up the party.

But, afterwards, I hoped that Oliver hadn't thought me rude.

This worried me while I was getting ready for bed – and even whilst reading my book. Then common sense prevailed. The following day I could explain.

But, as it turned out, I didn't have to wait until the following day.

Soon after one there came a tap upon my door.

6

'I saw your light on. Can't you sleep?' He spoke from the doorway – a bit offhandedly, I thought.

'I haven't even tried.' I held up 'The Long Goodbye'.

'I'm afraid it must have been dull for you tonight. You clearly don't care for card games.'

'I don't know how to play them. I had a good time, though, listening to Mrs Millwood.'

'Bridge can be useful – besides, I think you might enjoy it.' He paused. 'I saw you talking to Elizabeth Sheldon. I wondered if you needed rescuing.'

'No. It was fine. She's not difficult to get away from.'

He had now folded his arms and was leaning against the doorjamb. He looked dashing in his dinner jacket; several times during the evening I had wished that I possessed one. 'Did you know she was adopted?' he asked, with a yawn.

I shook my head. 'Another little orphan Annie, then, who's found her Daddy Warbucks.'

'Yes. Not that I go for Sheldon in a big way. Unpleasant type, I'd think, if you should ever cross him.'

This hadn't occurred to me. He went on: 'Well, I'd better leave you. It's late. But I was wandering in the garden and, as I say, I saw your light and I suddenly wondered. . .'

'Wondered what?'

'Whether you weren't feeling well.'

'You mean – you noticed the quantities of salmon I tucked away at dinner?'

'No, I don't mean anything of the kind.'

'Anyway, it was a nice thought. Considerate.'

'Yes, wasn't it?'

We smiled at one another. I said, 'By the way, I'm worried. 'You weren't affronted, were you, when I didn't come over to say goodnight?'

'Affronted? No, why in the world. . .?'

'It might have seemed I'd been neglecting you. We don't appear to have spoken very much since this morning.'

'And did that bother you?'

'Well, let's say I'd have had an even better time if there'd been more chance to chat. Possibly the best part of the day was when we were sitting together in the library. Just you and me and Canaletto.'

I could see him trying to conceal his pleasure.

'That's nice,' he answered. 'Besides being a tactful reply to a tactless question.'

'A truthful reply, too – although disturbingly selfish. Or should that be, truthful *because* disturbingly selfish? How in God's name could I expect exclusive possession, at a time when you had a whole houseful of guests? Talk about arrogant!'

But apparently he didn't choose to debate the philosophy. 'Well, at least you've exclusive possession right now.'

'Ah, yes! So I have! And I'm not tired. So if you'd like to come in properly to have that chat – ideally, you see, one which is local, rather than long-distance. . .?' I gave him a broad smile. 'Save waking up the neighbours?'

'No immediate neighbours,' he said. 'It's a big house.' But he closed the door and came to sit on the side of the bed. As usual, I thought how pleasant was his aftershave.

'Good. In that case I'll be able to sing in the shower again.'

We were quiet for a moment.

'You know, I feel like your mother. Sitting up in bed and graciously receiving. Though – again, how presumptuous! – she was far better dressed than me.'

'Wearing her diamonds?'

'Well, naturally – if you're referring to her necklace and tiara?'

I couldn't stop myself.

'Or was it her crown?'

He gave a smile but made no comment. He only asked, 'What did she want you for?' Patently, his tact of the previous morning hadn't survived into the small hours of the current one. In a way I liked him all the better for it.

'Oh, nothing much. I think that – like us – she just felt like a little chat. "Getting to know you, getting to know all about you. . ." ' I raised my hands and let them undulate as though conducting.

'I saw Gertrude Lawrence do that, in New York.'

'And no doubt found it excruciating. I saw Deborah Kerr do it in Folkestone – and found it enchanting.'

He nodded. 'That figures.'

'What's more, my mother and great-aunt *also* found it enchanting!'

'Then I retire, defeated.'

'What made you go to see it, anyway? Oh, come to that, what made you see *My Fair Lady*?'

'Well, I like to think I'm open-minded. And if everybody raves over something. . . Besides, I'm very fond of opera; there *ought* to be a kinship.'

'*Porgy and Bess*?' I queried.

'Yes – absolutely! I suppose I'm always hoping for another *Porgy and Bess*.'

'*Carmen Jones*?'

'I'm not sure whether, in this context, *Carmen Jones* can count.'

He reached across and took my hand. We neither of us commented. I gave his own a gentle squeeze.

'Would you mind,' he asked, 'if I undressed?'

'No. On the contrary. Revenge is sweet.'

'Revenge?'

'For what you did to me on Thursday. I felt such an idiot when James walked in and saw me naked.'

As he didn't respond immediately, I added, 'I'm not claiming it was *altogether* your fault.'

'Actually, it may have been,' he conceded – unexpectedly – bending to untie a shoelace. 'It wasn't strictly necessary to have you undress. Not at that point. And I can't even put it down to prurience. . .which might have been a shade more acceptable. No, to tell you the truth, I was being cussed.'

'Cussed?'

'Yes. I realize this doesn't absolve me, but at the time I was brooding over a suspicion that you might have lied to me. I repeatedly tried to bury it – and think I succeeded fairly well, especially in the restaurant – but it *would* keep on resurfacing. Rankling. About your having been to my exhibition.'

I hesitated.

'Oh, Christ. Was it as easy to see through as that?'

'For someone supposed to be interested in art,' he observed, 'you weren't evincing much desire to talk about it. That's all. It wasn't until last night, though, that I knew for sure. By then, I might add, it wasn't so important.'

'Trick question as we left the car?'

'Move over now,' he said.

I did so. We slipped down in the bed and he put his arms about me. I laid my head on his chest and it was amazingly comfortable.

'I'm sorry for that lie. It was completely stupid. But I wanted to attract your attention and couldn't think how else to do it.'

He was running his finger over one of my ears. 'Well, looking at it in perspective, I suppose that it was hardly such a crime.'

'No – and, looking at it in perspective too, it wasn't completely stupid, either. In fact, it was pretty astute. It succeeded.'

'Why did you want to attract my attention?'

'Because I thought you looked nice. Handsome, sexy, sympathetic.' He stretched over to switch out the lamp. 'Which only goes to show what a perceptive nature I have – how right your mother was! But why do you work so hard at seeming bored, and giving the *less* perceptive among us such a false impression?'

'Is that what I do?'

'Yes – even she told me it was a total sham. The world-weary Mr Cambourne. At heart, she said, you're still a baby.'

'I shall speak to my mother about that.'

'Yes – and so you should!' I had no fear of repercussions.

'But for the moment,' he said, 'tell me a little about yours. So she actually enjoyed 'The King and I'. . .?'

He encouraged me to talk even before discovering this was my first time in bed with a man. . .or, indeed, with anyone. I told him silly things – like about my mother's working in a café on the seafront and getting bullied by the manageress. Like about how disappointed she'd been when I had turned down my place at university. I told him about my father's aunt who had lived with us since long before his death and about my mother's anxiety that she, Aunt Clara, whom I loved perhaps more than anyone in the world, might be going senile. I told him about my fear of the bomb. About my exemption from National Service on account of being deaf in one ear. About my tiny flat in Gloucester Place and how hard I had worked on this. And through it all I could hear my voice going on and on and I kept telling myself I ought to stop, find out more about *him*, but I felt there had never been anyone to whom I could speak so freely – and, frankly, I relished it. That isn't to say I didn't enjoy the rest of what was going on, but for much of the time it was gentle and unhurried, and might have been little more than a background to conversation. Or to monologue! Certainly it seemed like that at the beginning – say, for the first hour – while we were getting used to the experience; or, at least, while I was; coming to accept the feel of him, the slight roughness of him, as something wholly natural. He stayed with me about two hours. . .the bed wasn't a wide one and if he'd spent the night in it, neither of us would have had much rest. 'And don't forget,' he said, 'that in the morning we've a date on the tennis court – bright and early!'

'So we have.'

He told me he'd bring down the necessary equipment when he came to the library for his coffee. Fortunately, we wore pretty much the same size in everything – even shoes.

Partially dressed, he now stood beside the bed for a minute, resting his hand on my shoulder.

'Ça va?'

'Ça va,' I said. 'Ça va?'

Thankfully – because I wouldn't have called it all *that* bright and early – our 'date' had been fixed for eleven. We played two sets. Oliver won them both, though not easily; he'd needed to put up a fight. My reaction surprised me. I'd have thought I would care about having lost – care enormously. Especially before an audience.

But, no, I didn't. Not at all.

Each game had been a good one. Exciting. Exhilarating. I felt satisfied. Victory, I told myself, could come along some other day.

As we left the court he made a suggestion. He offered to ring the shop the following morning, tell Personnel I was ill and would be laid up for about a week – well, at the very least, a week. 'You *did* hand in your notice, I take it?'

'Yes.'

'Then I'll ask them to send your cards to Gloucester Place.'

I nodded, now feeling far more confident on that score. . .as well as every other. 'But I'm glad it will be you who's making the call! As you know, little George Washington here finds it so difficult to fib.'

He answered more seriously – although, somehow, it didn't come out sounding pompous. 'Normally I do my best not to tell lies. Yet in this instance I believe I have a good reason.'

I asked what that might be and – despite the fact he didn't at first respond to this question – was relieved to hear him speak more lightly.

'Henceforward, you'll be able to write to your heart's content – occasionally, of course, taking time off to compose effusive dedications to your august and noble patron.'

'All right. I always wanted an august and noble patron.'

'But I warn you: I'll be a hard taskmaster. I shall expect between two and three thousand words a day.'

'Struth!'

'However,' he added, 'for us both to gather enough strength to embark on this enterprise, I thought that tomorrow we might pop off to Biarritz for a short while. I have a friend there. A writer. I feel it could be beneficial for you to meet her.'

'In Biarritz it could be beneficial for me to meet anyone. Who is she?'

'Marnie Stark.'

'Ah, yes! 'Daisy and Sybella'! Well, *now* I understand.'

'But it was interesting to put you through your paces. And it gave you a fine chance to show what you were made of. Which, I might add, you grabbed hold of with both hands!'

'Are you meaning to imply that I still came across like a fresh wind? Invigorating?'

'No other word for it! But afterwards I did feel a touch of compunction. Am I forgiven?'

'Totally. To err is human.'

'Thank you. To forgive, divine. I'll try to bear that in mind.'

'Yes, please do. For all future occasions.'

He laughed.

'But back to our muttons. Marnie's book. Have you read it?'

I hadn't. What made this particularly annoying was that I'd meant to skim through it during my lunch hour on Friday. But I'd been caught up in conversation with two of my colleagues, and hadn't liked to snub them.

'Then you can borrow my copy – perhaps make a start on it this afternoon? As you're aware, it's only slim. I'll also let you have 'The Moving Staircase', likewise attractively brief. She'll feel flattered to know that you've read them. You could even let her think it was before we met.'

'Oh, no! That would be such a falsehood!'

He ignored this. 'I'm hoping she might give you a private master class. The thing is, if we don't go tomorrow she won't be there for a while, and I admit to being impatient. I don't suppose the bookshop will collapse without you.'

'Oh, don't you, indeed?'

'And I assume your passport hasn't expired since all those madcap jollities in Paris?'

'By *expired* you mean *given up the ghost,* don't you? *Turned its face to the wall.* No, it has not! On the contrary, it sprang into boisterous life simply on account of them.'

'I'll phone the airport right away. It could be fun.' He gave a wry smile. 'Besides, who knows? This time, it might even teach you a little French.'

7

We caught an Air France flight to Paris, and Air Inter for the second leg. On the former we travelled first-class. The stewardess recognized Oliver. 'We haven't seen you lately,' she smiled, handing us champagne.

I asked afterwards: 'When was the last time they did see you?'

'There was a fellow I went to Paris with last April. A musician. It didn't work out. Matt was just the last in a very long line.' He looked at me ironically. 'I don't know if that answers your question?'

'Yes – thank you – all-embracingly. Are you so *terribly* difficult, then?'

'I'm honestly not sure. Difficult? Demanding? Unlucky? Perhaps a combination. . . Always, however, optimistic.'

'Careful! The jaded aren't permitted optimism.'

He sipped his champagne and disregarded small gibes. 'On our return we'll go VIP. I think you might enjoy that. Little men trotting about pretending desperately they've heard of you.'

Earlier we'd driven straight from Merriot Park to the Embankment. It was from there that Oliver had phoned the shop. Then we'd taken a taxi to my place, where he'd left me at the front door, saying he'd be back in twenty minutes. Actually it was nearer forty – I began to think we'd miss our flight. But he laughed at this, pointing out that I wasn't *yet* a seasoned traveller. He had bought me a suitcase: pigskin, beautiful, fit for a king or a dandy, about half the size of the one I'd taken into Surrey. 'We'll have it initialled when we get back,' he said; brushing aside my appreciation almost before I had started to express it.

So I hurriedly repacked, and while I did so he glanced around the flat. For fully forty-eight hours (maybe longer; maybe ever since Thursday) I'd felt apprehensive as to what his comments were going to be: he was practically the first person to have seen it, this recently redecorated home of mine, certainly the first person whose reaction I cared about, and for a moment I remembered some of the blemishes.

But after he'd walked all through it (it certainly didn't extend that far) looking first at the bathroom, then into the kitchen and the sitting room, he came back only to exclaim:

'Well, haven't you finished your packing yet?' My pleasure in my new gift instantly disappeared.

After all, *I* hadn't had the Renshaws to do it for me!

'Yes, I'm ready.' I closed the lid and turned round; was about to lift the suitcase off the bed, when suddenly he caught me to him.

'I think it's magnificent!' he declared. 'You're obviously a highly talented young fellow.'

My pleasure in my new gift – and in everything else – returned full-strength. (I was glad I hadn't had the Renshaws do it for me.) 'I only wish,' I said, 'I'd taken photographs of what the place looked like before.'

'I can guess, you braggart, just from looking at the state of the entrance hall.'

'And you see that little yard through the window? It's not quite the way I want it yet, but it was I who cleaned it up and whitewashed the walls and put that bench out there and all those tubs. . .'

'You must give me a complete rundown on the way to the airport.'

We went by taxi to Heathrow, had lunch on the flight as well as the champagne, and reached Biarritz (travelling from Bordeaux by self-drive car) early in the evening.

The hotel was tremendous: opulent and heavily rococo. Oliver said it teetered on the brink of vulgarity – and was saved from toppling only by its abundance of period charm.

'So obviously it toppled once,' I remarked, 'but somehow, over time, managed to regain its footing?'

Oliver smiled. 'I've found myself a fool,' he said. 'And – I'd bet on it – one a lot more enticing than any Lear acquired!'

Flattered and happy, I retorted that he had delusions of grandeur.

He told me he was already thinking of revoking my licence.

But all that was after we'd gone up to our suite and I had spent a fair while being impressed by its magnificence. As soon as the porter had departed, I first threw myself onto the bed and then tested the comfort of the sofa and the armchairs, and was able to report that appearances weren't in the least bit deceptive. 'One sometimes forgets,' observed Oliver tolerantly, either to the ceiling or, far more likely, to the mildly protesting chandelier, 'that he *is* only eighteen!' Following this, we stood on the balcony and drank white wine; and then we bathed and changed and went to look around the town.

Sunshine, sea, sand and sparkle – even in November and not too long before dusk. White buildings, fresh paint, clean streets. When viewed from the beach, Biarritz truly did resemble a wedding cake.

First, though, when arriving on that beach, we had been struck by something different: by several interestingly shaped rocks a short way out to sea, and by a miniature humpback bridge which connected one of them to the shore.

However, what made this particular rock important was neither the fact of its being central nor the fact of its having a link to the mainland. What made this particular rock important was the statue it provided a base for.

It was a statue of the Virgin Mary.

'My goodness,' I said. 'I don't suppose *that's* something one comes across very often.'

'Not to my knowledge.'

'How motherly she looks.'

'Yes, doesn't she?'

'And how welcoming. . .to any sailor returning from the sea: some poor, homesick fellow who might have been away for months, if not for years!'

I mentioned the terrifying storms he must have had to face. Possibly, the pirates and the men-of-war.

'Though don't forget, you romantic old thing, that she's looking in this direction. Which suggests it was more the mothers, wives and sweethearts who sought her comfort – her protection for their loved ones.'

'I like it,' I said. 'Protection for their loved ones.' I glanced at him. 'I may have to retitle my novel!'

'And, anyway, in view of all these rocks, that lighthouse over there might have seemed a shade *more* welcoming, don't you think? I mean, to your homesick sailor returning from the sea!'

With some reluctance I agreed; but by then he'd turned away and was gazing at the wedding cake.

Shortly afterwards we got back in the car and drove to Fuenterrabia – just across the Spanish border – to have dinner: prawns and squid and ice-cream. Oliver told me it was the custom, on leaving, for a well-bred young man to pinch the waitress's bottom as a token of respect. She would feel herself slighted if such a courtesy should fail to be observed.

'All right,' I said. 'Thank you for warning me.'

While we awaited her next approach I made a show of flexing my thumb and forefinger – we looked at one another seriously.

She arrived. Oliver asked for the bill.

'Now?' I asked.

'When she brings the change,' he said.

She came back with the change.

'Now?'

'When else, for heaven's sake?'

'Right!' – and my hand was already touching the black material of her skirt when Oliver cried out. *'Don't!'* The waitress went away unpinched, all smiling affability and buxom sprightliness.

'Coward,' I said.

He answered: 'I really think you'd have done it!'

'Of course I would have done it.'

'You're dangerous,' he stated, in a tone that seemed to fall midway between amusement and awe.

The next night we had our dinner with Marnie Stark. She wasn't at all what I'd expected. Far from being the fashionable dresser I'd have thought Oliver only associated with, she was a woman of about fifty who had let her figure run to seed and who slopped about in a down-at-heel pair of Dr Scholl's sandals and a smock covered in dog's hairs. Furthermore, she had a coarse laugh and the kind of forthright manner which would have seemed more at home in a smoke-filled London pub than among the tamarisk trees and hydrangeas of a modish French resort. Yet at the same time she gave off a sort of unforced sexuality I had never come across and which – in small doses! – was warm and earthy and endearing.

Although her villa seemed far from small, she still had to push magazines and newspapers off one chair and a Pekinese off another before she could accommodate us in her living room. 'Servant problems,' she said.

'What nonsense,' answered Oliver, 'I've never known you any different! And certainly shouldn't like it half so much if I did. Have you still the same cook?'

'Of course.'

'That's all that matters, then. And your martinis are just what they always were. Enough said.'

'So this is the new boyfriend?' observed Mrs Stark. 'You were so bloody cagy on the phone I knew he must be special.'

Oliver pulled a face at me. 'I deliberately didn't warn you about Marnie.'

'Just as well,' I said.

'I hear you want to be a writer,' she remarked. 'What sort of thing do you hope to write?'

'At the moment I'm working on a love story.'

'Between men?'

I was surprised. It hadn't occurred to me there could be homosexual love stories.

We talked about writing for the next half-hour. Although I afterwards told Oliver I had found it enlightening, I was glad he didn't press me to explain how. She several times used the words 'obsession' and 'persistence' – apparently she had completed ten novels before at long last having one published – and counselled me to write solely of the things I knew. (Oh dear. In 'Where Two Roads Meet' the plot not only hinged on a kidnapping, half the book was set in Hollywood!) I disagreed with much of what she said – also found it discouraging. But for Oliver's sake I remained humble and was able to hold my tongue. Annoyingly, it turned out I needn't have read either of her novellas (which I hadn't especially liked – although, again, I had hidden this from Oliver). Yet I managed to praise them convincingly and I wasn't called upon to give examples. Thank God.

After that, we had dinner. As we ate she inquired whether we had known each other long. Long enough, said Oliver, to be very sure we went together well. Then I asked when and where *they* had met. Marnie Stark gave one of her noisy laughs. 'Oh, you tell him, Oliver.'

'About fifteen years ago, at some particularly hideous party. People kept jumping into the pool fully clothed. Mamie's current beau had just left her. She spent most of the next few days crying on my shoulder.'

'And we've been crying on each other's shoulders,' she asserted, 'ever since. *Misfits Anonymous*! Oh, it's pathetic. The eternal quest for love!'

Then she stopped looking tragic and took another forkful of paella.

'You see, Oliver would do anything – absolutely anything – to help out a pal! He was sane, wholly non-judgmental, endlessly encouraging! Restful, too: you realized *he* would never make demands. So whenever one of my little amours was exploding into tiny pieces – probably about once a week! – I knew I could run straight to Oliver for sanctuary.'

This meant apparently – as Oliver told me on the way home – that Marnie Stark had often been attracted to the kind of man who rapidly grew violent. Divorced from a husband who had frequently beaten her, this hadn't taught her to avoid other such combustible relationships. 'What's the feminine form of Icarus?' I asked. He looked at me and nodded.

Now she patted his arm lovingly.

'And, of course, it wasn't all one-way, pet? I used to make *you* look respectable. When all the pure young things – and their mothers! – were chasing one of London's most eligible bachelors, you could always suggest you were helplessly in love with yours truly. Fifteen years ago,' she turned her head briefly towards myself, 'I was at least three stone lighter and could even appear glamorous. So the debutantes sighed and went off searching somewhere else. Now that I'm no longer in Blighty I don't doubt there are other equally knowing ladies who are happy to fill in for you, Ollie – at all those dinners and parties and functions.'

'Not,' he said, 'that one wants to be overly hypocritical about these things.'

'Maybe not, love. But if you go to prison it really needs to be for something worthwhile. And take it from me: no man's worth going to prison for!'

She gave her usual grating laugh. It was starting to irritate me.

'No man,' I said, 'nor woman either.'

'Ah, there speaks the voice of youth,' lamented Oliver. 'Just wait until you've experienced it, my lad: the feeling that somebody's actually worth dying for – let alone serving time for!'

I took exception.

'As happens so often, I'm not sure if you're being serious or not. But, in any case, it's hardly only the voice of youth that speaks. A couple of seconds ago Mrs Stark made precisely the same comment.'

'I shall always treasure that little gallantry,' murmured Marnie Stark.

I smiled. 'I didn't mean to imply that yours was the voice of the Ancient Mariner. Just of maturity and wisdom. And surely you'd rather be the spokeswoman for maturity and wisdom than for callow adolescence? Come on – admit it.'

She winked at Oliver. 'I must say he extricates himself with aplomb. *I* have so little finesse it makes me appreciative when I meet it in others. It's quite a charmer you've got there.'

'Yes, he's not bad, is he? I mean. . .for a callow adolescent.'

I said: 'Did your parents never tell either of you that it's rude to discuss somebody in the third person as though he weren't present?'

'Ollie, I have but one piece of advice,' continued Mamie Stark, paying no attention to this interruption. 'Just you make the most of your young Johnny Rarebird there before he flits away. There'll be plenty of others in pursuit of that honeypot.'

It was a strange thing to say, even a hurtful one, and her tone sounded only mildly humorous. But we were in the midst of a good meal, we'd already drunk lots of wine and it was easy to laugh and pretend it was merely a joke which had misfired. And, on reflection, I decided that's exactly what it was. She must have known Oliver would scarcely thank her for a warning and that my own possible resentment of it could easily make trouble. Everyone said things on occasion which came out sounding wrong.

Yet nonetheless I was prompted to reach round the table and momentarily take Oliver's hand. I was suddenly conscious of a strong upsurge of affection for him – a wish to look after him and make him happy.

I didn't know if Mrs Stark had noticed this movement. I hoped not. It wasn't meant for show.

8

We went to San Sebastian. We drove to the top of a high hill and looked down over a natural harbour which made me think of South America. I felt gratified when Oliver said yes it was like a miniature of the view one enjoyed at Rio de Janeiro. But I eventually realized he was lingering some six feet behind me – behind me and of course the parapet – and for a moment I forgot all the splendours of the panorama. 'Oliver, you're not scared of heights, are you? No! That's absurd. You can't be.'

He smiled. 'Oh, damn you – yes, I can be. I hoped you wouldn't notice. I suppose I might have known.'

'But that isn't logical. You were a pilot in the Battle of Britain.'

'I agree. It *isn't* logical. Yet being inside a plane gives you a sense of protection from the drop. As being inside a car does, driving on a mountain road.'

'And here you have a good strong wall which reaches to your waist.'

'I assure you that it's not the same.'

'Poor Oliver. I don't understand it, but I'm sure it must be awful.'

He shrugged. 'Oh, it's liveable with. I've never had the least desire to be a window-cleaner or a steeplejack. It does mean that, if I walk across the Thames, I inevitably feel I'm being pulled towards the parapet – and it also means I don't much care for platforms on the London Underground. But as I haven't walked across the Thames since childhood, and as it must be at least five years since I travelled anywhere by tube, you can see these problems aren't exactly insurmountable.'

'Yet it seems so silly. Why don't you just come here a moment? I'd hold on to you, I promise you I would!'

But he only shook his head. 'No thank you. Even with an inducement of that sort, I think I'll remain where I am.'

I certainly didn't believe people should give in to their phobias but I didn't press it and a minute or so later – after a bit of clowning to do with the wall beginning to crumble and the commencement of a landslide – we returned to the car.

We drove for a while, then had some tea and looked at the shops. When it grew dark I was surprised by two other things: first, by the dingy quality of the lighting, even in the busy centre of a town where the shops were all excessively smart – Oliver said the dimness reminded him of post-war London – and, later on, by the numbers still out on the streets at nine o'clock, ten o'clock, beyond: the liveliness, the gaiety, the air of relaxation, even of carnival: the crowded taverns, the children chasing round the squares (many in grotesque animal masks) – above all, by the good-natured tolerance of their elders.

Folkestone High Street had never been like this! Nor yet Gloucester Place. It was exhilarating.

Exhilarating also was the ride back to Biarritz; or some of it, anyway. Because, that night, we became involved in the smuggling trade.

Drink was so incredibly cheap in Spain. During the afternoon we had concealed in various parts of the car some Benedictine, Cointreau, Marie Brizard, sherry, Armagnac ('You see?' said Oliver. 'You can never say I don't remember!') and two bottles of Rémy Martin; in short, a little more than our allowance. And that still left us with two bottles apiece for which there wasn't any hiding place.

As we drew closer to the frontier Oliver suggested we tuck these inside our coats, clamped against our sides. 'But for heaven's sake,' he smiled, 'if we're made to get out of the car don't forget they're there!'

'Do you think we *shall* be made to?'

'Always possible.'

'Christ.' As we approached the barrier I could feel my heart thumping and my upper lip beginning to sweat. Despite the fact that I wasn't alone.

He said, 'Don't worry too much. It's not important.' He laid a hand briefly on my knee – his bottles seemed scarcely to impede him.

'Who's worried?' I asked. 'This is fun.'

He glanced at me.

'Or perhaps we ought to declare them all?' He brought the car to a gradual halt.

'No!'

I almost shouted the word. His tone had held no trace of 'Chicken!' yet from the strength of my reaction the accusation could certainly have been implicit.

'No,' I said, more quietly. 'Please don't. You mustn't. This *is* fun.'

'Okay.'

The first part of our inspection made total nonsense of that little drama. The Spanish customs official, without coming out of his box, gave a shrug and waved us through.

'It's a fairly cold night,' said Oliver, as we drove on a short distance, 'and that might well be our salvation.'

But the French were possibly a hardier breed. A large-nosed man with a moustache regarded us first from his little window and then indicated that he was coming out to speak to us. 'Perhaps he doesn't consider we have honest faces,' whispered Oliver, with a smile, in the brief period we had to wait. 'What a frog! *What* impertinence! But never mind. Hold on to your bottles, remember you're British, and say a couple of Hail Marys – to the mother we're now quite eager to get back to! Besides, think what a good story it'll one day make.' I didn't know if he meant around the dinner table or between the covers of a book.

As the *douanier* came towards us we saw he was a short man – 'a miniature de Gaulle,' I thought. I didn't follow everything he said but after about a minute he asked us to get out of the car and from the looks of him he meant to stick to procedure. The vehicle would be searched; we would be frisked. I felt practically clammy with apprehension. The telephone that suddenly rang inside the office seemed like the bell that called the contestants out of their corners: us, in the role of knock-kneed little Charlie; *him*, the swaggering bearlike champ. I reached out to open the door – already not a simple movement, with one's elbows not allowed to leave one's sides – and thought how ironic we should so recently have been talking about prison. (Though at least we'd be together; they surely wouldn't split us up!) At the same time a colleague inside the office, holding up the phone receiver, spoke urgently to de Gaulle through the window hatch. . . whereupon our fellow abruptly appeared to lose interest in us and waved us on with a quick, imperious gesture. It was nearly enough to make me think our Hail Marys had worked; or, rather, the mere mention of our saying some. Oliver drove off swiftly and we neither of us said a word for at least thirty seconds. We both removed our bottles in silence. Then finally he looked at me and gave his forehead an exaggerated wipe with the back of his hand. 'Phew!' he said. 'How do you feel, Dr Syn?'

'Oh, thoroughly cock-a-hoop – now,' I assured him.

'Well, don't be *too* cock-a-hoop,' he warned. 'They could yet come after us. They have the right to do so while we're still within a reasonable distance of the border.'

'But is it likely?' I half expected wailing police sirens, a squad of armoured cars. I looked to him for reassurance.

'No. Nothing would surprise me more.' Then he laughed. 'I don't feel either of us was cut out for this life of crime.'

'It seems not. Solid citizens – that's us. Respectable and law-abiding.'

'Well,' he answered, doubtfully. 'As Professor Joad might have said, it depends on what you mean by law-abiding.

But I'll tell you one thing. I vote that when we return to England we declare it.'

'All of it?'

He nodded.

'Well,' I said, 'if not actually all of it. . . definitely most?'

'Some?' he suggested.

'A bottle or two.'

'You mean, if we have to?'

All this reminded me of Jane Austen: was it 'Persuasion'? 'Oliver, I'm sorry that I was such a scaredy-cat.'

Again, he put his hand on my knee, though only for an instant. 'In fact, I found it quite endearing.'

'One learns about oneself.'

'With any luck.'

But I felt uncomfortable – remembering his mother saying that *he* had never learned. I remarked quickly: 'Oh, I think it must be something similar to childbirth!'

'You do?'

'Well, they claim that if a woman didn't forget what *that* was like she'd never agree to have a second baby.'

'And Nature gave the same merciful dispensation to liquor smugglers? That was certainly thoughtful of her. You,' he said, 'are most obviously pregnant again.'

'Yes – and blooming with it!' A minute or so later I was singing as lustily as if I'd been in the midst of my morning ablutions.

'My goodness,' he exclaimed. 'A touch of the Charles Coborns, too! Is there no end to your accomplishments?'

'None whatever. But why Charles Coburn?' I thought he meant the American film actor.

'Well, wasn't he the man who made that song famous?'

'Was he? Still, I'd rather have a touch of the Howard Keels. But it's true: I really do feel as if I'd just broken the bank at Monte Carlo!'

'I'm glad. So do I.'

As we drove on, he began to sing as well – we made a harmonious team! We sang for the rest of the way back to Biarritz and featured songs far more contemporary than the one I had begun with.

'Oh, she wears red feathers and a hula-hula skirt. . .'

'Open the door, Richard!. . .'

'She was afraid to go in to the water. . .'

It was quite a revelation to hear him give expression to such models of esoteric sophistication. I wondered how his mum would feel if she could see him now.

Happy. . . may be?

9

Our only proper row had to do with my flat. Oliver wanted me to give it up but I saw it as a symbol of my independence: something I could proudly point to as my own, wholly and utterly my own, not a by-product of Oliver's generosity or of anybody else's (other than for the small bequest made to me by my father): a refuge I could always retire to when I felt the need to reassert my own personality or – more accurately, perhaps – rediscover it.

It was a Friday morning and, unusually, neither of us was working. We'd been lounging around with the papers when – apparently apropos of nothing – Oliver had brought up the subject. 'But supposing we were to separate?' I asked.

'We won't.'

'Supposing?'

'Good God! I thought you said you loved me.'

'Well?'

And I had said it, too: on the evening we had seen 'Nabucco'. The opera was interminable. My only interest had been in the splendour of the opera-house, the novelty of the opening scenes, and the rousing quality of 'The Slaves' Chorus' –

otherwise, I had felt bored. And what had made it especially difficult, afterwards, to keep up the pretence of having had a good time was my discovery that actually Oliver was none too keen on this particular work and had only booked for it because there was nothing else available. But he didn't admit this until considerably later, when we were sitting over dinner in a small out-of-the-way restaurant; and, as with our very first encounter, I knew he would think less of me if I retracted. . .or, anyway, never again be sure he could trust my initially expressed verdict. Besides, on this occasion, it would seriously have diminished the gratification my lie had given him – entirely defeating, of course, much of the original motivation of that lie. (I had also not wanted him to think I could appreciate only American musicals.)

'So this evening,' I had teased him, 'was all in the nature of a noble sacrifice?'

'Not at all. It gives me enormous satisfaction to introduce you to new pleasures.'

'Brings a touch of freshness into an otherwise totally sated existence?'

'Precisely.'

He smiled at me and I didn't know what it was: it could have been his habitual niceness or the attractiveness of his smile (which invariably made him look so handsome), it could have been the ease and contentment I always experienced in his company. But I said something which I'd had no intention of saying and which had somehow been surprised out of me by the sheer enjoyment of the moment. I said: 'I love you, Oliver.' And the instant I'd done so I fervently wished I hadn't.

He stared at me for several seconds. Then:

'My God,' he exclaimed softly. 'Am I imagining things?'

Well, what could you reply to that? I felt trapped – committed – helpless. The look in his eyes was nearly enough to light the restaurant. He said, 'Naturally you're aware of how I feel about *you* – and have done almost from that very first weekend? But somehow I couldn't believe...'

'Why not?' After all, I had to say something.

But he didn't tell me. 'No. It doesn't matter. I think I must be the happiest man on earth at this moment.'

He said now, in the sitting room at the Embankment:

'Well, if you love me there's no reason why we shouldn't be happy together for the rest of our lives. Other people seem to manage it.'

I should have liked to ask how many of those were unmarried.

I should have liked to remind him that he was twenty years older than me.

I should have liked to say that I didn't believe I was homosexual. Nor regard our liaison as anything but the very pleasantest of prologues to my one day getting married and having children. You had to be realistic. In the past I had often wondered about the type of girl whom I would fall in love with. It seemed to me odd that at the moment I should know absolutely nothing about her: what she was doing, whether she was presently in London – even in England – whether she felt contented with her situation or alone and faced with overriding problems. I didn't like to think of her as unhappy. Later she'd be the most important person in my life.

But, clearly, I couldn't say *any* of these things. I shrugged.

'And what does that mean?' he asked.

I gave no answer.

'Look,' he said. 'I didn't think the young were supposed to care that much about security. But I make you a promise. Here and now. If ever we do split up I'll see to it that you're not left homeless.'

'Oh, that's nice. You think, then, if we do split up, I'll be in the right frame of mind to accept your charity? You know, other people besides you – though I realize this may come as something of a shock, I'm glad you're sitting down! – other people besides you may sometimes have their pride.'

'Ah, really? There – I must admit – you do surprise me.'

'And what does that mean, exactly?'

'That means, exactly. . .' He gazed at me for a moment but then his expression softened. 'Do you realize you've just stolen one of my lines?'

He must have seen my perplexity. He enlightened me.

'I said 'And what does that mean?' about half a minute before you did.'

'Oh, is that so? I'm afraid I don't keep check. And I suppose you feel you own the copyright?'

Then his expression softened still more: he actually smiled. 'Regarding copyright? Did you ever hear what Groucho Marx said to the Warner Brothers?'

I had thought about Groucho Marx while I'd been talking to his mother (though how often, in the normal way, did I think about Groucho Marx?) and the fact that he should now reappear like this was perhaps a feeble attempt on the part of providence to remind me of life's basic absurdity.

But I was hardly in the proper mood to speculate on life's basic absurdity, or on the meaning of trifling coincidence – and, after all, although it didn't feel like it, that *had* been several weeks before.

'Oliver, I do wish you wouldn't try to change the subject! I want to know –'

'Apparently Warner Brothers were threatening to go to law over 'A Night in Casablanca', claiming that it parodied their own title. Would you believe it? They actually hoped to copyright a *place-name*!'

'Oliver, can't you please, *please,* stick to the point?'

'Well, there was a meeting between Groucho and Jack Warner. It seems that Groucho chewed on his cigar a bit. 'And talking of copyright, Jack, isn't there one word you yourselves make pretty free with?'

"Yeah? What's that?'

"Moreover, we've consulted lawyers – Chico, Harpo, Zeppo and I – and been advised we have grounds for a counterclaim. Pretty foolproof grounds, too!'

"Jeepers! What fucking word you talking about?'

'Groucho looked at him pityingly for a while. 'And you don't even know! In law that wouldn't be any excuse, but personally I feel inclined to take pity on you. I'd better write it down so you can practise not saying it."

I supposed that, like Oliver's mother, I couldn't bear to have anything left unfinished – whether arguments or anecdotes. 'So what *was* the fucking word?' Apart from the adjective, I felt I was humouring a child, although my tone remained sullen.

Oliver laughed – and practically with a child's own glee in the presentation of a punch line.

'Brothers!' he said.

I hadn't meant to register amusement. But the story was new to me and his impersonations were good. Possibly more than that, his persistence was virtually irresistible. I had to smile.

'I do wish you wouldn't try to change the subject,' I repeated, if only for the look of it – the sullenness was largely gone.

Oliver shook his head, sadly. 'That's bad,' he said. 'Quoting me seemed to offer up hope – an indication of good taste and humility and a readiness to learn. Quoting yourself can only be seen as a sign of falling standards.'

I sighed. I wasn't proof against such determination.

'Oliver, why must you be so bloody nice all the time? Queers have a reputation for being bitchy. Can't you occasionally live up to it?'

'I always think I do rather well on that particular front.' He added abruptly: 'You don't really see it as charity, do you?'

'Huh! Charity, indeed! I work damn hard for every penny. I warn you, I soon mean to put in for a rise.'

He laughed.

'In any case,' I said, 'I was using the future tense. Pity, if your own hold on grammar is so slippery you failed to notice!'

'I love you,' he said.

'And I love you too.' Unsurprisingly, it grew easier every time.

'I'm sorry you think I squash your personality.'

'Is that what I said?'

'Something of the sort.'

'Well, you must know by now I usually speak first, think afterwards – no one's supposed to examine the things I come out with. Also, you must know by now, I have a totally unsquashable personality.'

He appeared satisfied.

'And listen,' I added. 'About the flat. I'll think about it. I really will. It's just that. . .well, you know how much it means to me. . .'

'Yes,' he said. 'Apparently more than I do.'

It was incredible! Incomprehensible! (*Nearly* so, at any rate.) All that patient cajolery, all that striving after harmony – and then what? 'I love you' followed at once by such a neurotic need for permanence that peacemaker became warmonger. Part of me could sympathize; part of me felt riled.

'Oh, for crying out loud! Is it the expense or something? Have you suddenly gone mean? Shall I see to the rent out of my own money?'

'What money? That charity you spoke of?'

'I told you, I don't see it as charity. I reckon I earn every penny!'

'So you're saying, then, it's really *such* hard work to come to bed with me each night?'

'Oh, Oliver! For fuck's sake!'

'Well?'

'I was referring to the modelling. You know damned well I was. Is it charity or isn't it charity? Do please make up your mind, and then I'll try to act accordingly!'

Unable to remain seated any longer I began restlessly to pace.

'And anyhow. . . those contacts which you mentioned? I think you spoke about an escort agency. Why can't I pay the rent out of the salary I'd get working for that?'

He, too, got up. I thought he was about to leave the room. 'If you really believe I'd allow you any more to take on *that* kind of a job –'

'My, my! Possessive, aren't we?'

'Don't be so camp! It doesn't suit you!'

We stood there glaring at one another.

It felt like at least a minute. Probably it wasn't fifteen seconds.

Oliver was standing near the mantelpiece. Suddenly he turned and gave a vicious kick to one of the burning logs.

And then it was just as if – through his well-polished toecap – all the tension drained out of him and went flying up the chimney in a shower of sparks.

'My dear sweet idiot, I hope you know it's not a question of the money.'

'What's more,' I said, 'I don't like James!'

To say the least, this statement was a non sequitur. Such a non sequitur, indeed, that after an instant of utter stupefaction we started to laugh. We grew practically hysterical. We laughed so much it hurt and by the time we collapsed together on the sofa we were gasping for breath.

It was impossible to argue after that.

10

Then we made love but really nothing was resolved. For the rest of the morning we kept carefully away from anything which might prove controversial – in fact, Oliver stayed in bed, while I, following a nap and another shower and two large cups of black coffee, went back to the sitting room and tried to get on with some writing. We had lunch and it was fine; but we remained careful. Towards three I decided to go to the gym for an extra workout. I had a pretty gruelling one, which meant ending up in even more of a sweat than usual. Yet after some thirty lengths of the pool I felt reinvigorated and if Oliver had been at home when I returned I'd have gone straight to him and put my arms around him and apologized. I might even have promised to give up the flat. But frustratingly he'd left a note telling me he was having tea with Rachel Millwood. So I lounged in front of the TV and half-watched children's programmes, flipped through the *Standard*, drank a couple of gins – and then changed for my dinner at the Savoy. Elizabeth had phoned the previous evening.

Oliver, who liked the Sheldons less than I did, had pleaded an engagement but on my giving him a languid nod had said he felt sure that I was free. He would make certain I received the message.

And the evening turned out pleasantly. Mr and Mrs Sheldon still weren't loquacious but they were easily amused and Elizabeth was lively. We spoke at first about their odyssey through Britain and their enjoyable if largely unsuccessful attempts to trace their forebears; and afterwards, although I hadn't originally been going to mention it, I told them of my trip abroad with Oliver and gave them a spirited account of our brush with the French authorities. As they too would shortly be visiting France and Spain, they declared they would be careful at all costs to avoid Customs Officer de Gaulle.

'Did you say you'd be going in just a couple of days?' I asked.

Mrs Sheldon nodded and then commenced to talk – for her, quite volubly. Paradoxically, when this occurred, I felt at something of a disadvantage – for I was never strong on geography and her recital of all the places they'd be seeing left me with so little to say that my mind began to wander. I started by thinking how entertainingly Oliver could have chatted about each town on their itinerary, even if he hadn't been to it, and then went on to wonder where and with whom he was spending the evening (he had mentioned only tea with Mrs Millwood) or whether he might be spending it alone – and, if so, whether he was perhaps feeling a bit under the weather on account of what had happened earlier; and I suddenly thought how pleased I'd be if by some piece of magic he were now to appear in the doorway of the grillroom, wave and walk across. This brought me up with a little start of surprise: it was the first time I had consciously missed him. But also – and very fortunately – it alerted me to the end of Mrs Sheldon's recital. She said: 'Then we come back here for two last weeks before leaving for the States on the twenty-fifth of March.'

'My word, but what a tour you're having! The trip of a lifetime!' I was afraid I might have put too much emphasis on it, in sheer relief they hadn't caught me napping.

When the evening ended, Elizabeth and her father came to put me in a taxi and Elizabeth said quietly, while her father was joking with the doorman, 'You wouldn't mind, would you, if I wrote to you while we're away?'

'Why should I mind? I'd be delighted. And maybe if you have the time I'll be able to see you when you come back?'

'Oh, I'll certainly make the time,' she said. 'And, by the way, I call it really exciting about your book. I do admire your courage.'

No need to disabuse her. As the taxi drew away and I twisted round and waved before we turned into the Strand (and before I gave the cabby his new destination) Mr Sheldon was already engaged once more in hearty, democratic discussion with the doorman; but Elizabeth was still standing there, hopefully, hand upraised. I felt a sudden pang of something – *for* something – although I wasn't quite sure what. The sensation quickly passed, however. I settled back into the comfort of the cab.

Oliver was in bed when I got to the Embankment. It was after midnight but even so this was unusual. He was reading, though, and not pretending to be asleep, which I'd feared might be the case.

'Hello,' he said. 'Had a good time?'

I was so thankful he wasn't brooding that I bound, fully clothed, onto the bed and gave him a big hug. 'Not bad,' I answered, 'but I'm glad to be back.'

'I'm glad to have you back.'

'I've missed you this evening.'

'Get on with you! You've had the gamin-faced Elizabeth to bill and coo with.'

'Yes, that's definitely the right word, isn't it? Gamin-faced. At first I thought her plain.'

He didn't answer. We lay there in contented silence.

'Shall I let you in to a secret?' I asked, eventually. 'I came back from the gym this afternoon just *itching* to see you. I was prepared to make all sorts of concessions, too. Now you'll never know what you missed.'

Somehow, he managed to bear up. 'Rachel sends her love. Hopes to see you soon. I told her we'd fix something up during the next week or two.'

'Yes. She's nice. Did you stay with her after tea?'

'No. She was getting too exuberant; talking about phoning friends and having cocktails. So I hurried off to a theatre.'

'I hope it was something suitably gloomy.'

'It was. 'Ghosts', at the Old Vic. Gloomy but absorbing: absolutely what I needed.'

'And I suppose you never gave me a thought from start to finish?'

'Flora Robson is one of the most riveting actresses I know.'

I knelt up and swiped him across the shoulder with one of my pillows. 'Now I'm tempted not to make my great renunciation.'

'You don't need to make your great renunciation. There's one little point we've overlooked. You signed a tenancy agreement; you're committed till the end of August.'

I really had forgotten.

'And even apart from that,' said Oliver, 'I suppose a fellow must have his odd occasional whim.'

I felt touched. My eyes glazed over and he must have seen it.

'Idiot! Perhaps *you* should be committed until the end of August.'

'I'll tell you what,' I said. 'Why don't we look upon it simply as my pied-à-terre? And this will be my country seat. Naturally I intend to pass most of my time in the country.'

'Good. But why don't you stop talking rot and come to bed? Those fine new evening clothes must be getting fairly rumpled. Old Davidson would throw a fit.'

'Oh, never mind that,' I said airily. I had lain down again with my head now resting on his chest. 'James can press them in the morning.'

There was a pause. Oliver continued stroking my hair. But I knew what he was going to say.

'Why don't you like James?'

'Well, at least in part, because *he* doesn't like *me*.'

'How can you tell?'

'Darling, are you joking?' I nearly sat up again but felt too comfortable. 'It oozes out of every pore. I think he's probably in love with you himself.'

'What nonsense. In any case I shan't get rid of him. Not even to please you.'

'Now, have I *asked* you to get rid of him? I assure you – the last thing I'd want on my conscience!'

'Fine.'

'But all the same. . .I think he's the wicked housekeeper in 'Rebecca'. And only very thinly disguised at that.'

'Mrs Danvers went up in smoke, as I remember.'

'There you are. Her reincarnation.'

'You're a reincarnation!' said Oliver, laughing. 'And when are you going to come to bed?'

'I'm too sleepy. And far too happy as I am. Of whom, anyway?'

'Of whom what, anyway?'

'Am I a reincarnation?'

'Why – naturally! – of your illustrious namesake from the court of King Charles.'

I gave a groan.

'Oh, no! Not him! There was this history man at school. He thought he was a wit. 'Being difficult again, Wilmot? You'll grow as evil as *he* was, mark my words."

'Evil?'

'That's what he said.'

'I'll tell you what somebody else said. 'I know he is a devil but he has something of the angel yet undefaced in him."

'Pardon?' I sat up again and looked at him. Absently removed a hair from my mouth.

'Well, that's the way Etherege described him in one of his plays.'

'And you can reel it off just like that?'

'Are you impressed?'

'Tremendously. I really am.' I continued to gaze at him. He was now propped up against the pillows. 'But you impress me all the time. From the moment you set me right regarding Epicurus. I thought, 'Crikey – an intellectual!' And from then on there's hardly been a day when I haven't been impressed by something that you've said. In anybody else, I'd think this might be frightening but in you it isn't frightening in the least.'

I added: 'Or been impressed by something that you've done. Yet that's a little different.'

'And to think I could have quarrelled with you even for an instant!' He reached out with both arms and pulled me down again. 'But I'd better tell you the truth. My parents couldn't afford to give me the whole encyclopaedia: I only had the volume D to F. Epicurus – Etherege – even Mrs Danvers. For heaven's sake don't ask me about Xenophon.'

'Oh, you poor thing. It must have been the cost of all those tutors!'

At length, reluctantly, I drew away and started to undress.

'Oliver?'

'Yes?'

'Seriously. Do you suppose that without believing in God one can believe in reincarnation?'

'I know Buddhists do. But, I have to confess, I'm not sure how they manage it.'

'Pity.'

'Unless one could say it's a question of nothing in nature ever getting completely lost; merely changing its form. No wastage of energy or matter.'

'Go on,' I invited, dubiously.

'Well, why should life – whether human or animal – be the only thing which comes to an end, the only manifestation of energy for all time done away with?' He paused. 'It's odd when you come to think of it: nature being so profligate with all those thousands of good ready-made personalities which she tosses away daily, when in some way she keeps on using every other molecule on earth. You'd imagine, wouldn't you, that minds and souls would be recycled automatically, along with everything else? The Law of the Conservation of Matter. Are you impressed again?'

I threw my shirt at him – and went to pee and clean my teeth.

'Honestly,' he said, when I came back, 'there are times when I even impress myself. Ten minutes ago I had no ideas whatever on reincarnation or the continuation of mind and soul. Now I find I could almost be convinced by my own immensely cogent argument.'

His tone was flippant but I sensed that, underneath, he was quite serious. Yet I was now too tired for my interest not to have dwindled. The Law of the Conservation of Matter couldn't make much impact – chez moi – at five-past-one in the morning.

He said: 'So, mark you well, my love. Assuming I die some twenty years before you, I may be keeping an eye on everything you get up to during those final twenty years of yours! Continuously at your side.'

'God, that sounds threatening! I don't know about rational, or logical, but most certainly threatening.'

'Oh, the sadness of it! It was supposed to sound comforting! I only meant I'd be watching out for you – watching *over* you – not spying or anything.'

'Well, that's all right, then.'

I got into bed and snuggled up against him. We put our arms around each other and the topic died. Reincarnation, survival of the soul, watchfulness, the whole caboodle. 'I'm glad that you intend to pass most of your time in the country,' he said.

'Mmm. Me, too,' I replied.

11

It was as well I wasn't at liberty to give up the flat. The second Sunday in December I made my weekly phone call to my mother – as usual from a public box. On the following day it was my birthday. 'Clara and I were just saying how much we'd love to be spending it with you.'

'Why don't you, then? The café's closed on Mondays.'

'Oh, darling, don't be silly. *You*'ll have to be at work.'

'Well, as it happens, I've got some time owing. I'll ring them in the morning and ask if I can take it off.'

'Oh, but do you think you should?'

'Give me one good reason why not.'

'Perhaps if they knew it was your birthday. . .?' I could picture her sitting in the hall looking uncertain but willing to be convinced. 'Naturally, I'll have to consult Clara. . . We'd get cheap-day-returns, of course.' Decision reached. 'Could you ring to confirm it before a quarter past nine? Or half past at the latest?'

I met them at Charing Cross and we first had a cup of coffee at Lyons and then took a taxi back to Gloucester Place. My mother was appalled at such extravagance.

But we arrived at the flat and her exclamations of joyous approval were everything they should have been. She went on a tour of inspection before she'd even taken off her coat.

'Oh, what a difference to the way it was! It's become every bit as charming as you said! Darling, you *have* worked hard!'

'Did I say it was charming? I don't remember that.'

She brushed my cheek fleetingly with the back of one gloved hand. 'Not in so many words, perhaps – but you can never hide from a mother how her little boy feels about the things which are important to him.'

My great-aunt also expressed her admiration.

'No, I've never seen anything like it! Norma, I think we can admit it now: weren't we both a little dismayed when we first set eyes on it in August? But tell me – what other boy do you know who could have done all this?'

I said: 'I am nineteen, remember.'

'Oh, you sound as though you think you're very old at nineteen!' declared my aunt. 'Well, listen to this, Master Methuselah. You're not even on the threshold of life! You've hardly been born yet! Ah, my dear, what wouldn't I give to be nineteen again. . .except, possibly, my smart new overcoat?'

I helped her out of that smart new overcoat – which I'd already complimented her on, sincerely, almost as soon as she'd stepped off the train. She was wearing her old but still elegant dove-grey costume, which together with her matching hat and pretty, high-heeled shoes had the usual effect of making my mother, about thirty years younger, appear dowdy by comparison. My mother had the looks; Aunt Clara, the élan. And now, having sat down, my aunt opened her handbag – her equally well-worn handbag – and took out an envelope containing a cheque for three pounds. 'You can use it to start decorating your flat with.' She made a bulge in her left cheek.

'Bless you. How timely! I was planning to begin on it in just a day or so.'

'And I thought the best thing *I* could do,' said my mother, 'was take you to the shops this afternoon. As you know, I'd been meaning to wait until you came to Folkestone but this would be nicer. Oh, I see you've received our cards. When did they arrive?'

That was anybody's guess. I'd not been at the flat for at least a week and since I'd recognized the writing on the envelope I hadn't thought to study the postmark.

'With impeccable timing,' I declared. 'This very morning!'

'Oh, I am pleased. It occurred to me after I'd put the phone down that you hadn't mentioned them. How lucky that I sent them early!'

Before she finally took a seat she looked at the inscriptions on the few other cards I'd put out and she briefly asked a question, or made a comment, concerning each. 'You didn't mind my sticking our two into the one large envelope, did you? It seemed so silly to pay twice the postage when they were coming to the same address.'

'It would have vexed me most terribly if you had.'

'Well, it's all very well to pull my leg, you rascal, but if only you *knew* how much we've spent on sending out Christmas cards – it's really no laughing matter! Already we've received thirty-five, haven't we, Clara. . .half of them from people who probably find it just as tiresome as we do. It's such a foolish practice. We say so every year.'

She went on to explain that they wouldn't be sending *me* a Christmas card unless I'd truly like to have one; and that the assorted boxes from W.H.Smith's were surprisingly good value if I still had many to send out myself – 'although, of course, I've been including your name on most of those *I've* been writing. And I warn you: don't leave everything until the last minute as you generally do. The post really is worse than usual this year.'

When the subject of Christmas cards had been fully exhausted – which wasn't the case for a while yet – and it had also been explained that they'd both forgotten to put in Clara's cheque until my birthday envelope had been licked down and the stamp stuck on (and then my mother had thought I'd be as happy to have the cheque in Folkestone as I would in London) – after all this I gave them a glass of sherry and started putting the lunch together. From a nearby grocer I had bought a lot of their favourite things (and, quite unknown to me, Oliver had sent James out early that morning to buy a quantity of smoked salmon – he had also supplied two bottles of wine) and they repeatedly enthused over all of it. Everything was perfect. 'Except that I'm sure you'll be living on nothing but bread-and-scrape right up till Christmas! You said a *simple* meal. I wouldn't have come if I'd known it was going to put you to so much trouble and expense!'

'More fool you!' exclaimed Aunt Clara. 'I, on the other hand, am seriously considering staying.'

'No, I'm not joking, darling. You really must allow me to contribute.'

'And I'm not joking either, Mother dear. I should be dreadfully insulted if you did – please put away that purse! Now tuck in, enjoy your lunch, and stop being quite so daft.'

However, I didn't produce any of the liqueur we'd smuggled back from Spain. I'd felt that this *might* have been overdoing things.

But I'd bought real coffee. We left the table and settled back in the three more comfortable chairs with our cups and saucers resting on our knees. 'Do you realize something? This is the first time, the very first time in my life, that I've ever done any real entertaining.'

'Is it, darling? Well, I do feel flattered. Don't you, Clara? And, Johnny, do *you* realize something! You never need do it a jot more beautifully than you have today.'

'Yes,' agreed Aunt Clara. 'As to the manner born!'

'Good gracious,' sighed my mother. 'Isn't this an occasion! I shan't want it ever to end.'

'Well, it's scarcely begun,' I told her. 'But what I was really trying to say: it's so very nice to have you both here. A place you haven't yet entertained your family in, no matter how pleasant it may be in every other way, is somehow still missing one key ingredient. It hasn't wholly come to life.'

I was aware this sounded schmaltzy but I meant it. It must have been the mellowness of the after-lunchtime mood – with the gas fire hissing peacefully and the plants outside the window looking green and soft against their white distempered wall and Oliver's good wine – of which, naturally, I'd drunk by far the largest share – being happily absorbed into my system. The world seemed extremely kind and gentle.

'Oh, what a sweet thing to say!' exclaimed my mother. 'You make me want to cry.'

'Well, for heaven's sake, please don't.'

'How old is he?' suddenly inquired Aunt Clara.

'Nineteen,' I said, 'as you perfectly well know! But why?'

'I was just thinking how mature you seem. . .much older than your years. And how lucky, too! What wouldn't I give to be nineteen again! You're hardly yet on the threshold of life. You've hardly yet been born.'

I saw my mother frown. She looked at me significantly but I pretended not to notice. I stood up, ostensibly to refill the coffee cups, yet then I gave a small start of surprise.

'Oh, my goodness! I've forgotten the Cointreau! I thought we'd all like some liqueur.'

'No, no – not another thing!'

I coaxed but they were adamant.

'And when we accompany you to the bankruptcy court,' added Aunt Clara, 'it would hardly do for us to totter.'

'This afternoon? That *would* be fast! I wonder – shall I get time off for good behaviour?'

'Yes, of course. It's your birthday.'

I wiped my forehead, in evident relief, then sat down again.

And fortunately my mother had now remembered something else.

'Your manager didn't mind giving you the day off?'

'No, not a bit.'

'What did he say?'

'He said, 'I don't mind giving you the day off. No, not a bit."

'I mean, you silly chump, when you told him it was your birthday. What did he say then?'

"Many happy returns!"

'But didn't he ask how old you were or what you were planning to do with your day?'

'Nope.'

'That would have been friendly. But at least it was lucky for us you should have had all these hours owing. How did it happen?'

I was prepared for this.

'There's been a lot of stocktaking. I've had to give up my last three Saturday afternoons.'

My mother turned to my aunt.

'Of course! *That's* why Johnny hasn't been able to get home recently! I said there was bound to be a good reason.'

'But, Mum, it's only been a month or so.' I'd gone to Folkestone the weekend following our return from France.

Her remark, though, had been somewhat ill-timed. It made me feel even guiltier than I already did – being mindful of the news which I still needed to impart. 'In any case,' I said, 'I'll be coming home this Friday.'

'This Friday? How lovely! I hadn't expected that.' She did some rapid calculations. 'So, afterwards, only a matter of three days! You'll be travelling down again on the Wednesday evening?'

I then had to explain that I'd be spending Christmas elsewhere. To find the courage, I'd needed to keep remembering how dreary past Christmases had sometimes been at home, how different and exciting this one promised to be in London. But such reminders couldn't stop me feeling wormlike: I knew that neither my mother nor my aunt had ever thought of Christmas as being in the least bit dreary, not so long as I'd been there to help them celebrate. However, I broke the news as gently as I could and hoped to heaven that it wouldn't ruin our day.

'But Johnny. I was counting on your being at home!'

Yet it wasn't half so bad as I'd imagined. My mother rallied. 'Then what will you be doing instead, while we couple of old hens – ?'

'Speak for yourself,' said Aunt Clara. 'You can be whatever you like. *I* admit to being nothing more than a spring chicken!'

'And quite right, too,' I grinned. I was truly aware, at that moment, of how much I loved them.

'I've already ordered the usual-sized turkey,' remarked my mother.

'An old hen, a spring chicken and the usual-sized turkey,' commented Aunt Clara. 'Did you ever hear of such a delicate trio?'

There was a lengthy pause.

'I have these friends, you see, and it's not for a single instant that I place any of them above yourselves –'

'But one of them at least happens to be a little younger and a little prettier than we are?' Aunt Clara patted the back of her well-coiffed head, in which there wasn't even a glimpse of grey. 'Hard though that is to imagine.'

I smiled but didn't say anything.

'Younger and prettier than your mother is, anyway. Norma, my dear, didn't I always say he'd leave a trail of broken hearts?'

'Is there anyone in particular?' asked my mother. 'Darling, you would tell us?'

'No one in particular,' I said.

'You won't go and do anything silly now, will you? Remember, the very last thing you'd want – at your age – is to be tied down.'

'You're telling me!'

'Isn't it ridiculous? I feel I want to cry again. It seems only yesterday you were my little boy.'

But then – it struck me as a miracle – she suddenly cheered up.

'Yes, only yesterday! Do you remember how we used to go to the cinema on Saturday afternoons? Your father didn't like the pictures. We always went to Fuller's for tea, then caught the four o'clock performance. *I* was your girlfriend then.'

"Kind Hearts and Coronets," I said. 'I saw it again quite recently.'

"Miranda," she answered.

'Was that the one about the mermaid?'

"Spring in Park Lane'!'

'Oh, not that thing which –' I suddenly jumped up; I put my hand to my heart. "The moment I saw you, I heard a skylark sing. . ."

'Fancy your remembering that!' My mother also jumped up, in evident delight. "November was April, and down the street came spring. . .' They danced to it on the balcony; I can see it clearly. Here. Pretend you're Michael Wilding.'

'Oh, spoilsport! I wanted to be Anna Neagle.'

Twenty seconds later we were giggling like children, too helpless to continue in our waltz. Aunt Clara watched us indulgently. 'Sometimes I think I'm the only sane person in a crazy world. Besides, Norma, you weren't his only girlfriend. What about 'Peter Pan'? What about 'Where the Rainbow Ends'? What about 'Goody Two Shoes'? Eh, Methuselah? Just tell me that!'

'Oh, kid's stuff!' scoffed my mother. She looked pretty and full of sparkle and about ten years younger than she had looked a minute ago.

We sat down amid the remnants of our laughter, and I again held out the box of Bendicks.

'I couldn't! I couldn't! No. We must now go and do the washing up.'

'No, we mustn't. There isn't much. I'll see to it later.' I laughed. 'Oh, God! I'm getting to sound like you!'

'And you could do a lot worse for yourself!' pointed out my aunt, with mock severity.

'What a treat this is – eh, Clara?'

'I can't recall when I last enjoyed anything so much!'

I hoped this wasn't true. During the next couple of seconds, however, I actually thought my mother was setting out to remind her.

'Do you remember,' she asked slowly, 'do you remember how he used to throw his pyjamas out of the window and as often as not they'd catch in the branches of the apple tree? You and I would do everything we could not to be seen laughing but it always made Nickie so *very* cross.'

'Well, he was the one who had to get them down!' Aunt Clara turned to me. 'Oh, you naughty boy! I remember how you found that pathetic fledgling. The way you sobbed all night when the poor thing died.'

'Oh, stop it, *please,*' I cried. 'You're breaking my heart. Both of you.'

'And that other time you just sobbed and sobbed, after no one came to your birthday party.' My mother again. 'We'd invited at least three of your little friends, yet for one reason or another...

But then you seriously thought there was no one in the whole wide world who really liked you.'

'And look at him now – that great strapping lad who's so much in demand he's not even coming home for Christmas.'

'Good gracious, Clara! Can you believe it? Fifteen years ago, to the very day!'

'And then seven years ago – or was it eight? – we weren't either of us very happy, were we, when he had to go off to boarding school for the first time?'

'The first time? *Every* time! We always dreaded the end of the holidays even more than he did!'

It was a lovely afternoon. We went shopping and my mother bought me a stunning crystal bowl. It cost her well over ten pounds – which was at least twice as much as she had spent on me the year before – and I thought this was her crafty way of paying me back for the meal and for the taxi. Although at first I tried to stop her, I eventually gave in.

'Which is what we all knew was going to happen right from the beginning,' observed Aunt Clara, with a moue.

I ignored this, loftily. I kissed my mother on the cheek and said, 'But, of course, this present has to be for Christmas, too, not just today – absolutely the finest I've received in ages!'

Which wasn't quite the case. At breakfast Oliver had given me an engraved Rolex wristwatch. 'With so much love, for all time.' ('Look,' he'd said anxiously, whilst watching my expression, 'somehow, in the shop, that seemed like an amusing notion but now I can't think what possessed me! But every word of it is true.') At first I hadn't been going to wear it immediately, yet then found I couldn't bear not to. Naturally I'd been very careful to keep my cuff down.

Aunt Clara had wanted to take us to tea after we left Selfridge's but everywhere was so crowded we went back to the flat. No sooner arrived, though, than she offered to sally forth again in search of cakes. I set the table and made toast while, after all, my mother did the washing up.

'Tell me, darling, how do you find her?' The question came the moment I had returned from closing the front door.

'Absolutely as normal. In brilliant form.'

'Oh, thank God.'

'Don't you?'

'Yes, I think that maybe – when I wrote you that very gloomy letter – I *was* imagining things. I was a bit run down, possibly. But you did notice, didn't you, how she repeated herself after lunch. I tried to catch your eye.'

'Well, but everyone repeats themselves on occasion. *We* certainly do. I recall this exact conversation when I was last at home. Or, no, not the last time – the one before it.'

'Perhaps we're all growing senile.' She laughed.

'Perhaps we are. But honestly, Mum, I don't think you need worry. I really don't.'

'No, I'm sure you're right. Yet it's such a relief to hear you say so. It's good to have a son like you.' She spread the dishcloth on the drainer and turned around and smiled. 'And try to forget what I said earlier. I'm glad you've found a girlfriend. One of these days – although there's certainly no rush! – I look forward to your providing me with grandchildren. Is she nice?'

'Very! She's a bit like you.'

'Ah,' said my mother. 'Flatterer!'

'Not at all.'

'Mutual admiration society.'

'That's right.'

It was nearly five o'clock. With the curtains drawn and the lamps lit it was even cosier than before. I put on some records: evergreens from the thirties and forties: the sort of thing we all liked. We had tea and toast and then the lemon curd tarts and Eccles cakes which Aunt Clara had picked out at the U.D. Watching them both sitting there, wiping their mouths one last time, in each case an almost reluctant, vaguely wistful gesture, I was suddenly engulfed by an ache of sadness for the pair of them. In a couple of hours or so, while I'd be sitting next to Oliver in a warm theatre, with the prospect of a good dinner in an expensive restaurant still in front of me, followed by a comfortable taxi-ride back to a modern, luxury, double-glazed apartment and a finish to the day which would embrace sex and togetherness and lazy conversation, they, my poor mother and great-aunt, would still be travelling home in a rattly, cheerless train, thinking of that cold walk down from the station, their celebration all behind them. I wondered if there wasn't any way of our soon repeating this outing – on a regular fortnightly basis, maybe. Or monthly at any rate. I pictured my mother filling their hot water bottles, in a sparsely heated house.

'Well, Clara, I suppose... It's been a gorgeous day, my darling. Many, many, *many* happy returns.'

'Yes, for all of us. But don't start to say goodbye here. I'm coming with you to the station.'

As I watched their train moving out across the lighted river, long after it was possible to distinguish any waving hands at windows, I felt a continuation of this melancholy – this empathy with the emptiness of other people's lives – which wasn't altogether unpleasant. I walked back along the platform; and thought that, on the one adjoining, none of the hurrying footsteps, raised voices, door-slamming – jocularity, even – could disguise the air of general dissatisfaction, general disillusion. The only joyous individuals seemed to be those belonging to a group of carol singers in the main body of the station. So while the yearning was still on me to try to do something, however small, to alleviate this emptiness, I crossed the Strand and went into the Civil Service Stores – open late in this pre-festive period. I bought my mother a large bottle of the scent I knew she liked – not simply the toilet water but the actual perfume – and for my aunt I chose a smart leather handbag, into the purse of which, before I should forget, I dropped a sixpence. I paid for these purchases by cheque. I felt intensely happy again – just as I had done when we'd moved away from the lunch table with our cups of coffee. Glancing at my new watch I saw I had only four minutes in which to cross Trafalgar Square and reach Her Majesty's – we'd arranged to meet in the foyer by seven, to have a drink at the downstairs bar. I started to run but decided I didn't want to arrive looking flushed, sounding winded, appearing wholly unsophisticated. Preferable to be late.

Oliver would understand.

Well, come to that, if I'd arrived late *and* flushed *and* winded – *and* swinging my newly acquired carrier bag! – Oliver would still have understood.

The only time, to my knowledge, he had ever been disapproving of me, or downright cross, had been over that question of the flat.

So I began to run. He was probably there already. He always took good care to be punctual.

And it wasn't fair to keep him waiting.

Just because he had a generous nature.

12

We didn't spend Christmas in London, after all. I should have realized – of course I should! We drove down to Surrey on the Wednesday afternoon. This time there were to be no other guests, however, and the notion of being in such daunting proximity to Mrs Cambourne over four whole days – with only Oliver as buffer – certainly didn't fill me with elation: four whole days during which any sign of reclusiveness, let alone enmity, either on her part or mine, would clearly be questioned by her son and cause him a great deal of distress.

No. I made up my mind that I should have to be extremely sweet to her. Whatever the cost.

But I began to think I'd have been better off in Folkestone. Except that, naturally, Oliver wouldn't have been in Folkestone. It was all a bit disappointing.

In the car I felt glum.

'What's the matter?' he inquired. 'Missing James already?'

'Oh, most amusing! Where does *he* spend Christmas?'

'In Shropshire, with his parents. You should have asked.'

Even though I'd at least made the man a small gift, this rebuke was so well justified I preferred not to think about it. 'Don't try to kid me James has parents! You'll tell me next he had a childhood.'

'What *else* is the matter, then?'

'If you must know, I was wondering whether I, too, should have gone home for Christmas.'

'Oh, damn and blast,' he said, 'I was afraid that might be it. Again, I think, I've behaved badly. But I promise you there was a special reason I wanted us to be together – I mean, apart from the obvious one of just liking to be with you.'

'What special reason?'

'Surprise.'

'No – tell me.'

'It's one of my greatest pleasures in life to give people surprises. Surely you wouldn't wish to deprive me of it?'

He was always saying something of that sort – and meaning it, as well.

We arrived at the house much earlier than before.

And Mrs Cambourne could scarcely have been more affable. It was astonishing.

Indeed, by the time she went to bed I was prepared (almost) to admit I might have done her wrong. There was no summons to her room on this occasion, no sad, impassioned tête-à-tête. Such a summons wouldn't have been necessary: more than once Oliver had left us for longish periods and there would have been every opportunity for hostilities to recommence. But instead I received polite inquiries after my mother's health and reminiscences of a holiday in Folkestone when she herself had been a girl. I even wondered if there could have been a veiled apology about her saying to Oliver, *twice,* how extremely well he was looking.

Also, the bedroom I'd been given was the one next to his own; there was even a communicating door. So, all in all, I was glad I had bought her a decent present – although it was mainly with the aim of pleasing Oliver I'd done so.

I'd had much greater difficulty choosing what to get him. At first I'd thought of a signet ring but then he'd unwittingly foiled that by making a disparaging remark to do with men who wore signet rings.

Naturally, he already had a wallet and pen and all the other things a man might carry on him – plus, even, a silver medallion he always wore beneath his shirt or jumper; so I'd been pleased when in the window of an antique jeweller's in the City I'd caught sight of some unusual cufflinks and following discreet inquiry had found he currently possessed only one pair. . .and not a very interesting pair at that. I'd also bought him a box of fudge, a couple of paperbacks, some soap, a tie, handkerchiefs, socks, and five or six other equally small items, each done up in one of three strikingly patterned papers, so as to make a colourful display at the foot of the bed on Christmas morning. I made a special point of staying awake until Oliver was asleep so that I could place them there.

It was worth it. It was a lot of fun, his opening of the presents.

But there wasn't any mention of anything for me.

Some early morning tea arrived. I was sitting in my bathrobe, cross-legged on the end of the bed, more or less where the presents themselves had been. It was fortunate the maid had reached Oliver's room first, because I'd totally – and uncharacteristically – forgotten to rumple the bedclothes in my own.

When we were dressed we went downstairs together. I was a little way ahead and slipped into the dining room an instant before he did. Our breakfast places were laid but there was nothing on the table of the kind I was looking for.

'I say, Oliver – haven't you forgotten something?'

'Forgotten something?' He seemed puzzled. He looked down, made a rapid inventory. 'Jumper, trousers, socks, shoes. . . I can distinctly remember that I brushed my hair. I know I had a good shave. Now what else could there possibly be?'

'You know: festive greetings, compliments of the season, peace on earth and goodwill to all men. . . Something along the lines of 'I wonder what old Eeyore would like this year; there must be *some* little bit of junk lying around which nobody else would ever want. . .''

'Oh, merry, merry Christmas, John! Hadn't I wished you that before?'

'I do so much appreciate my cufflinks – *exactly* what I wanted – how clever of you to guess – and isn't 'reciprocity' a difficult word to say quickly?'

'Yes, it is,' he replied, 'but my mind's quite easy on the question of the cufflinks. You *Know* how much I appreciated them. And every other of your thoughtful gifts.'

There were no sounds in the passageway outside. I went up to him and put my arms about his waist. 'You,' I said, 'Mr Oliver Thornton Cambourne, R.A., are – infuriating! Perfectly infuriating. Do you realize that?'

'And you,' he said, 'Mr John Nicholas Wilmot, G.L., are obviously going gaga.' After a moment he gently pulled away. 'Come on – what you clearly need is a short stroll before breakfast to help you think straight. This way.' And he really did start walking to the front door.

'You should have warned me. I'd have brought my sunhat.'

'That's the trouble with all you Health and Strength aficionados: you want to wrap yourselves in cotton wool. Afraid of a little frost on the lawns or a bracing bite of country air.'

'Ah. Talking about wrapping things. . . And, incidentally, what does G.L. stand for?'

'Greatly Loved,' he called back. He was already striding briskly round the corner of the house. By the time I caught up he was starting to open the doors of the double garage.

'That's the trouble with all you Lazy and Degenerate Layabouts. Your idea of a bit of exercise is simply to get in the car and pull the starter.'

I was joking, of course, but even then I hadn't twigged. Oliver gave me a long sardonic stare. I stood there with my feet apart, my hands on my hips and stared right back at him. 'Well, don't just pretend to be a tree,' he suggested. 'Why don't you do something useful and help me with this door?'

Inside, next to his own car, stood another, which I hadn't seen before.

'Happy Christmas!' he said. 'Compliments of the Season! Peace on earth and goodwill to all men!'

'What?'

'*Now* you see why I didn't put the Jag away when we got here yesterday. That's a Jaguar too, in case you don't yet know about these things. An XK 150. It came out last October. Drophead coupé – that means you can open the roof in fine weather. British Racing Green is all the rage at the moment but if you don't swant green you can have it sprayed whatever colour you'd like.'

I was scarcely listening.

'Oliver! Is that. . .mine?'

'Sorry it's not done up in stunningly attractive paper. I went round all the shops and heard that Mr J Wilmot had hijacked every sheet.'

I started to cry – started actually to cry. 'Oh, you idiot!' he said, and held me for the ten or twenty seconds this ridiculous fit lasted; he wiped my eyes on one of his new handkerchiefs.

I advanced towards the car in a state of numbness. I think it was nearly a surprise when, shyly reaching out to touch it, I felt the smooth metal underneath my fingers. I turned my head to gaze at Oliver. 'Tell me that this isn't a dream.'

'This isn't a dream.'

'And it really is for me?'

He nodded, silently.

'I honestly think,' I said, slowly, 'you must be a saint.'

'Yes, so do I. The trouble is, none of us ever found a more successful incognito.' He handed me the key. 'Now why don't you just try it on for size?'

I followed his suggestion. No driving seat of any other car could ever have felt so completely right.

'Does your mother know?' I asked him at last.

'Naturally.'

'But what did she *say*?'

He answered, 'Didn't you already remark on her enormously changed attitude?'

'Yet even so. She must have made some sort of comment.'

'Yes. "Tell him to be careful!"' He put on an old lady's voice, wildly exaggerated.

I said, 'Entirely what I'd have guessed! I can hear her saying it.' I was now running my hands sensually around the steering wheel. 'Oh – and to think! I only gave you cufflinks.'

'Don't be such a nitwit. I shall still be treasuring those cufflinks long after you've traded this in – for what will by then be the latest model.'

'You're wrong, you know. You really are. I shan't ever – *ever* – want to part with it!'

I may have spoken with greater vehemence than I'd intended. It made him laugh. 'Well, I'm not going to cross swords with you. After all, only time can tell.'

'*I* can tell, too – tell you something that you don't have to wait for. If giving surprises is honestly one of your greatest pleasures in life you must think you've been the happiest man on earth for these past ten minutes.'

I then remembered he'd used a very similar phrase following the opera; but this was scarcely the time to worry about originality.

'Yes, that's so. Except. . .I don't merely think it.'

'How, then, can a man of your intelligence be so oblivious to the competition?'

'All right, then, we'll call it a draw. Which suits me. But now you know why I wanted to have you here for Christmas. Any other time and it mightn't have felt quite the same.'

'I think it would always have felt quite the same. Though, anyway, I wouldn't have wished to be anywhere else this Christmas – not if you weren't there. However, there is one very *minor* snag.'

'No,' he said, 'I'll give you your first driving lesson this morning. And, yes, we do have an L-plate!'

Dear God, he seemed to have thought of everything. He'd taken out a provisional licence. He'd enrolled me for a course of lessons at a driving school. He'd also arranged for someone to drive his own car back to London so as to enable him to drive mine.

'By the way, I had to forge your signature. I didn't think you'd mind.'

Finally we went in to breakfast. Mrs Cambourne was having hers in bed, so I had to wait until our pre-lunch cocktails to double-check her reaction. There was none; at least none discernible. On my first trying to express to her my incredulous delight she serenely replied that, yes, Oliver had thought it was likely to give me pleasure – and then talked about the first car which *he* had ever owned and how much more real enjoyment he'd derived from that than from any other he'd possessed. From there the conversation moved on to what driving was like in the early days of the motor, before the Great War; the charm and beauty of all the veteran cars; the old crocks' rally from London to Brighton; the film 'Genevieve'. End of comment about the two-thousand-pound present her son had made me – and from a woman who had not so long before been on the point of writing me a cheque for that same amount, to entice me out of that same son's life!

Also, she seemed sincerely grateful for the vase I'd chosen. She had a gift for me, too, three long-playing records which almost certainly Oliver would have selected on her behalf: one of Noël Coward in cabaret – another, from the soundtrack of 'Oklahoma!' – and the third, taken from this current London production of *My Fair Lady*.

I was able to reassure her that, up until then, I hadn't owned any of them – but how very pleased I was to realize I now did – and that honestly I'd been meaning to buy myself the third as a souvenir.

She no doubt thought I meant simply as a souvenir of the show. . .and naturally I didn't enlighten her. I should have been surprised if she knew she was commemorating the occasion on which I'd first seen Oliver.

13

In the afternoon I had hoped to be taken out for a second lesson but Oliver wanted to go for a walk. Though we set off along the roads, we soon left them and took to the footpaths, ending up in a large and sombre pine wood, possibly the one the Sheldons had explored that morning seven weeks ago. The wood sprawled over a gently sloping hillside and standing at the edge of it we looked down across a valley in which there wasn't the smallest sign of human occupation – I hadn't realized that in the Home Counties there were still such vast areas of wilderness. 'The world is very big,' I said, 'and we are very small in the world.'

'Comforting or otherwise?' asked Oliver.

'Oh, otherwise. Definitely. I should like to be very big in the world. Wouldn't you?'

I added: 'Of course, you already are. Prints – if not paintings – hanging in countless homes across the globe!'

But he didn't bother to answer. We stood and surveyed the great rolling landscape at our feet. There was still a remnant of pale sunshine, which must have boosted the loveliness.

'I could feel a bit fed up,' he said.

I was amazed. 'What! You? The second happiest man on earth?'

He made a harsh, dismissive sound and gave a wan smile. 'That,' he said, 'was this morning.'

'Well, it didn't get much of a run! No real threat to 'Chu Chin Chow'! Did your dinner give you indigestion?'

'No.'

'You're sure you didn't swallow a sixpence?'

'Threepenny bit,' he corrected me, mechanically.

'Well, there you are, then. That explains it.'

But all he said was: 'Do you want to turn back yet or carry on?'

'I know: you're piqued because I wouldn't let you be the first happiest man on earth. Okay, I relinquish the title. Anyhow I wouldn't want it, not unless you're feeling the way you should, when standing here on top of the world!' As I said this I put my arm affectionately through his. 'You see, I can make terrible puns, as well!'

He didn't respond, but neither did he draw his arm away. 'What's the trouble, love? Surely you don't have vertigo again?'

'A kind of vertigo, perhaps.'

'What kind?'

'The kind you get when you look behind you at all the years you've wasted, and look ahead and know the remainder of the way will surely be downhill.'

'But that's ridiculous. You're not even forty. You're still on the very crest.'

'That's what I mean. And do you realize something? By the time *you're* forty I shall be sixty.'

'Though *fantastically* well-preserved, I have no doubt. Sylvia Renshaw won't have stopped gawping at you on the tennis court.'

'Maybe not. But, somehow, I don't find that tremendously reassuring.'

'And I thought life was supposed to *begin* at forty!'

I was speaking humorously but nevertheless was starting to feel angry (what, with that man who this morning had given me an XK 150?), possibly because I could now sense the walls of the prison threatening to close in – *and where will you be in another twenty years*? – possibly because I felt this hitherto perfect day stood in danger of becoming spoilt. Possibly because I always grew swiftly impatient of self-pity.

'Well, yes,' he said, 'for some it may begin at forty. But you'll seldom hear a homosexual tell you that.'

I pulled my arm away and turned up the collar of my sheepskin jacket. 'Shall we head back?'

And if it's really so terrible to be a homosexual, I thought, why have you done your damnedest to turn *me* into one? Again, I recalled that just a few hours earlier I had said he was a saint.

'Admittedly,' he went on, 'for 'normal' men – for men who have a family – it could all be rather different. By forty you're more or less established, the children are becoming less of a millstone, the future's reasonably secure. Not so many fears of a lonely or a loveless old age. I sometimes think it must be very satisfying to have a family to work for.'

'In that case, matey, I'd say there's only one solution.'

'And what's that?'

'You'd better go looking for a wife. You're rich enough. You're attractive enough. Just say the word; I bet the women would come flocking!'

'You sound as though you're serious.'

'Well, damn it, if you're really that anxious to wallow in long-term emotional security!'

But then I heard what I was saying – and at once felt guilty.

'In any case, why in heaven's name do you need a family to work for? You have me to work for. I'd have thought that would be enough for anyone!'

It was extraordinary to see the change in his expression when I told him that. One moment he was wooden-faced – dull-eyed – aloof.

The next he gave a laugh.

I said: 'You're a nut, Oliver Cambourne! You really are.'

'Yes, I suppose I am.' Already he spoke in a far more lively tone. 'It's just that a person gets so tired. He can't go on and on being positive. He loses his vitality.'

'Oh, balls.'

'No, it's true.'

'Then there's one very obvious comment, concerning the things people get up to, either late at night or early in the morning. You won't win much sympathy from me, complaining you feel tired!'

'That has nothing to do with it. Good sex is one of the few things which increases your vitality.'

'Oh, really? Well. my word! Anyway, remember this. 'Philosophan Fortifies the Over-Forties!"

That slogan was on every tube train – although he would probably never have seen it there, and even I, since we had met, hadn't used the underground.

'So just hold out for another eight months,' I said, 'and all your problems will be over.'

Oliver made as if to give me a clip across the ear. I dodged. Then, laughing, I ran back along the track.

'Come on, Granddad! Puff, puff, puff!'

But after a while I let him catch me and we had an energetic tussle on the pine needles. These days Oliver seldom went to a gym (I was trying to get him back into the habit – as company, and competition, for myself) yet otherwise we were fairly evenly matched. As I brushed the dirt off my trousers, I remarked, 'Well, not too many signs of advancing decrepitude *there!* And – rather annoyingly, if I'm aiming to keep up – I can't believe there ever will be!'

The rest of the day held no such downswings. We returned home ready for tea – and Christmas cake – in the library; then moved a table closer to the fire and played a lengthy game of Monopoly. Mrs Cambourne was the winner, with Oliver coming in second. As for me, I fell a long, long way behind.

'And I always assumed,' I said, 'that the Cambourne Empire was just another music hall!'

'Well, now you realize your mistake,' answered Mrs Cambourne pithily, waving a wad of paper money underneath my nose.

But soon she was talking gaily of Albert Whelan and Ella Shields and Lily Morris – 'people I don't expect either of you foolish boys have ever heard of.' Yet she was wrong. She, Oliver and I spent the next hour happily capping each other with half-spoken snatches of song: 'Why am I always the bridesmaid?', 'My ole man said follow the van', 'I'm 'Enery the Eighth I am.' And also – no malice aforethought here, since I was the one who raked it up – 'She was a sweet little dickie-bird; cheep, cheep, cheep she went; sweetly she sang to me, till all my money was spent. . .' And so on. . . Between us we must have resurrected more than twenty of these old music-hall anthems, interspersed with charming little footnotes from Mrs Cambourne on where she had first heard some of them or what they reminded her of. Altogether, it was fun.

Afterwards, we ate turkey sandwiches and watched 'Top Hat': despite its inexpressibly silly story, the sort of thing we all felt in the mood for. The song title 'Isn't this a lovely day?' would have matched my sentiments entirely – if it hadn't then gone on to talk about the rain!

Yet the next morning it did indeed hit the household like a downpour.

Oliver's depression.

My God! He was morose from the moment he got up, but was obstinate and wouldn't return to bed – although at first I'd thought the problem might be tiredness. He ate no breakfast, spoke to me either in monosyllables or not at all, and retired after only a few grudging sips of coffee to the drawing room, where he hid behind the latest 'Paris Match'. I felt restless and aggrieved. I couldn't make him out. He had seemed in such high spirits the night before and wholly recovered from the few dismal moments of the afternoon. But now there was no question about it. He was behaving like a sulky little boy.

And in fact it was far more entertaining when, halfway through the morning, Mrs Cambourne came downstairs. She and I grew practically conspiratorial. We drank coffee in the library.

'Oh, he gets these attacks,' she said. 'The only wonder is, he hasn't had one for so very long! But I've learned it's best if we ignore them. Or do I mean – ignore *him?*'

She gave a crooked smile.

'Lots of artistic men, they tell me, are subject to these black periods. The dark night of the soul, I think they call it. It's very trying for the rest of us.'

'You can say that again! I was going to suggest you come for a drive this afternoon – in *my* car – but not if these blackout conditions still prevail.'

'At any rate, John, I'm glad to know you can retain your sense of humour.'

But I hadn't been feeling particularly humorous. I'd been thinking: *I*'m artistic and *I* don't carry on like this!

I noticed she had called me John. Of course, when speaking of me to Oliver in my presence she had often used the name; and also on the tag to my Christmas gift; but never whilst addressing me directly. And it went through my mind how ironic life was:

only two days earlier I'd have been considerably alarmed at the idea of sitting alone with her over morning coffee – and yet here we were now, getting on wonderfully. We had a stimulating ninety minutes. At the end, our talk returned to Oliver.

'It makes me very happy,' she said, 'to see you show such tolerance – such sensitivity.'

Christ!

But there it was, I reflected. Her apology. Out in the open.

It assuredly gave me a good feeling – but caused me to think that I, unlike Rachel Millwood, could *never* be a soothsayer.

Not even in prose.

Sorry, Oliver.

14

New Year's Eve.

Chelsea Arts Ball.

Its golden jubilee, to boot.

Ten minutes to twelve. We're sitting in a large party of Oliver's friends, all of whom seem very merry and some of whom appear quite drunk. Oliver is dressed as a French aristocrat, circa 1780. I'm a pirate from the Spanish Main. At various times I've been mistaken for Errol Flynn, Tyrone Power and Cornel Wilde. Shall I fly off to Hollywood, I wonder, and see if similar mistakes arise.

Yet despite the fact I've been looking forward to this since Christmas, now that it's here I'm not honestly enjoying it, I think chiefly because I, like everybody else, have been drinking. But unfortunately it hasn't made *me* merry.

Just queasy.

Also, although perhaps merely in keeping with the theme of the ball (says he, charitably!), nearly half our party is wearing female attire and could probably, even in daylight, pass for women. We boast a couple of apache dancers, one of whom, Gerald, is made up to look like Cyd Charisse in 'Singin' in the Rain'. He could almost be her double – his legs are perfect. I can't help it but I find this, too, a mite nauseating. I know it's intended as a joke.

One of the girls, however, actually *is* a girl: a petite blonde called Melissa Stanton, who's the daughter of a diplomat. (Oliver sold a painting to her father.) It's a pity she isn't Elizabeth.

It's also a pity that she keeps talking like a character out of a book and saying things like, 'Isn't it lovely about Sir Alec?'

'Sir Alec whom?' I ask.

Her baby blue eyes express astonishment. 'Why, Guinness, of course! Oh, didn't you know? New Year's Honours List. Out tomorrow.' Giggles; puts a hand to her mouth. 'Oh, naughty me, I shouldn't have told you! Please don't pass it on!'

I take her word for it about Michael Somes and Stirling Moss and Freddie Grisewood. She appears to have them all off pat: her CBEs, her OBEs, her OMs.

She says, 'That's Felix Topolski over there; he's a very dear friend of Philip's. Thirty guineas those boxes cost but I wonder if *he's* had to pay for his. I don't think I have to tell you – he's the person who painted this lovely canvas!'

'Mmm. I believe they did allow him a small discount,' I murmur. 'Twenty-five percent.'

She doesn't quite know how to take this. Can't be sure whether I'm serious or not. Gives another little laugh. 'I mean! Who sums up Chelsea better than Augustus John?'

'Yes, who?' I ask. 'Who on earth?'

For Augustus John, my informant tells me (and I suppose reliably), will be eighty next Sunday and – clearly in honour of this – has been made the central figure in Topolski's panoramic design. 'Oh, isn't it wild!' enthuses Miss Stanton. 'Just look at the 1958 girl. Gosh, has he painted one mean girl in *her*! Wouldn't you say that girl is really mean?'

Because the enormous canvas under which we're all doing the cha-cha when she says this – it must be at least sixty feet by a hundred – depicts Twentieth Century Woman at ten-yearly intervals, from 1908 until the present time.

'Oh, absolutely!' I reply.

That mean 1958 girl is thin and angular and wearing a sweater and black stockings. She's certainly no glamour puss. No rival to Mae West.

But this year's costumes according to my partner are quite as brilliant and saucy as ever – and as far removed from any trace of trying to economize. The only thing that's different this year is the peaceable behaviour.

'Because, well, haven't you noticed all those marvellous specimens of manhood dotted around the Hall?'

When I answer that, no, I haven't – because I'm sure she doesn't mean Gerald – she tells me that amongst the fifty stewards there are a dozen barrel-chested gymnasts from the London Polytechnic Weightlifting Club. I only hope this girl never goes over to the Reds; she's plainly in the Mata Hari class.

'So much less *rowdy* this year,' she repeats, shaking her head in bewilderment. 'Honestly, John, you wouldn't believe it – you would not believe it!'

'Tell me,' I say. 'I'm interested. You've obviously been here before. Why do you keep on assuming *I* haven't?'

This throws her, it truly does throw her. For about a minute she becomes confused – apologetic. Afterwards she doesn't twitter on half so merrily.

Then I feel sorry and suggest she possibly heard it from Oliver. Too late I discover she isn't really such a bad girl; too late I discover I didn't *need* to be unkind. But now Miss Stanton appears to be avoiding me. How tiresome when people show themselves sensitive!

As I say, it's ten to twelve.

'Happy 1959!' Though Oliver's sitting next to me he still has to raise his voice.

'Thanks,' I say. 'And you.'

'It's going to be a splendid year.'

'Yes. But I'm sitting here deliberating if I ought to get a job.' (Elstree? Shepperton, Pinewood? Or straight out to California?)

'Why? You're busy enriching the heritage of the British novel.'

'Not very fast I'm not.' 'Where Two Roads Meet' is in the doldrums. There was a strong, invigorating wind some three weeks back; but this abated well before Christmas.

'Well, who cares about speed?' asks Oliver.

'I can't live off you forever.'

'Why not?'

Why not? I'll tell you why not. Because I want to go to Hollywood. I want to smile down from cinema screens across the world, be mobbed in the streets, give press and television interviews, be recognized by head waiters in all the luxury restaurants. I want to be known as both an actor and a sex symbol. I shouldn't mind being the new James Dean. I shouldn't mind acting with Gregory Peck or Rock Hudson or Jean Simmons or Henry Fonda. No, I don't even want to be the new James Dean – let alone the new Errol Flynn, the new Tyrone Power, the new Cornel Wilde. I want to be the new John Wilmot. Me. Me, in my own right. Top Box-Office Draw of 1959. And '60. And '61. Et cetera.

But not so easy to convey all this in one pithy sentence at the top of your voice. Not so easy to convey all this in any way at all – not to Oliver.

For instance: when you have your friends in. . . Either they're queer (and I don't like mixing with queers en masse, although individually, I suppose, most of those I've met have been all right) or they're not queer – and then what sort of position does that place *me* in? I wasn't born, Oliver, to be viewed merely as some extension. Subservient, the hanger-on, the one who has to be included in all those invitations you receive. I wasn't born to be patronized. Or overlooked.

And, anyway, I want to go to Hollywood.

But how *can* you convey all this when your head hurts and you have to shout and the very last thing you want to do is cause him any pain?

Why, of course, you convey it in a shrug.

I shrug.

'Besides,' says Oliver, 'a job would only get in the way of things. I want to take you travelling. And you remember we spoke the other day about our sailing round the Greek islands? Up to now, you haven't even *seen* the 'Sarah', let alone sailed on her!'

Corks pop. Balloons are bursting. Two monstrous pink elephants float above our heads.

'I must say'. . .I temporize. . .'that would be very pleasant.'

'Well, yes, it would.'

And I don't temporize for long. 'Oh, to hell with all those petty bourgeois scruples!' (Is that what they were? Not quite but never mind.) I unexpectedly revive a little. There has risen up an image of our sailing round the Greek islands, other places too, sunning ourselves on deck – perhaps naked, a deep overall tan – putting into port to spend peaceful languorous evenings drinking and eating and singing in small tavernas off the tourist routes. And after all, damn it, I *am* only nineteen. Hardly born yet! Hardly yet standing upon the very threshold of life! I move in a little closer – we were already pretty close. 'Okay. Eat, drink and be merry, for tomorrow we die. That's my New Year's resolution.'

'I thought it was your Old Year's resolution.'

'Aren't I allowed to reaffirm?'

Now it's nearly midnight. Everyone is wanted on the floor. There are a few seconds of comparative quiet; the M.C. has his right arm raised and his eyes on his watch. . .the arm comes down, lights flash on and off, couples kiss and – atypically in public – I, too, lose my inhibitions: Oliver gets a long and robust hug, one that dislodges his feathered hat.

"Should old acquaintance be forgot and never brought to mind, we'll drink a cup of gladness yet, for the sake of auld lang syne..."

The great linked circles come in on themselves, right in, then retreat, advance, retreat again, break up. There's something about it that always makes me feel emotional.

But when it's over, the throbbing in my head – which has so far been bearable – starts to accelerate.

'What now, Ollie? Back to your place? Let's have an orgy!' Lucien, a dashing musketeer – but with the kind of almond-shaped, highly buffed fingernails I don't suppose d'Artagnan ever had – begins to organize everyone. 'We're all going back to Ollie's!'

'But not for any orgy,' says Oliver.

The grace with which Oliver gives in to the suggestion – or, rather, the readiness with which he seems to meet it – coupled with the undeniable good looks of Lucien, however effeminate, provokes in me a rush of jealousy. But I clench my fists and determine not to show it.

Thirty minutes later we are reassembled at the flat, some dozen males in all (whatever happened to Mata Hari – did she feel so *very* much offended?), and we're sprawling about with yet more drinks. Even I have another; I'm not sure how it found its way into my hand. James appears in his element – I have never known him so convivial – passing round the glasses with an almost skittish air. Either he senses Oliver's new interest in Lucien *(is* Oliver interested in Lucien; can there have been anything between them in the past?) and will be glad to see *my* much-hated nose put out of joint – or else he's looking for a new master. That's my own view of it. Not that I care much any longer. All other, smaller aspects of my misery are abruptly pushed aside by one that demands instant, absolute obedience. I rush towards the lavatory.

In the corridor, whom do I meet but Lucien, returning from the same place.

'John, my pet, you're looking fanciable.'

'Not feeling it.'

'So very butch, with all that open shirt and acres of yummy torso. How about coming round to my place one evening this week? Rick's away till Saturday.'

'Take care, I'm about to be sick!'

'Now you mustn't act coy, my poppet. Don't play hard to get. I know dear Oliver's inclined to be a dash possessive, a bit old-fashioned at times –'

'Lucien, I warn you. If you don't let me past –'

'Let him past!' says Oliver, coming up behind.

But, even so, I don't quite make it. I hear Lucien in the background saying peevishly, 'Oh, surely you can take a joke, Ollie *dear*. . .' I throw up over the floor instead of into the bowl. I hang over the lavatory, sweating, dripping, retching; feeling I may be very close to death.

A moment later Oliver arrives. 'Come on, my love, the place for you is bed. Is that the end, d'you think? Or not quite yet?' He hands me a wad of tissues.

'I'm sorry about this,' I say, eventually. I'm beginning to feel a degree better.

'Not your fault. If that fool hadn't. . .' He adds grimly, 'Well, now I'll send 'em all packing. They were starting to get on my nerves, anyway.'

'I'm not sure what you heard but I promise you I didn't –'

'I know that, idiot. In any case you wouldn't have to tell me, but I saw you leave the room looking pale, then I came out after you. . . I'm so relieved I did.'

I allow him to cosset me: to plump the pillows and to bring hot water bottles. 'Please tell James I'm sorry for the mess.'

'Don't worry about James. Knowing how you feel about him I've seen to it myself. Now try to get some sleep. I love you, my angel.'

He adds, 'I'll be in soon.' The door closes. I am comfortable now and warm; the shivering's stopped, I taste only mouthwash. I imagine I'll have a hangover in the morning, yet for the moment I feel pampered and tranquil and secure. It's a nice feeling. No jealousy. Not even much regret. Just a sense of wellbeing.

But shouldn't there be at least a smattering of regret? After all, not the *most* auspicious start to a New Year. Brought in on a wave of vomit.

*

As if to show, however, that this doesn't bode ill for 1959. . . not a trace of a hangover! I actually wake up feeling hungry. I eat a good breakfast. Oliver says it's incredible, and what it is to be young! Life begins at nineteen, I tell him – because we're not going to have any taboo phrases in *this* household! He frowns; looks petulant; then wants to know why – for me – life didn't begin at eighteen.

And later in the day, also, Oliver gets a note from poor Miss Stanton: it has been truly the loveliest of evenings – utterly perfect in every way. And how absolutely super John is!

So even this appears to be all right. I no longer need to have her on my conscience.

Not that I've ever fallen *too* great a victim to my conscience. My name is not Raskolnikov. Thank heaven.

15

Two months afterwards, on an evening in March, I returned late and found him sitting in partial darkness, having nothing but firelight to illuminate the room. My immediate fear was of another attack of the blues. This proved unfounded.

'How was 'South Pacific', my darling? No' – he hastily held up his hand – 'you needn't tell me! How was your driving lesson, instead?'

I kissed him on the temple, put my arms around his shoulders and laid my cheek against his. 'Fine.'

'No collywobbles yet?' He pressed the back of my hand.

'About the test? Gracious, no, there's more than a week until the twenty-third. Besides, it's going to be a walkover.'

'Yes, I think it probably is – thanks to that *excellent* extra tuition you've been receiving most evenings.'

'Not to mention having to regurgitate the Highway Code at practically every meal.'

'Talking of which. . .have you eaten tonight? If not there's chicken in the fridge. And Mrs Danvers has already gone to bed.'

'I'll get something in a minute.' I poured myself a drink and flopped down into the armchair opposite his. 'Old stick-in-the-mud! What have *you* been up to?'

'Mainly listening to the wireless. 'Scrapbook for 1940'. And then sitting here thinking about it.'

'So that explains the Daylight Saving. . . You know something, Oliver? You've never spoken much about the war.'

'Perhaps it's not a period one normally wants to dwell on.'

'Okay but – now – what would you say was your worst experience?' I uttered an exclamation. 'Grief! Is this me or is it Wilfred Pickles? 'Give 'im the money, Mabel!''

He replied without hesitation, and put my levity to shame.

'My worst experience? Listening to a man's screams as he burned to death in the cockpit of his Spitfire – the radio still on, of course. . . He was someone whom I knew quite well.'

I didn't say anything. What could one say?

But it occurred to me – apart from the sheer horror of it – there might have been the hint of something else in his tone; something a bit too deliberately casual about the utterance of that last sentence?

'Yet when you were flying bombers,' he said, 'can you really home in on the death of a single man as being your worst experience?'

He picked up his glass of whisky.

'However, that was the night I lost my faith in God.'

There followed a further pause. 'I didn't even realize. . .,' I began, tonelessly. But it seemed irrelevant. I stared into the fire. 'What was his name?'

At first it seemed he hadn't heard. 'Sorry,' he answered, slowly. 'Edmund Marshall. Why?'

'No reason. Just interested.'

'Oddly enough, in appearance, he wasn't dissimilar to you. And he also wanted to write. I often wonder whether he'd have been successful – achieved a lasting reputation.'

'Do you think he might have?'

That wasn't the question I had wanted to ask.

I had wanted to ask, *Did you love him?* But I hadn't the temerity of Mrs Cambourne. And, anyway, I wasn't sure I wished to hear the answer.

Then Oliver shook off his reverie. He yawned and stretched and said, 'Forgive me, it's not the past which ought to be concerning us. No; it's the. . .potentially. . .much brighter future.' And he lifted his glass and pointed it in my direction. 'May yours now be the lasting reputation!'

'Yours, too. Here's to lasting reputations!'

'And here's to the brighter future! Let lasting reputations take their own chance on salvation!'

We drank to it and then I went into the kitchen and raided the refrigerator – on both our accounts – and everything was fine again.

16

'I'd give anything,' he said – he was standing in front of the wardrobe pulling at the ends of his bow tie – 'to be stopping in quietly by the fire with our books, listening to a few records, and then getting a reasonably early night.' He sighed. 'But I suppose it's altogether too much to ask: the avoidance of punishment *twice*!'

'We stopped in quietly last night,' I pointed out, with severity. I could have added: *Are* you growing old? 'And one gets an excellent meal at the Savoy. Besides, the floor show's fairly entertaining.'

He groaned. 'Do we really have to stay for that?'

'After all, they're your relations!'

'Very distant. I hadn't met them until the day you did.'

'That doesn't alter a thing.'

'And it's certainly not me that Elizabeth fancies!'

I grinned. 'So is that the reason we're being asked?'

He came across to help me with my own bow tie. 'Nothing,' he said, 'would surprise me, my sweet *shepsel* – nothing!' He gave my cheek a fawningly sadistic pinch.

'And in that case,' he added, releasing my troubled flesh, though now administering a small hard pat, 'we know exactly where to lay the blame.'

'What does *shepsel* mean? And why this whole Jewish-momma act?'

'It means little sheep.'

'Oh, does it? Well, thank you.'

'Am I mistaken then? Is it only the clothing you wear?'

And standing back a little to admire my tie, he expressed his satisfaction, and finished by giving me a quick kiss on that same maltreated cheek.

'Come on,' he said. 'Enough of all this nonsense. We'd better hurry to our doom.'

But, of course, he found the evening much less of a penance than he'd expected; and – for me – having Oliver there to take his share in the conversation made it even pleasanter than before. 'You could write a book on all your travels!' I said to Mrs Sheldon.

And as I'd half intended, Oliver explained to her why this should have occurred to me.

'Goodness!' she said. 'We didn't know you wrote.'

'Have you had anything published, John?' asked her husband.

'Not yet. But I live in hopes. I've very nearly finished my first novel.'

He nodded, appreciatively. 'And now I understand why you want to run a chain of bookstores – to promote your own novels! Good thinking, I call that. But if you'll take a little well-meant advice from someone who's been around, young man, you won't let the sideline get too much in the way of the main goal. Are bookstores a really paying proposition in this country?' – he turned to Oliver rather than to me.

It was the first time I had seen Oliver even mildly at a loss.

But it was Elizabeth who answered.

'Daddy, that wasn't *exactly* what I said. You asked what John's ambitions were and I told you I thought he might like to own a large and important bookstore, or maybe even a couple.' She smiled at me without any trace of embarrassment. 'Or did I misunderstand the whole thing? I sometimes do, you know.'

Oh, the wide-eyed innocence of it!

I said, 'Well, whilst working in Wigmore Street I may have had some rather humble notion of that kind – which possibly I did allude to in November. But since then I've started to think big. I've actually given up that job in the bookshop.'

'Well, I have to confess it to you, John, I did wonder what sort of a future there could ever be in books. . .'

'Oh, a tremendous future, Mr Sheldon. There can't be any doubt. But I agree with you: not on the retail side, more on the creative.'

'The creative. . .?' he repeated. 'You mean – ?'

'Think Edna Ferber,' I said, 'William Irish, John O'Hara, James M Cain – the number of *their* novels which have been filmed.

Look at Daphne Du Maurier. Practically all of hers have! I could cite you positively dozens of wealthy writers.'

Mr Sheldon seemed still more puzzled. 'You mean you gave up your job just to write a novel?'

I answered lightly: 'Oh, don't say 'just'.'

'But what are you living on? If that isn't too indiscreet a question.'

Oliver laughed. 'Oh, didn't you know, sir? There are no such things as indiscreet questions. Only indiscreet answers.'

"An Ideal Husband", supplied Elizabeth. 'Lord Goring.'

'Yes, that's right,' said Oliver.

'I wonder which is more ill-bred,' asked Elizabeth. '*Your* sounding surprised or *my* remarking on it?'

'Oh, your remarking on it – definitely. *My* lapse was involuntary. I hadn't realized Wilde was so well-known in America.' I knew he was lying.

She said, 'But that hardly improves matters. By implying he is so well-known in America, you're detracting from my own little triumph, surely?'

'Yes, you're right,' said Oliver again. 'I'm behaving very badly. You'll have to forgive me.'

I felt pleased. Elizabeth had never shown this side of her to Oliver. They were practically flirting.

Nor had they finished yet.

'No, I was the one behaving badly. I got what I deserved. I'm afraid I'm a hopeless show-off.'

Oliver said: 'I wonder what the third defect will be.'

'Hey,' I butted in. 'Shame on you! I'll have to call you out, if you can't justify that remark.'

'Oh, these things, you know, always happen in threes.'

But I also protested at this. 'What was the first?'

'Hasn't it already been let fall – and from the lady's own lips – that she sometimes misunderstands things?'

But, for the lady's father, such badinage had lasted long enough. He hadn't been diverted. 'What *are* you living on?'

'I've almost forgotten,' I answered, cheerfully. 'Oh, yes – my savings. And meals at the Savoy.'

Mona Sheldon gave her husband's arm a pat. 'That's what they call dedication, sweetheart.' To me she added, 'I'm afraid Theo isn't artistic.'

Mr Sheldon appealed to Oliver. 'Is this book of his any good?'

'First-rate,' replied Oliver. . .who hadn't read so much as a single line.

Yet – in my own view astonishingly – Theodore Sheldon didn't appear impressed. 'All the same,' he said, 'to give up your job (even though, I agree, it mayn't have been such great shakes to begin with) without first making sure of another one. . . Not even to be *looking* for another one. . .'

'Actually, sir,' said Oliver, 'I think it's incredibly brave. Shows an enviable singleness of purpose! And if you can't do that sort of thing while you're young – well, when can you, for heaven's sake?'

'How old *are* you, John?'

'Fifty-nine,' I said.

'And wearing very well, too,' applauded Mrs Sheldon. 'Honestly, Theo, you've no right to go round asking people how old they are.'

'At twenty-five one isn't sensitive about one's age. I hope.'

'The thing is,' drawled Oliver, now at his most languid, 'so often one meets these unimaginative types who tend to stick people in boxes – boxes labelled twenties, fifties, eighties – and, when they've done that, think they have them pegged. Like me, you'll say it's immature, but I assure you there *are* those sufficiently blinkered.'

Thanks partly to this – partly to Mrs Sheldon – the subject was dropped.

Between the main course and the dessert Elizabeth and I danced.

'It's nice to get you on your own,' she said.

'I was about to say the same.'

'Thank you, Johnny, for your letters. They were neat.'

'Neat?'

She nodded.

'Elizabeth, call them models of epistolary elegance – call them edifying, rib-tickling, satirical, crazy. Call them shocking, call them barbaric. But *neat*? Can't you do a little better than that?'

'Oh, neat incorporates all those things – and several more besides! It's not really an assessment of your handwriting.'

'Ah, well, *then* I understand. Oh, and by the way, I received your letters, too. Entertaining little notes.'

She had written to me three times, the second and third time being more about her life back home than about her current travels. I had written twice. Possibly my original letter had been responsible for the autobiography in her next two. After talking for a couple of paragraphs about 'Where Two Roads Meet' and some of the films and plays I'd seen, I had gone on to describe the time I'd spent in Folkestone immediately prior to Christmas (although allowing that weekend and Christmas conveniently to merge), painting a vivid picture – *hopefully* a vivid picture – of my mother and aunt and their circumstances, to which she had responded with great sympathy.

We danced for a while in silence.

Then she inquired if I might let her read my novel.

'Yes, of course. I was going to ask you, anyway. My hero's an American; I'm sure his speech will need some vetting.'

Then I said:

'A chain of bookstores, indeed!'

'Oh dear. I was hoping you'd forgotten.'

'Hmm.'

'You see, I wanted Daddy to think well of you.'

'And you could only accomplish that by gross deception!'

'I guess you may now have seen why.'

Later on, after I'd had a courtesy waltz with Mrs Sheldon, we danced again. Elizabeth said casually, 'I've two tickets for a show tomorrow night. I wondered if maybe you were free and would like to come.'

'I'd love to.'

'It's 'Auntie Mame', with Bea Lillie and Florence Desmond.'

'Better and better.'

After a moment's pause: 'Johnny? How old *are* you?'

She, I remembered, was twenty. 'I'm twenty-one.'

'Is that all? I'd have said twenty-three or twenty-four.' She paused. 'If you don't mind, I'd like you to choose the restaurant we could eat at afterwards – somewhere nice, no matter how expensive – but I want you to understand the whole evening's going to be on me. . .including any drinks before the play begins. Yes, no objections, please! Right now you don't have a job.'

'You, neither.'

'But I'm on vacation. One's entitled to be extravagant on vacation.'

'There are those who might claim *I'm* on vacation!' Naturally, I didn't name any names.

'Okay, then.' I thought for a moment she was going to give in. (Poor Oliver!) 'But there's something you don't know as yet. My grandfather – my adoptive grandfather – left me a twenty-five percent share of the company. In trust. For when I come of age. Beat that.'

'You're just so vulgar,' I said.

'Aren't I?'

'But in the circumstances. . .all right, then, I pass!'

'And what did I tell you?' said Oliver, an hour or two later – we were on our way home in the taxi. 'That girl's after you.'

'I think perhaps she is. And she's loaded. It could turn a young boy's head.'

'Is this young boy's head in danger of getting turned?'

'Well, what do *you* think?'

'I think I was right about that third failing of hers.'

'Which is?'

'Tenacity. She's tenacious, like her dad.'

'Failing?' I queried. 'Or virtue?'

'Oh, in this case, make no mistake about it. . .*failing*! She's a lot softer and more intelligent than he is – I'll give you that – and in fact I do like Elizabeth; you mustn't get me wrong.'

'But?'

My hand was resting between us on the leather seat; he laid his own upon it. 'But,' he said, 'you'd better spell it out to her loud and clear. That if this goes on, she'll wind up at the bottom of the river, with a knife between the shoulder blades. I don't suppose she'd care for that.'

'I'll mention it tomorrow night. While they're striking up the overture.' Not that 'Auntie Mame' was a musical.

'Tell her it's cold at the bottom of the river.'

'And dark,' I said.

'And wet.'

'And all the little fishes go goop-goop-goop! All right – I'll see what I can do.'

Late though it was when we got in I stayed up, inspired, and wrote a further three pages of the book. Which left me with only the short final chapter to attend to. After that I couldn't sleep for a long time. I went through the novel mentally, almost incident by incident, one favourite passage following another. I kept thinking of how surprised Oliver and Elizabeth were both going to be, and of the pleasure my book was going to give them.

17

I finished 'Where Two Roads Meet' on the nineteenth of March – not, as I'd hoped, before breakfast but very soon afterwards. It was one of the happiest and most satisfying moments of my life when I placed the typescript in Oliver's hands; there was an element of ceremony about it and recognition of a work completed.

'Well, writer?'

'Well, painter?'

'Does this call for a spot of celebration?'

'What – at ten o'clock in the morning?'

'Why not at ten o'clock in the morning? Will there ever be a better ten o'clock than this?' He caressed my cheek with his knuckles. 'Last night I put some Dom Perignon in the fridge.'

I floated through the day in a haze of excitement. Oliver was going to do no painting – meant to sit comfortably in his studio, with a Thermos flask beside him, and to read solidly, without interruption. A twenty-minute break for food – that was all.

I couldn't bear to stay at home; I couldn't bear to have lunch with him, his task unfinished, his opinion unexpressed. I went to Kew Gardens, and wished my mother and aunt could have been there too, on one of those outings which, mainly due to the rigours of the winter (mainly – not, unluckily, *altogether)* had never taken place.

In two days' time, though. . .spring! What better moment to try to resuscitate the idea?

But no regret could spoil the heady magic of that day. Every ten minutes I wondered where Oliver might have got to *now* and sometimes I imagined I was reading with him, looking down over his shoulder. Even when I ended up at a cinema, I was still as conscious of Oliver as I was of the film.

I returned to the flat at seven. And he had finished my book barely half an hour before. He had moved into the sitting room and had the typescript on his lap.

'Well?' I demanded.

'Says he – feigning blithe indifference!'

'Don't keep me in suspense.'

'All right.' He went to the drinks cupboard in order to pour me a sherry. 'Then let me say before anything. . .congratulations on your having completed your first novel! Two hundred and eighty-one pages – on its own, no mean achievement!'

He handed me my glass. 'And even more of an achievement, clearly, when it's a novel so very full of good things.'

I felt a cold trickle of sweat run down the side of my body. I put my sherry on the mantelpiece.

'But you didn't like it, did you?'

He proceeded with the thought he'd had in mind. 'That very long chapter, for instance, when Ella realizes Jean-Paul is attempting to kill her. I found the tension brilliantly sustained.'

'Jean-*Philippe*,' I said.

'Jean-Philippe.'

'And that's really what strikes you first? At that point my main worry, in fact, was that it might be turning into melodrama.'

'And what's wrong with melodrama? Nothing – when it's skilfully written.'

'Well, all right, then. . .but talk to me about Blanche! I want to hear about Blanche.'

He laughed. 'Oh, quel monstre!'

'Yes, but despite that – and of course she was often referred to as monstrous – didn't you sometimes feel a sneaking sort of affection?'

He said, 'Well, I can see *you* did. You obviously had a lot of fun writing Blanche. I loved it when she went to Timmy's speech day.'

'And, in her honour, the headmaster arranged a showing of her first movie? Did you appreciate the parody?'

'Was it based on something real?'

'Oh, yes. 'Peg of Old Drury'. And Cedric Hardwicke really did play Garrick. But the film was English, not American.'

'Ah. . . I didn't know.'

There was a pause.

Oliver picked up the typescript again.

He started to leaf through it.

I said: 'You didn't like it. Did you?'

He picked his words with care. 'I think the parts are better than the whole. I also think there's no doubt whatever that you're going to make a fine writer – already *are* a fine writer. But you'll need to find material which suits you. Not always so easy as it sounds!'

'And this sort doesn't?'

'It's too divorced from life. And remember Marnie's advice: write about the things you know – not the things you've seen in the cinema or read about in other books.'

'But you said you liked the chapter where Ella discovers Jean-Philippe is planning to murder her.'

'Yes, I know. I ought to be consistent. Tell you what, my love. Let's regard 'Where Two Roads Meet' as an invaluable and very necessary exercise – you shouldn't regret even one second of all the months you spent on it! And let me now help you find a storyline which would make far better use of your talents. I'd enjoy that, wouldn't you? We could stop going out so much, and spend our evenings working out a wonderful synopsis.'

I didn't answer. Fully a minute went by as I paced about the room. When I sat down he smiled.

'We'll dream up something so exciting you'll be able to think of nothing else for days and days! But this time with real character development. . .and with each event initiating the next, in such a way that your story will reveal a tightness – an *inevitability* – which even George Eliot or Jane Austen might have envied.'

I also gave a smile, though mine was probably more strained. 'Perhaps you shouldn't have read it all at one sitting. Could that have made a difference?'

He shook his head, silently.

I suggested cutting it.

Again he shook his head. 'I think you'd do a whole lot better to start afresh – and on something which bears the stamp of truth right from the start.' He reached out his hand, in a helpless gesture of empathy. 'Oh, my poor love. You don't look very happy.'

'No, I'm all right. A bit disappointed, naturally. Who wouldn't be?'

'And I'm disappointed, too. But doesn't that show what idiots we are? There's so much in this book to rejoice at! Why, only a year from now –'

'But is there nothing else you can say about Blanche?' I didn't want to hear about only a year from now.

'She was fun.'

'But that's it? *Fun*?'

'My darling, let's face it. Blanche is overwritten. She's amusing in small doses but you've let her run away with you. As I say, you probably had a whale of a time creating her, but then you became a mite self-indulgent.'

And what else? He said that both my hero and my heroine were insipid; and that, with Timothy especially, one had no idea what kind of person he really was, what drove him on, what made him tick. And another way of stressing that same point: there appeared to be no connection between Timothy the child and Timothy the man, and not one of his boyhood experiences need ever have taken place, so far as Oliver could see, for all the influence they'd had upon his adult character.

Oh, he was thorough – my august and noble patron; once he'd started he plainly sought to be inclusive! And I could have sworn the exercise was giving him enjoyment. Superficially it may have seemed he was occasionally trying to comfort me – a picking out of odd passages, satiric or perceptive, which honestly gave a foretaste, as he kept on saying in one form or another until I genuinely felt I might shout at him if he did so once again – a foretaste of the fine and important book I clearly had it within me to produce; but then, at the slightest prod, he would immediately rush off again on his pleasurable crusade of destruction. I had read recently that well-nigh any conversation, no matter how apparently innocent, was basically aggressive; an attempt to gain the upper hand. And I could well believe it. I didn't know what long-repressed resentments Oliver might be in the throes of releasing that night, but I could only hope he found it therapeutic. He certainly deserved to – with all the energy he was expending!

But I derived my consolation: it was actually I who had the upper hand. Not in my endless self-indulgent flow of words (who was *he* to speak of self-indulgence?) but in my silences, my weary nods, my pretence of acquiescence. Okay, I was thinking all the while, all the while I was enabling him to carry on with the great purge – okay, let him say this, let him say that, let him pick holes, let him demolish. But wasn't it, in truth, a little pathetic: this compulsion he had to dominate, to play Pygmalion, to mete out money and knowledge and approval with always the same barely concealed air of condescension? A father-figure, head of the household, undisputed boss! No wonder, I thought, he pined so feebly to create a family. It was of course a need that all essentially weak men had: to appear strong. Yes; poor Oliver. It was certainly a bit pathetic.

And so the joke was – the ultimate irony of a sad, sad situation – that when we went to bed at a ridiculously early hour and he believed that *he* was reassuring *me*, it was far more the other way about.

Poor Oliver.

The next morning, however, I no longer felt so tolerant.

From the moment I awoke, shortly after five, unable to return to sleep, I felt bleak, in some fashion bereaved – but definitely not tolerant.

I asked myself what right he had, first to encourage me, then to use me as something on which to take out his frustrations, all his pitiful frustrations. Did he suppose that, just because from time to time he so luxuriatingly owned up to how complex and cussed he was, this automatically exonerated him? The divine right of kings: such is the way I am; how can I help it if I am deeper and more finely wrought than others?

Oh, damn him! Damn him! Damn him!

But at least I wasn't a masochist – I needn't just sit there and endure it. Thank God, I had my bolt-hole. Thank God it wouldn't be a sign of any weakness if I now rushed back to that.

Therefore, straight after breakfast, I made a most grateful escape to my own flat.

It had been several days since my last visit: I usually went to air the place, and sweep and dust and even polish. But this morning, rather strangely, I had been there for scarcely fifteen minutes when there came a ring at the doorbell; and outside stood a lad with a telegram.

18

URGENT STOP PHONE TONIGHT STOP MOTHER

My instant thought, naturally: Aunt Clara. Rendered stupid by shock I sank down in a chair and gazed further at the message. She was either dead or as good as dead or. . .worse than dead. I said, Dear God I don't believe in you. But make Aunt Clara well and I swear I'll try to.

Yet gradually my mind started to clear. Of course I didn't have to wait until this evening. I could telephone right now. I hurried to the phone box.

But the phone box was occupied and, impatient for action, I ran to where I knew there was another. On my way to it, however, it occurred to me my mother wouldn't be at home; she'd be spending the day at the hospital; hence her instruction to ring in the evening. Though the second phone box was empty I ran past it. I'd seen a bus for Charing Cross and managed to catch it at the lights. A taxi would have been quicker but the bus was there and a taxi wasn't.

The journey to Folkestone was the slowest I had ever known. I arrived at half-past-twelve and went straight to the house rather than the hospital. Just in case. The distance was too short to regard the time as wasted.

Faintly to my surprise, when I rang the bell I heard movement. To my further surprise, the door was opened by Aunt Clara. For several seconds we simply stood there, like two ill-informed meerkats.

'By all that's wonderful!' she said at last. 'I thought you were the postman.'

There was obviously not a lot the matter with her. I felt tremendous relief, clearly – but also a sense of anticlimax, almost annoyance. She had managed to give me a very bad couple of hours.

'But why were *you* looking so astonished?' she asked. 'You could hardly have thought *I* was the postman.'

It was the relief that proved the stronger. 'Oh, you'd be surprised. The postmen are getting sexier each day. Where's Mum?'

We had by this time gone into the house.

'Why, at the restaurant – where else? But she forgot to tell me you were coming home. How on earth did you manage to get away in the *morning*? Has the shop burnt down? I do hope so.'

I followed her dazedly into the kitchen. Abruptly she turned and said, 'You're not ill, are you?'

'No, I'm fine.'

'And you haven't had the sack?'

I shook my head. We laughed a little. I said: 'And you two are keeping okay?'

My aunt grew serious. 'Well, I am, thank you; but honestly I'm not so sure about your mother. She came home last night looking extremely peaked. And she didn't seem any happier this morning. But when I ventured to suggest she spend the day at home she fairly snapped my head off. If you ask me, I think that job's getting a bit too much for her.'

Cancer, I thought. The anxiety returned, practically as strong but, this time, directed towards my mother. She must have found a lump; in addition to everything else – early widowhood, straitened circumstances, boredom, worry over Clara – now this! Why was there no fairness to this life of ours?

'Anyway, John, it's as well you *are* here this weekend. It will cheer her up.'

'Yes.' I'd been going to another concert with Elizabeth that evening but I could always telephone.

'Sit down and tell me what sort of sandwiches you'd like,' invited Aunt Clara. 'I'm having cheese. I could offer you cheese. In the cupboard there's some nice cheese.'

'Oh, decisions, decisions,' I cried. But my heart wasn't in it. 'Listen, if you don't mind, I won't stop; not for the minute. You see, I'd like to speak to Mum as quickly as I can.'

'Such urgency!' she said.

She was half laughing, but still looked puzzled.

'You do know, John dear, that if you're ever in any kind of a scrape...?'

'You'll be the first to hear about it.'

'No, I don't necessarily ask that. But naturally you realize how very fond of you your old aunt is? Anyway,' she added, with sudden brusqueness, 'I'll see you later!' I kissed her on the cheek – answered, 'Ditto!' – and left.

The Copper Kettle was, for me, less than a ten-minute walk away. Its regular clientele was elderly and mostly female and its decor was the sort you would expect: a long row of copper saucepans, of graduated sizes, hanging from nails in the mock beam above ye olde fireplace...but with the eponymous kettle sitting in state upon the hearth. Every table always had at its centre a jar of wild flowers.

It was one o'clock and in all likelihood – this being a Friday – the customers would be eating delicate portions of steamed fish in parsley sauce, with apple crumble and custard, or ice cream, to follow.

The place was full. When I opened the door my mother was sitting at her cash desk. For the moment, she was alone, and looking in my direction.

Yet she didn't see me – not until I was standing right before her. Then she focused and gave a start.

'Hello, Mum!'

But it wasn't easy to appear cheerful. Her expression had brought back the awful scene there'd been in January, when inadvertently I'd mentioned my driving lessons and had then been unable to keep my grand new car a secret. After which – very unhopefully – I had been obliged to invent an Oliver who was a widower of sixty-five: an improbable benefactor who regarded me in the light of one of his own sons, of whom there were four.

However, since then, that mutual admiration society, whose final meeting had been in December, had utterly disbanded; since then, things hadn't been the same between my mother and myself.

'We can't talk here!' Those were her first words.

'Where can we, then?'

'This evening. After work. I told you.'

'But nobody can hear us here. Can't you tell me what the trouble is? I've been so worried since I had your wire.'

'Have you? Yes, I'm not surprised.'

'Are you ill?'

'Ill? Yes. . .ill. I feel quite ill.'

'Then you shouldn't be working. I'll speak to Mrs Watson. I'll ring for a taxi and take you home.'

'No! I don't want you to! In any case – can't you see how busy we are? You could hardly have chosen a less convenient moment!'

'I don't care how busy you are. If you're not fit to work –'

'What are you doing here, anyway? I didn't want you to come –'

'The telegram said urgent. I decided the best thing would be to take the day off and catch the first train down.'

'No, you didn't.'

'Didn't what?'

'Decide to take the day off. You didn't need to. You see. . .I *know*!' Even in this extremity there was a note of triumph in her voice and – at least equally disconcerting – a gleam of it in her eyes. 'Why do you think I sent that telegram? Because I couldn't reach you at the shop, that's why!'

'Oh. . . Oh, yes. I see.'

'I'm not quite the fool you thought me.'

'I never thought you a fool.'

'Excuse me. I must attend to this customer.'

When she had finished I said, 'You know, it still involved my taking the day off.'

'We really can't talk here. It's impossible.'

'I've been writing a book, you see. I told you about this book. I've been working on it every day – more or less keeping office hours. Now it's nearly finished. . .and I think it's going to make me money!' I was speaking rapidly, and with urgency, trying to cram it all in before she could tell me to stop, or before there should come another business interruption. 'I realized you wouldn't like me giving up the job and that's why I didn't tell you. But I wanted to give you a surprise by getting the book done quickly and having it accepted. You've always known it was my aim to be a writer.'

'I suddenly feel I don't know anything about you at all.'

'Why did you ring the shop?'

I had meant to ask the question calmly, matter-of-factly, but it came out sounding sharp. Accusatory. Of all the questions, I thought, which shouldn't have sounded sharp or accusatory!

She looked at me as if we couldn't be speaking the same language. And then she said, 'Yesterday morning, before coming in here, I went to the library. I sat down at a table to look at my novels and there was a big book about modern artists lying on the table.' Her tone was utterly flat. 'I remembered your man's name and I looked him up.'

Incredibly, for the first second or two, I didn't take in the implications.

'He was born in 1919,' she said. 'And he doesn't have four sons. The book said he was a bachelor.'

'Oh. . .? Oh, did it, now?' There didn't seem much else to say.

'So you admit it? You lied about that, as well?'

I shrugged. Said bitterly: 'Congratulations on your new job!'

'Have you gone mad – in addition to everything else?'

'My mistake – I thought you must have joined the CID!'

For a moment she looked almost sorry for me. 'It didn't say he wasn't married or that he had no children. I just put two and two together.'

'I see. How clever. I thought you'd already done that, when I told you about the car.'

'I was still hoping against hope.'

'That wasn't the way it appeared.'

'All yesterday I couldn't get it off my mind. At three o'clock this morning I decided to have it out with you. I rang the shop at five-past-nine and imagine how I felt, when. . .'

'Well, yes, and now you *have* had it out with me! I hope it's made you very happy.' It felt as if I hadn't any fight or energy remaining.

'Happy? I should like to kill myself – that's how happy it's made me!' She had unintentionally raised her voice. She looked about her quickly and lowered it again to an intense whisper. 'We can't go on like this,' she said.

'All right. What do you suggest? A divorce?'

She didn't answer; she didn't have the chance. I was suddenly aware of a small and busy presence: bouffant-haired, sharp-eyed, inquisitive. 'Why, if it isn't *John*! How *are* you, John? I thought your mother had a new boyfriend. I'll swear you grow bigger every time I see you. Doesn't it seem like that to you, Norma?'

'Oh, yes!' It was ludicrous, grotesque, to see the way my mother's manner altered. 'Yes, it does, Bea! I suppose that one day he may actually stop!'

It shouldn't have fooled anyone, I thought – least of all this shrewd little manageress – and yet the woman prattled on as if she'd noticed nothing.

'I'm sure he must eat you out of house and home. Whatever do you do? How's life in the great big wicked city, John?'

'Fine,' I said. 'Just fine! Couldn't be better!'

'Oh, Mrs Karminski, you'll never believe it, this is Mrs Wilmot's little boy. I knew him when he used to wear short trousers. Isn't it amazing that she could have a son so tall?'

'And so handsome, too,' nodded Mrs Karminski, fumbling with her bill, and her handbag, and her shopping basket.

'Yes but – hush! – it never does to tell them that.'

I could see that the waitress and the cook and everyone else on the premises would soon get drawn in to the act. I murmured my thanks to Mrs Karminski and then – gratefully – saw her turn towards the shiny black hairdo and heard her whisper, 'I am sorry, dear, but I don't think the fish today was quite up to standard.'

'I'm off,' I said to my mother.

'Yes,' she said. 'We'll talk later.'

'Not today we shan't! I'll be catching the next train back to London.'

'No – I forbid you to go back until we've spoken about this! And don't forget to say goodbye to Mrs Watson,' she added in the same fierce undertone.

I disregarded this entirely; Mrs Watson was in conference with Mrs Karminsky.

'Oh, and by the way,' I said, 'you'll have to think up some sort of story to tell Aunt Clara. I went to the house first.'

That was my parting shot.

*

In a florist's window I saw:

This year, on Mother's Day, why not let flowers convey a message that's sometimes hard to put into words?

'Wish you'd caught my eye earlier!' I told the window.

*

The train wheels pounded out an insistent, infuriating melody.

> 'The moment I saw you
> I heard a skylark sing;
> November was April
> And down the street came spring. . .'

I closed my eyes but couldn't stop the tears dribbling out beneath the lids. What *was* the matter with me? Had I forgotten how to be a man?

Had I forgotten the art of self-reliance?

Was this one of the side effects of being a kept boyfriend: of having all the usual economic difficulties lifted, all the boring household jobs removed, many of the everyday decisions – decisions bound up with becoming a responsible, dignified, self-respecting adult – taken from my shoulders?

A boyfriend. A gigolo.

Was I getting spoiled? Soft? Was the place I had my hair cut called *Delilah's*?

In short, I wondered. . .was I gradually, if very gently, being emasculated?

19

On leaving Charing Cross I went straight to the gym for what I hoped would be another gruelling workout. But my performance was distinctly below par and it didn't offer me release. When I called for Elizabeth my despondency was still strong. I hadn't even bothered going home to change. By 'home' I meant the Embankment.

But it was incredible how swiftly I recovered; not like *some* you could mention – *some,* who could be thrown into a day-long (week-long) gloom, without having half so good a reason.

And, believe it or not, this was currently what was going on. I'd rung Oliver when I left the gym and was soon surprised that he'd even managed to drag himself to the telephone. Hearing the lifelessness in his voice, and the brevity of his responses, I immediately thought Oh God, what now? But I knew, of course. It must be the disappointment of my book.

Except that, if this were indeed the case, how typical that *I* should have been able to suppress my feelings, whereas he. . .! And which of us, would you have said, had the better right *not* to suppress them?

Well, I assumed it was the book but – who knew? – it could have been anything. Yet, whatever it was, you'd have supposed that on *this* occasion he might have done his utmost to hold back.

But, anyway, I felt determined to put it all out of my mind; the whole lot; everything. I felt determined to have fun.

So Elizabeth and I went first to a pub and then to a new and fashionable restaurant; she was lucky to have got a table. Although I had only one Scotch at the pub, this affected me rapidly – well, admittedly it was a double and I'd eaten scarcely anything since breakfast (and *then* not very much, either). Added to which, we each drank several glasses of wine and afterwards

I had an Irish coffee. Moreover, Elizabeth seemed extra sweet – she must have sensed that something was the matter.

But finally it was Rachmaninoff who set the seal on my recovery; for ever since I had seen a revival of 'Brief Encounter' his Second Piano Concerto had been unquestionably my favourite piece of music. Leaving the Festival Hall I was as full of resilience as ever. Oliver was certainly mistaken about my novel. . .the Danish soloist, both during her performance and after, had provided the perfect accompaniment to every major incident in Timothy's childhood and early twenties – sometimes a passionate and tumultuous score, sometimes a touchingly wistful one – and elicited all the pathos inherent in the comedy; all the poignancy to which Oliver had so plainly been oblivious. Even that unhappy episode in *The Copper Kettle* now appeared less intractable, and mercifully remote, and once more life was most emphatically for getting on with. As we strolled back across the bridge, holding hands as always, I felt like a brave little orphan who had battled his way head-high through the storm (and found the golden sky and sweet silver song of a lark which Mr Hammerstein had promised). I remembered that Elizabeth had really been an orphan; and that made me feel protective and still more Olympian.

Oddly enough, though, the more cheerful I became, the less so did *she*. Perhaps she'd thought I was unhappy about her imminent departure. . .which actually to some degree I was. When we were halfway across the bridge, Big Ben started striking, and we leant over the parapet and faced towards Westminster. Everything seemed unnaturally quiet when the last of those eleven booms had faded. I was about to say, 'Can you imagine *anyone* not being able to stand here like this, to revel in such a view?' when Elizabeth suddenly gave a sigh.

'I like London,' she said. 'I like it better than anywhere.'

'Paris? Vienna? San Francisco?'

'Better than anywhere.'

My hand rested on hers. It felt companionable. I listened to the soft, mesmerizing slap of the river as it washed against the bridge. Elizabeth gestured to a path which the moonlight had made across the water.

'Five days from now,' she said, 'it may be looking much the same. But I shan't be around to see it.'

'A hundred years from now it may be looking much the same. But neither of us will be around to see it.'

'That's different.'

'Why?'

'Because this is possibly my last time.'

'No, it isn't. I'll bring you here tomorrow! And Sunday – and Monday – and Tuesday! But yes,' I said, more seriously, 'I do know what you mean.'

'I reckon I'd better try to catch some rare fever. Sufficiently bad I can't be moved, but not so bad my parents feel they have to stay. The trouble is – that sort of fever hasn't yet come on the market.'

'Do I detect the signs of incipient rebellion?'

'I love my parents. But sometimes I wish I were freer.'

'Ah, yes. . . The story of *all* our lives!'

'Though, obviously, it isn't just the place I'm going to miss.' She was still gazing at the water.

'It isn't?'

'But I guess that's foolish. Aren't places usually all tied up with. . .with the people whom you've met in them?'

Her voice caught on that second half of her sentence, and I realized she was crying.

'Here! What's this?'

I touched her shoulder and the next moment she was in my arms.

'You know,' I said, 'you don't absolutely *have* to leave, do you?'

As I spoke I was rhythmically stroking her hair. It smelled good.

'Don't I?'

'You could always tell your parents you want to stop here for some reason. Want to stop here, say, to get married. Or something else equally trivial. Guess what, you poor scrap? *I'd* marry you! You could always tell your parents that.'

I said it lightly, of course, expecting her to smile through her tears, before replying in similar vein. ('Yes, that would be nice... Why didn't *I* think of that?')

But for a long time she didn't reply in *any* vein. I was on the verge of adding in a rallying sort of way, 'That was a *joke*, you know,' when she again forestalled me. She drew back and gazed into my face. By the light of a nearby lamp I saw her cheeks glisten...('gossamer tracks of Stardust' was a phrase I'd written in my book). She looked young and trusting. Vulnerable. Gamine.

'Were you being serious?' she asked.

I instantly realized two things: the first, that Elizabeth clearly couldn't have been regarding these many past weeks simply in the light of some fly-by-night holiday romance; and the second, that – astoundingly – at this very moment a sum of well over a million dollars might be winging its way along the wire to meet me...winging its way, *singing* its way...I had merely to say the word!

'Astoundingly' hardly covered it. The only time I had given the matter so much as a minute's thought had been during the weekend of our first encounter; and even then I had assumed she would be unattainable.

But, my God! The life now beckoning was a life of luxury and ease. (No – I had luxury and ease already.) The life now beckoning was a life of independence.

Master in my own house. No further need to play second fiddle.

Not to anyone.

Plus...the most perfect escape from that whole sorry situation in Folkestone.

You almost had to wonder whether – in the complete, unexpurgated history of the universe – anything else could ever have been quite so fortuitous.

'Serious?' I said. 'Serious about what? That *I'd* many you, if that was the only way you could contrive to stay in England?'

'Yes.'

I waited a few seconds before answering.

'My goodness, Elizabeth! I didn't think I stood a chance, not in a month of Sundays – but if I hadn't meant it, do you really suppose that I'd have said it?'

'Maybe you were feeling sorry for me? I was being an awful sap.'

'I don't *often* propose out of sympathy.'

Then suddenly she was laughing and hugging me – I was laughing, too. Three old men who'd been approaching had to make a detour. They muttered and stared.

And, for the next sixty minutes or so, it was all giddiness and unreality. Plan-making and protestations. We began sauntering in the direction of the hotel and then – roughly opposite the spot where, last November, Oliver had sat waiting in the parked car – we spontaneously whirled round and started back towards the other side. Reckless about the lateness of the hour. . .or, at least, all ready to be. But then Elizabeth said: 'No, there's no point in making them cross. On the contrary! We must do everything we can to keep them sweet.'

She was sweet, I told her. She was sweet and she was sensible and she was loving and she was loaded. 'And you're mine. Isn't that sensational?'

So I serenaded her. "Because you're mine, the whole world sings a melody. . ." I held my arms out, in an attitude of beatific welcome. 'Come back, Mario Lanza! All is forgiven!'

So I sang and danced and played the fool; kept up an incessant flow of nonsense. And she joined in – we even waltzed together

– yet all the while she was steering me, resolutely, towards the hotel.

At the entrance I said: 'I'm coming up!'

'No, not tonight, Johnny. It's better I prepare the way. Come back tomorrow. As early as you like.'

'Five a.m.?'

'Suits me.'

'We're getting married,' I said to the commissionaire, who was standing nearby, pretending not to notice.

'Congratulations, sir. Congratulations, Miss.'

'I'm not doing badly, would you say?'

'Not badly at all, sir.'

And it wasn't until I was on my way home – please God, to a more responsive Oliver – that my first mild misgivings started to appear.

20

I returned to the Savoy – not at five a.m. – but at eleven. I left about an hour later.

And the following day, Sunday, I telephoned Elizabeth from a callbox.

'Oh, thank heaven,' she said. 'I've been on tenterhooks.'

'Are your parents there?'

'No. Can I meet you? For ten minutes?'

'Obviously you can. I'll come to the hotel.'

'No, don't do that. Let's say the Adelphi. In quarter of an hour?'

I caught a taxi but she was already there. Although it was so short a time since we'd seen 'Auntie Mame', the photographs outside the theatre imbued me with nostalgia. How pathetic! We went into the first café we found open and I ordered coffees.

But it wasn't going to be hard to play the suffering hero.

(John Wilmot – one of the most exciting new stars ever to grace the Metro firmament – caught here in a tensely dramatic scene from this year's most distinguished hit, 'The Parting'.)

'I was so anxious,' she said, 'when you didn't call me.'

'But I did.'

'I mean yesterday. I didn't stir from the telephone all afternoon.'

I looked down at the table and for a moment chewed my lip. 'To tell you the truth I felt a bit shaken.' She reached across and took my hand. 'Also, I half promised your father that, for a day or two, I'd let you be.'

'So that was it,' she said. 'He wouldn't really go in to what happened between you – not with me, anyway. He told us you behaved like a gentleman and seemed very reasonable.'

'Well, that's something, I suppose.'

'But it didn't cheer me up a great deal.' She let go my hand. 'Darling,' she said softly – and I thought at first her hesitation had simply to do with the endearment. 'I want you to stop behaving like a gentleman.'

'Don't ask the impossible!'

She didn't smile.

'But what is it you mean?' Surely it wasn't bed she had in mind?

'I want us to elope.'

I stared. Suddenly the script had gone all haywire. 'Elope?'

She nodded.

'Elizabeth. . . Perhaps you haven't considered this for quite as long as you ought to?'

'On the contrary. I was already considering it on Friday night, while we were still on Waterloo Bridge. I love you, John Wilmot. And I'm determined to marry you.' She paused. 'And that's the only way.'

'Listen.' I groped frantically for the best manner in which to Renounce a Great Love. 'Listen, Angel Face. . .'

But *why?* I stopped. What had changed since Friday? I had allowed a few irrational qualms to escalate; to grow out of all proportion. Yet, otherwise. . .? And was I truly going to let a few irrational qualms stand in the way of everything which had then appeared so good?

'No, Johnny – *you* listen. It isn't as drastic as it sounds. On the nineteenth of April I shall be twenty-one. That's exactly four weeks from now. And after that there's not a thing which can prevent my grandfather's money from getting through to me. Nothing.'

I looked down at the table. Then I looked back up.

'I have to admit it – you certainly time things well!'

'Yes, don't I?'

'But. . .'

'But what, sweetie?'

'Are you sure you've *really* thought about it – all the unpleasantness there'll be? And are you sure you *really* think I'm worth it?'

'It'll be utterly miserable – I know that! But yes, Johnny, I really do think you're worth it.' She spoke with decisiveness and humour.

'My goodness. You're suddenly quite a girl!'

'Suddenly?'

Then she laughed and said, 'No, don't change that! Maybe it's because *you're* quite a guy – and I knew I'd finally found something worth fighting for.'

I liked the idea of my being quite a guy.

'Johnny? Shall I tell you when I fell in love with you?'

'The moment you saw me?' (You heard a skylark sing.)

'No. Though I think I was more interested in you than you were in me. And I did admire the way you stood up to Cousin Sarah and I thought you tremendously attractive. But it was actually some time afterwards.'

'That first evening I came to the Savoy?'

She shook her head. 'Oh, yes, perhaps a little. . .when I saw you drive away and I knew I shouldn't be seeing you again for such ages – I would have given a lot just then not to be going on the Grand Tour. But when it really happened you weren't even there. It was your letter which did it: the description of your mother and great-aunt and the time you had together over Christmas. And I don't know what it was – there was something in the way you wrote about them – and I thought I love that man, I love that man so much it hurts, I shall love him till the day I die. And from that moment I began to have an insane fear you might be knocked down in a traffic accident, struck by lightning, anything. I so much couldn't imagine what the world would be like without you that I grew quite superstitious and kept believing the Fates might force me to find out.' Involuntarily, she trembled. Then she smiled, as if apologizing for her foolishness.

I smiled, too – but a little uncertainly. I was almost shocked by her intensity. That anyone should feel this way about *me*. . . *could* feel this way about me. . . I was moved, naturally, yet at the same time found it disturbing. I recollected telling Mrs Cambourne I had never been in love, never experienced any depth of emotion remotely like the one Elizabeth had just described. Now, of course – if I was so soon to marry – it was unlikely that I ever would: the one glaring omission in my life which I knew I should regret more deeply than any other. I said confusedly:

'When had you in mind for our 'elopement'?' It needed the inverted commas.

'Darling, did I embarrass you just then?'

'Not in the slightest. Why?'

She continued to gaze at me searchingly. But then she answered my previous question. 'Next Tuesday. The day before my parents leave.'

'No chance of getting them to change their mind?'

'None whatsoever. Don't think I won't be trying, but my father's even more stubborn than I am.'

'Next Tuesday?'

'Gretna Green.'

'Oh, Elizabeth! How corny!'

'And, besides that, how unnecessary! By the time we've been up there three weeks – the three weeks are obligatory – I'll be nearly twenty-one. But at least it will give us a point to aim for; and once we're registered we'll feel completely safe. And in any case,' she said, 'I'd love to see some more of Scotland.'

I answered absent-mindedly – and as bitterly as though it were a matter for real resentment, 'Ridiculous you can die for your country at eighteen but not get married in it till you're twenty-one! Not unless you've got the consent of your parents – and we both know how we feel at the moment about parents!'

Apparently, though, she was somewhat disinclined to join me at the pillory. She merely said: 'I suppose it'll change one of these days.'

'Big deal.'

'Yes – think how easy it could all have been! We'd have taken out a special licence and then been flying off on honeymoon by Wednesday. Sailing round the Caribbean, or something.'

I had a fleeting vision of the Greek islands – of stretching out naked on the deck of the yacht 'Sarah'.

'I see you've done your homework,' I said.

'But, anyhow, we Yankees aren't quite as ignorant as you and Oliver would seem to think. Even in Massachusetts we've heard of Gretna Green.'

'I didn't mean that.'

'And in addition you'll never believe how organized I am. Nothing left to chance! I already have a list of train times and the stations where we'll need to change – all that kind of stuff. And I'll get the tickets tomorrow, make the reservations –

reservations for both the train *and* the boarding house. You, sweetheart, won't have to worry about a thing!'

It sounded comfortable. I felt tired. I expressed my gratitude.

'Though about those tickets...'

'Yes, Johnny?'

When I faltered, she proved herself a mind-reader.

'Oh, but wouldn't it be lovely to *drive* up to Scotland! Next month we'll get ourselves a car. After the money comes through.'

I said: 'Actually, I've had one these past three months. Since Christmas. As it happens – I take my driving test tomorrow.'

She stopped in the act of picking up her cup. 'I had no idea you were learning to drive! I didn't even know you had a car.'

'Oliver gave it to me.'

Her eyes widened. I didn't care. Let them widen. Let the whole thing swing whichever way it chose.

But all she said was – slowly and after a pause – 'Isn't he just the most wonderful person around! What make is it?'

I told her. She seemed excited. She knew about Jaguar XK 150s. For several minutes we talked only of cars.

Afterwards she said:

'By the way, how is Oliver?'

'Well, since Friday he's been wrestling with what your Cousin Sarah refers to – along with countless others, I suppose – as the dark night of the soul. I have to say, it *is* a bit tiresome, but at least when I left this morning he was beginning to show signs of improvement.'

I knew I'd made a faux pas. She did nothing, however, to suggest she might have noticed.

But again – either way – I didn't much care.

21

I passed my test. It didn't elate me particularly – I'd never supposed I'd fail – but at least it provided me with half an hour of complete escape while I thought of nothing but my driving. When I returned to the Embankment Oliver gave me a bear hug. His depression was over. In some ways – how selfishly! – I almost wished it wasn't. 'We must paint the town,' he said.

I'd envisaged an evening spent at home; I hadn't yet settled on how best to break the news. But on the other hand, I thought, it might be easier to do it some place where there would be bustle and bright lights.

'I've bought us both a small present,' he added, 'to commemorate your success. Come into my parlour. . .said the spider to the fly!'

'And supposing I hadn't been successful?' My state of mind turned me contrary. Why did he have to make me all these gifts? What would I have to do – return them? (I couldn't return the car; definitely not the car.)

'Then there'd probably have been more need of it,' he said.

'What is it?'

'Well, you remember that hour or so we passed in Hamley's. . .?' Oliver held open the door of his studio.

I stopped and stared and forced a laugh. 'You're crazy!'

Laid out on the floor was an extensive network of railway lines, bridges, stations. There were two electric engines and each one drew six coaches.

'Now don't pretend you didn't enjoy yourself that morning,' said Oliver. 'Remember how we decided we'd suffered deprived childhoods and I said we'd have to do everything in our power to correct this?'

'But I didn't think you meant it.'

'I didn't entirely. But then – hunting around for something to get you – us,' he amended, 'it all came back to me. You can buy hills and houses and lakes and churches and. . .oh, I don't know. . .masses of other things. . .and build up quite a little community, once you really get started. Look, my love: these are the controls.'

'Well, I would never have guessed that,' I said sarcastically.

But I ran the two trains round the circuit a couple of times and shunted them back and forth a bit. I couldn't show much enthusiasm.

'Again,' he said, 'I'm so sorry it wasn't all wrapped up in pretty paper, with ribbons and bows and tinsel; but one of these days, maybe. . .' He saw I had tears running down my face (of course!) and he must have supposed it was like when he'd given me the car. He tried to wipe them away with his thumbs but there were too many for that. Once more he had to use his handkerchief. 'Come on. I know what you need,' he told me. 'I'm such a thoughtless bastard: it suddenly occurs to me you haven't had anything to revive you since your big ordeal.'

But I was still being bolshie – perhaps this seemed to me a good means of defence? 'I don't want anything. . .and it *wasn't* an ordeal! In fact, it was by far the best part of the day.' I remembered my saying that the best part of another day had been when the two of us were sitting in the library studying Canaletto.

He made me sit down by the fire while he went into the kitchen. (Mondays were James's day off.) Soon afterwards he brought me a tall glass filled with a frothy yellow liquid. 'Orange juice, eggs and honey and a drop or two of brandy. Prepared with my own fair hands! Oranges freshly squeezed, too – and need I say, at quite appalling effort?'

I answered: 'If you'd told me the eggs were freshly laid at quite appalling effort, now *that* might have been something to boast about.' This retort had also started out as bolshie but somehow it ended up on a reluctant smile. Handing me the glass he bent over to kiss my forehead. 'Now, that's more like it,' he approved.

We didn't exactly paint the town. We drove into Sussex. It was the first time I'd driven without L-plates and it was a perfect spring evening, with clumps of primroses under the hedgerows. But it was not the experience I'd once been looking forward to;

and even my driving was erratic – had I made the same mistakes an hour earlier I should probably have failed.

Dinner at a pub. Only a few days ago I'd surely have found it delicious but tonight my appetite was poor. 'Oh, my darling,' he said. 'You must be in love.'

'Ha!'

'What time on Wednesday do the Sheldons depart? No association of ideas, naturally.'

'They leave Heathrow at ten.'

'In the morning?'

'Yes.'

'Going to see them off?'

This, I realized, was the time to speak. *Now.* If I didn't say anything now, it would be harder later on.

'I don't know. You?'

'I hadn't any plans to. But if you like we could go together, I don't begrudge giving up a morning's work in so excellent a cause.'

I sipped some coffee. Oliver put his hand on my knee and gave a sympathetic squeeze.

But I couldn't tell him. Not yet. For one thing – with the revelation made, how could I face the thought of our journey home?

'If we go now,' he said, 'we could still catch the last performance of something. Or are you weary?'

'Yes, a bit.'

'It's hardly surprising. You didn't sleep a wink last night. Shall I drive back?'

When we returned to the flat he suggested I have a drink and go to bed. I didn't want to go to bed. I wandered listlessly. I felt a ridiculous urge just to touch things. He put on some records: twice he played the Tchaikovsky 'Pathétique', aware of my fondness for it – I liked it nearly as much as the Rachmaninoff, which had recently been scratched and was now unplayable.

I sat opposite him in my usual place wondering if this would be the last occasion I'd do so. It struck me with great force how little security, true security, life ever offered you. These past few days, perhaps for the first time since the eve of my initial departure for boarding school, I'd been feeling nervous and unsafe; like a man leaving home in wartime for the unknown terrors of the front – a man who knew he hadn't made an especially good son, husband, father, but now saw clearly how he would behave if he could only have a second chance.

Yet for millions and millions there had never come that second chance.

At last I went to bed. After all, it wasn't imperative to break the news that evening. The following morning would do as well; in fact, rather better; I wasn't meeting Elizabeth till after lunch. (Before I'd got home I had telephoned her briefly with the result of the test.) In the morning I would write a letter to my mother and I would tell Oliver. The thought occurred to me for the first time: why not write a letter to Oliver, too?

I pushed it aside, as unworthy.

Half the night, though, I lay there composing letters. When I wasn't doing that I was several times being tempted just to wake Oliver and make a clean breast of it. Please get me out of this! Make everything all right! Once, I turned over and actually reached out my hand. But even as I did so the thought of all those thousands of dollars stopped me; together with a nightmare vision of growing older and more pathetic: a figure of fun clinging tenaciously to youth, keeping up pretences, shying from the prospect of imprisonment – yet, all the same, often discerning distaste or puzzlement in the looks of others. And what about the fathering of children? At the moment it wasn't important to me but I could well imagine that someday it might be. And the thing was. . .I wasn't even homosexual! Well, yes, to some degree, obviously, but certainly not completely so. Indeed, I didn't know *what* I was. Nor what I ought to be doing about it.

Doing about that, or – as it almost seemed to me now – about anything.

Then at around four o'clock I drifted into a deep sleep and when I awoke the worst of my doubts had gone. Or, at any rate, diminished. I made myself think about Elizabeth – about her niceness and her intelligence and her standing in the world – and the more I concentrated on those things the more strength did I derive from them. I saw again the disparity between the status of a husband and that of a kept boyfriend.

It was going to be easier than I'd thought.

Nevertheless when it came to writing my letters, which some hours earlier I had thought I had word-perfect, the phrases wouldn't return to me. Or when they did they seemed either too contrived or too emotional. I sat and stared at the intricate carving on Oliver's desk and at two heavy paperweights on top of it – ugly bronze Buddhas which had belonged to one of his grandmothers, who must have thought them interesting – and I made one false start after another. Then I had the idea of seeing to my mother's letter first. I didn't care so much about that. The words began to flow.

While I was writing, James came in, bringing me a cup of coffee.

'James, is Mr Cambourne in the studio?'

'Yes, sir. And he asked me to say he'll be having lunch at home; his appointment has been cancelled. Will you be eating in today?'

I hesitated. I had intended to be but I didn't feel that I could face it now. Much though, simultaneously, I was very much drawn to having lunch with Oliver.

'No thanks. And thank you for the coffee, James. That's nice of you.'

'Not at all, sir.' Was there the slightest hint of surprise in his tone – at what, I supposed, might have seemed like uncustomary warmth? 'Is there anything else you'll be wanting? Before I go to the shops?'

'No, thank you, James.'

A moment later he was back. With an inquiry totally unprecedented.

'Nothing you'd like me to get you while I'm out, sir?'

It seemed a real shame I had to decline such an offer. Perhaps I had misjudged him all along.

But if so it was now a little late to be discovering it.

'My dearest Oliver,' I wrote when the door had closed for the second time (I would finish off my mother's letter afterwards), 'I'm sorry I haven't been quite my usual self recently. The reason is, there was something I had to tell you, which I kept putting off. Now I've funked it altogether and am writing you instead.

'I'm going to marry Elizabeth. (Though absolutely *not* with her parents' consent!) We are running off this afternoon – heading for Scotland! I realize you'll have read this by the time we leave, but I realize equally that you would never try to stop us.

'Oliver, I just don't know how to thank you for everything you've done. My own – my own, my very dear – Pygmalion. These past five months have been, without reservation, the happiest I've ever spent. And that's because of you and not Elizabeth. You've been wonderful – right from the beginning – and will always occupy a very special place in my heart. You've given me so much. I shall always be so grateful.

'Obviously, this is far from being a letter of goodbye. I'd have liked you for best man if circumstances had been different. I shall most certainly be asking you to be a godfather. I shall forever need your friendship. You've been the best friend that anyone – anywhere – could ever possibly have had. I was aware of that almost from the start and it was something which I treasured deeply.

'Yes, hardly a day went by when I *wasn't* aware of your friendship and when I didn't feel intensely privileged to have it.

'I shall always feel intensely privileged. Simply to have been permitted to get to know you.

'To share your bed. To share your life.

'Perhaps you'll think of me, too, with something of the same affection? (And Elizabeth as well, of course – she's very fond of you.) Please do. Please do! And forgive me for everything. Do you remember. . .to err is human, to forgive, divine? You said you'd always do your very best to bear it in mind!

'Especially with regard to me!

'Isn't it strange how in the space of just two days I met the two people who would become the most important in my life? And that I should actually have met them in the order of their importance?

'Why don't you do what you said on Christmas Day that you might: look for a wife and start a family? Otherwise, it's such a sad, appalling waste. I know you'd make the very best of fathers. I only wish I had the slightest hope of ever discovering myself, even remotely, in the same league as *you*.

'In any case, don't be unhappy. I'm not worth it.

'With my deepest love – my *really* deepest love – and my sincerest, heartfelt thanks.

'John.

'PS. I've just seen the roll of banknotes in your desk and have taken a hundred pounds. I'll leave an IOU! I'm sure you won't mind – you being you. But I feel I shall probably need it to get us through the immediate future. (On second thoughts I'm going to make it *two* hundred.)

'PPS. It has only this very minute struck me that simply because I'm getting married there's no earthly reason why we shouldn't still meet up. On our own, I mean. And frequently. Did you ever see that Billy Wilder film, 'Love in the Afternoon'?

'After all, there's no need to become all moral suddenly – all tediously stuffy – just because I'm getting hitched.

'Anyway, I shall ring you the moment we get back. (And you must, without question, be our first dinner guest! We'll be living in Gloucester Place.)

'See you, then, *extremely* soon.

'John.'

I didn't really want to stop. Unexpectedly, once I'd begun, I had actually enjoyed writing it. And the last bit especially had made me feel more cheerful. I read the whole thing through and reckoned it was all right. Even rather good. I thought it struck a balance between being maudlin and matter-of-fact.

So I made a fair copy and put a row of kisses underneath my name – screwed up the sheet with all the crossings-out and shoved that inside the pocket of my jeans. At length I put the letter in an envelope, sealed it, wrote 'Oliver'.

But then I had a disquieting thought: could it have come across as sounding a shade literary – especially in the tidied-up version?

Yet what could I do? I was, in a sense, a literary person. Oliver was a literary person. And the content had been anything but insincere – dear God! – absolutely anything but the basis for some exercise in style. Every sentence, every sentiment, had come directly from the heart. I didn't want to think about rewriting it.

No. I left the envelope propped against one of the Buddhas. He would see it almost at once.

Following which, I finished my mother's letter; addressed, stamped and also stuck that into a pocket – but, this time, the breast pocket of my jacket, which was hanging over the back of my chair.

It took me ten minutes to pack: an unpleasantly suspenseful period. Twice I imagined I heard steps outside the door and once, when the telephone rang, it not only startled me, it made me break into a sweat. I had forgotten its bell would not be audible inside the studio.

At the end of those ten minutes I stood in the centre of the room, looking around as if for the last time and trying to imprint it on my brain forever. It was a strange and melancholy thought that I should never be seeing it again as its rightful occupant, never lie warm in bed on first awakening and gaze up only half-consciously at the splendidly convoluted mouldings on the ceiling, trying drowsily to trace patterns; never see again, at that hour of the morning, the tops of the trees that lined the river. It wasn't even half a year that I had slept in this room; and yet, somehow, it seemed more a part of me than the bedroom I had had since birth.

Then I went and stood in the sitting room. I remembered the first time I had walked into it; for an instant saw it again with fresh eyes, as if I was just at the beginning, not the end. I even felt the weight of those six books in my left hand.

I was about to go back into the study to take one last look at that as well, when I suddenly thought: no, this way madness lies. I turned abruptly, put on my sheepskin jacket, retrieved the suitcases and opened the front door. As I did so I heard Oliver call out, 'Is that you, James?'

I shut the door with frantic stealth and began to run (I hadn't time to wait for the lift), the older of the cases banging uncomfortably against my leg. On the fifth floor I listened. And on each of the next four floors, also. There was no sound of pursuit.

Outside the entrance I met James.

I saw the man's swift glance take in my luggage and saw the question mark flash in his eyes.

But I brushed past him with a quick nod and hurried on into the garage beside the flats. So much for our one brief moment of sympathy. I almost hated him again. Him and his tortured fingernails.

Once upon my way, however, amidst the seeming protection of the traffic, I began to feel more relaxed. I turned on the radio.

'Oh, Mr Porter, what shall I do? I wanted to go to Birmingham but they set me down at Crewe. . .'

Oh Christ, I thought. I hadn't thanked Oliver for the train set.

22

I put this right shortly afterwards. On reaching Gloucester Place I found his doorkey still in my pocket. I immediately wrapped it in tissue, then searched for a strong envelope. Before licking down the flap – and taping it – I added two lines: 'Forgot to leave your key. Forgot, also, to thank you for the train. It was a sweet thought. I love you very much. J.'

Hurried, badly written, totally unplanned, but I was glad I'd thought of it.

I put that and my mother's letter on the kitchen table, where I'd be sure to notice when I left the flat.

Having taken the clothes out of both cases, I repacked the pigskin one with the things I knew I'd need. For some reason I had an urge to travel light.

Even so, it would have been wiser to take the larger piece of luggage. Almost automatically, I chose the smaller.

I burnt the crumpled piece of paper from my pocket – without reading it still another time, although I'd felt strongly tempted to do so – and dropped the ashes into the otherwise clean and empty kitchen bin.

Then I had a simple lunch of honey, digestive biscuits and black coffee. It wasn't a lot, but even getting that second biscuit down proved difficult.

I had hardly finished, and was about to wash my cup and plate and spoon, when the doorbell rang.

It made me jump – almost literally – like the phone at the Embankment. My heartbeat quickened and I flushed. I knew that it was Oliver.

After ten seconds there was another ring: longer, more insistent: a finger left pressed upon the bell. The appeal of it was all but irresistible. Damn it, I *wanted* to answer. *How* I wanted to answer!

A third long ring. Pause. A fourth. Each an electric shock, snatching you up, flinging you down, yanking at your heartstrings. If there'd been a fifth, I might have lost control.

But no. After that. . .silence.

In its different, insidious way – second after second after second – the silence was as hard to endure. Maybe harder.

I couldn't believe that he had gone. I could feel his presence looming as if the door were made of frosted glass and his shadow spread-eagled across it and pushing its way through. I strained for the sound of footsteps. *Had* he gone? I thanked providence there'd been no parking space nearby and that I'd had to leave the car down a side street. But for this I should certainly have been trapped.

Half of me, that was, thanked providence.

I thought now that, after all, he might head for the Savoy. The first thing to do, then, must be to warn Elizabeth. I picked up my jacket and the case. I would phone her as soon as I reached the car.

There was another peal at the bell. It lasted for five seconds, maybe ten. It was agonizing.

Had he been standing there waiting or had he taken a turn around the block? He couldn't *know* that I was there, surely? Unless, of course, he had actually found the car.

Oh, Oliver.

Why are you doing this to me?

If it was instinct which told him to keep ringing – or instinct and desperation both – then *his* instinct wasn't the only one at work.

Mine told me that if I saw him again within the immediate future – had to look just once into his face – my resolve to leave him would not only weaken, it would disappear. I couldn't bear to meet him now and not go back with him.

In any case, I didn't feel that I could take much more of this.

Yet this time there was only the one ring. Nothing but the noise of the traffic – muted, usually unnoticeable – disturbed the silence after that.

The racking silence.

Five minutes later I began to move; no longer stood there irresolute. I again picked up the case, threw my jacket over my arm, and left the flat.

*

There was no sign of him. I stood in the centre of the pavement and stared in both directions. The pavement wasn't crowded. Then I walked steadily towards the car. No sign. I drove back to the callbox and double-parked while I telephoned Elizabeth. I asked her to leave the hotel at once; if possible by a back entrance. I said that Oliver might be arriving there at any moment in order to warn her parents.

She hadn't even finished lunch.

I said she was lucky to have been able to eat any.

While they'd paged Elizabeth (luckily the Sheldons had been having their meal in the Grill) they'd kept me waiting for at least a minute. But the only person I found by the car when I came out of the box was an admiring schoolkid.

'Sir, isn't that the latest model?' He asked it with round eyes and West One confidence.

'Last October,' I said.

'Automatic?'

'No. With overdrive.' I paused. 'I'd give you a ride but (a) I'm in a hurry and (b) your parents mightn't like it.' While I talked, my eyes searched the pavement on both sides of the road.

'I'm going to have a car like this one day.'

'Then you'd better start saving.'

'May I just sit behind the wheel a second?'

His second was more like a minute but he got out obediently enough the moment I requested it.

'I shan't forget this, sir. Thank you so very much.'

I didn't think that I should forget it, either.

*

Twenty minutes later I picked up Elizabeth on the corner of the Aldwych. Her eyes looked watery but in every other way she appeared calm.

She had two enormous suitcases. 'And even then I had to leave stuff behind. I've no idea what'll become of it.'

She said it quite matter-of-factly, yet, added to a momentary image I had, in which I saw her struggling determinedly across the Strand – for neither of the cases came with wheels – the remark caused her to seem a bit pathetic. Brave but pathetic. It was the best thing that could have happened. My initial sympathy gave place to a sensation of tenderness and warmth, almost of love. I again felt I wanted to take care of her.

Shortly afterwards we were doubling back the way I'd come. We drove up Gloucester Place – I pointed out the flat in passing – and soon we had reached the Finchley Road. Heading north.

It was about an hour later I remembered the two envelopes still sitting on the kitchen table.

I felt tempted to go back. Really tempted. More for Oliver's – only three lines though it was – than for my mother's.

Part Two

23

If their Stop Press hadn't been on the front page I mightn't have seen it. I'd been walking down towards the river, glancing idly at the headlines. I was about to turn the page when I noticed a green wooden bench and for some reason decided to sit. Perhaps a part of my brain had already registered – but not yet communicated – might have been preparing me. Delayed reaction. I saw the name 'Oliver Cambourne', almost illegible in smudged print, and thought at first it was an optical illusion brought about by my having Oliver so continuously in mind; then in a split-second of disbelief saw the words surrounding the name. 'Identified as. . .well-known society artist.' The rest of it built up in slow motion around that same hard core. 'Late last night. . . man's body. . .retrieved from Thames. Late last night. . . Mr Oliver Cambourne. . . Late last night. . .man's body. . . Late last night. . . Foul play not. . .' I let the paper slide from my knees; bent and picked it up. Read again: 'Late last night. . . man's body. . .Mr Oliver Cambourne. . .retrieved from. . .' It remained unchanging. I looked up and stared across the road. There was a whitewashed tollhouse with a hoarding in the garden: 'Late last night. . .' After a moment the words *there* did reshape themselves: '. . .house famous for Gretna Green runaway marriages.' There was another sign above the door. 'Over 10,000 marriages performed in this marriage room.' My eyes went from hoarding to front door. I couldn't seem

– quite – to make sense of either statement, although I read them both repeatedly, with dazed determination.

The paper had again slipped from my knees. Abruptly I stood up, stooped down, crumpled it. Savagely. My brain saw this as a ploy – savagery! A lifesaver, something to hold on to. I shoved the paper into a bin; viciously pressed it down. 'How feeble! How bloody feeble!' An old woman passed me with an umbrella – I became aware it was raining – it was only from the look on her face I realized I must have spoken the thought out loud. I didn't care. 'I always knew you were weak,' I cried at her bent, retreating figure. 'I never guessed you were *that* weak!'

I stood there for a moment – immobile, irresolute, numb. And yet not numb in the least. When I started back to the B and B I strode there as though only the rapidity of my motion, along with the anger which I clung to, could get me back at all. If I ran out of anger, ran out of speed – what then? Would I for all time simply moon about the fields and moors, the hidden byways: an endless wanderer, eternal tramp? Yes, fuck you, Oliver Cambourne! Fool! *Fool*! You spineless fucking fool!

So it got me back. I ran up the staircase, rapped on Elizabeth's door. It was half-past-eight. She was standing by the window, brushing her hair. When I went in she put down the brush and came towards me holding out her arms.

'Good morning, Johnny. Sleep well?'

'Yes. *Yes*! You?'

How could I mouth such inanities?

I stepped into her arms, largely because I didn't want her to look into my face.

'Darling, you're wet!' She felt my jumper, felt my hair. 'You've been out!'

'Went for a paper. Wondered. Anything about us.'

'Was there?'

'No. Didn't buy one.'

'Quite right – certainly not worth it if there wasn't anything about us! But you mustn't go catching pneumonia!' She touched my hair again and held me tight. 'What made you think the papers might get hold of it?'

'I told you: just wondered –

'But suddenly my voice broke.

She pulled apart, immediately. 'What's the matter, Johnny? What is it?'

'Nothing.'

'You're not disappointed, are you?'

'Oh, for Christ's sake! I choked, that's all.' I saw her face. 'I'm sorry. These past few days – they've been a strain.'

She accepted this at once. 'Oh, sweetheart, you do look off-colour. We'll try to take it easy for a while. Don't want you falling sick.'

She added brightly: 'Let's go down and have some breakfast.'

My God. Breakfast!

24

We'll try to take it easy, she had said. I didn't want to take it easy; couldn't bear to. That morning we went sightseeing, inspected the Sark Tollhouse. We paid sixpence each to be shown around the small, cluttered Marriage Room and view the relics of a bygone age: dusty stovepipe hats, black ties, creased certificates, prints of anxious runaways being chased by angry fathers. On the walls were notices declaring war on the blacksmith's shop a few miles away; it turned out we weren't actually in Gretna.

We went to see that blacksmith's shop. It was covered in posters. It had a turnstile that was clicking busily even at eleven on a Wednesday morning. We gazed at an anvil said to be the very one over which successive blacksmiths had formerly forged marriage unions. We listened to the tale of one so-called romantic escapade after another.

Most of the time I really did my best to concentrate, although I fleetingly wondered whether someday other eager tourists would hear about the young man who had come to Gretna with an American heiress and thereby driven his lover to suicide. Romantic enough for anyone.

Elizabeth voiced my own sentiments.

'I don't like this,' she whispered. 'It's claustrophobic. Let's get out of here.'

Outside it was still drizzling but now we had raincoats and umbrellas and she took a deep breath.

'All those fortune-hunters and abductors…and we're expected to feel glad they got away with it!'

'But they didn't,' I said. 'Not for the most part. I suppose it depends what you mean by 'got away with'.'

Then I bit my lip. *As Professor Joad might have said…* It was my first indication of the way attack could come. Without warning.

That evening Elizabeth phoned her parents from Dumfries. It was the prototype of several long conversations which only had the effect of tiring and distressing her. It consisted of a series of appeals and heated arguments on either side. Those of her mother, mingled as they were with tears and free of the abuse her father used, were naturally far harder to resist. By *Theodore* Sheldon I heard myself described as playboy, parasite, adventurer and – yes, obviously – as someone who was solely after her money. I heard all this because I was sitting next to Elizabeth on her narrow bed. At other times I knew I'd have been tempted to seize the phone and respond in kind but now, at *this* time, what did it matter? What could anything matter? It was rather touching to witness Elizabeth's indignation on my behalf, both on and off the telephone, and afterwards to have her pour out her apologies. Rather touching yet it scarcely touched me.

She admired me for my calm acceptance; said that all the time she was discovering in me new qualities.

From Dumfries – where we spent only that one night – I also made a phone call. Unlike Elizabeth, I didn't reverse the charges.

'Hello, Mum. It's John.'

'Oh, yes?'

'John.'

'I wondered if you were going to get in touch.'

'I wrote you a letter but forgot to send it. How are you?'

'Not very well, I'm afraid.'

'I'm sorry to hear that.'

'Are you?'

'Of course I am.'

'Where are you speaking from?'

'Scotland.'

'From *Scotland*? Then this must be expensive. I'd better say goodbye.'

'No! No! Don't do that! The money doesn't matter. I wanted to give you some news. I'll soon be getting married.'

'Oh?'

'Well, aren't you pleased?'

'I really don't know.'

'You will be. Her name's Elizabeth. She's impatient to meet you both. You're going to like her a lot. She's –'

'What did your man have to say about it?'

'She's sitting beside me right now. Would you like to talk to her a minute – say hello to one another?'

'Not really. No, I think it will be better if –'

I wasn't sure how much of this Elizabeth had been able to make out; my mother's voice was softer than her father's – especially at the moment – and for a lot of the time I hadn't heard Mrs Sheldon.

Anyway, I hoped for the best and handed over the receiver.

Hoped for the best? No. I no longer hoped for anything.

'Hello, Mrs Wilmot. This is just so nice! I'm sorry we had to spring it on you like this – that we couldn't have gotten acquainted beforehand. But we're going to put that right the moment we come south. Johnny's going to bring me down to Folkestone first thing. Aren't you, Johnny?'

As I had guessed would happen, my mother was a different person with Elizabeth. After all, Elizabeth might be tarnished by association, but it wasn't she who'd been at *The Copper Kettle* last Friday; it wasn't she who'd walked out without saying goodbye to Mrs Watson.

It wasn't *she* who had been living for the past five months with Oliver.

Besides. Whatever my mother's feelings about the way the news had been broken or at the hurried fashion in which the marriage appeared to be taking place – and heaven alone knew what she might infer from that – she must at any rate be glad I had now taken up with a woman. *Any* woman, practically. One who was nicely spoken and polite and warm and friendly could only be twice as welcome.

Surely?

Which isn't to say the going was completely smooth. Elizabeth spoke to my mother for about three minutes ('Yes, I like England *very* much... Oh, I think London's great... I met him at the start of November... Oh, no, we won't be going to America... For the time being we'll be living in his flat on Gloucester Place...') and after that she had a further two minutes – much easier – with my aunt. I also had a word with my aunt. 'Well, who's a dark horse then, who's the darkest dark horse I ever met? Was this the girl you were cavorting with at Christmas? Mind you, I'm not saying you haven't behaved a little badly: I get the feeling you've been causing your mother worry and I don't know why you couldn't have dropped her a hint or two. Anyway, end of lecture. Your bride sounds charming. Better than you deserve.' Before she rang off she said, 'Your mother wants me to tell you she thinks Elizabeth seems sweet. You're a dark horse, did anybody ever mention that? Quite the darkest dark horse *I* ever met.'

'I think I'm going to like them,' said Elizabeth, after I'd put down the receiver. 'Which doesn't surprise me in the least, remembering all that you wrote in your letter. At least we do have *some* family left,' she added lightly, with a brave smile.

I suddenly wondered what Mrs Cambourne was doing. How she was feeling. I even thought for a few seconds about James; alone in the empty flat.

That night I took four aspirin. . .and slept perhaps an hour for each. We left Dumfries the following noon, en route for Selkirk. Before we did, Elizabeth bought some postcards. One was of a fountain in the High Street – a strange, unlikely monument commemorating the arrival of water in Dumfries about a hundred years earlier. This rose in tiers like an elegant cake-stand; on the top there were three gilded cranes – below those, four gilded dolphins – and below those again four gilded round-faced negro children, each bearing a small alligator in his arms. A dreamlike and exotic edifice. 'We ought to get another,' suggested Elizabeth, 'and send it to Oliver. I'm sure he, if anybody, would appreciate that fountain.'

'Elizabeth,' I said. 'Listen.' I knew she had to hear it sometime and I thought for my own sake it would be better to tell her now.

'Yes?'

'You need to get ready for some bad news.' She looked at me inquiringly. 'I saw it in the paper yesterday but didn't. . .didn't want to spoil things for you right at the beginning.'

'What is it?'

'*Really* bad news.'

'Tell me.'

'It's about Oliver.' I paused again, fractionally. 'He's dead.'

Now she still looked at me inquiringly; but more as if she couldn't comprehend.

I went on, without expression: 'There was an accident. He must have been drunk. He fell into the Thames.'

And mightn't that be true? Mightn't it? The paper had said nothing about suicide. (Though what difference would it make?)

'Oh, God!' she said. 'Oh, God – oh, *God*! How horrible!'

She put her hand on my arm. We were standing in the centre of the High Street, by the Mid-Steeple, and its clock began to strike twelve as eventually we turned and walked back to the Jaguar. 'And you didn't tell me,' she said, when it had finished striking. 'But you should have. It might have made things easier for you. No wonder that. . .'

We went the remainder of the way in silence.

'I can't believe it,' she said, as we sat in the parked car. 'That night at the Savoy – he was so warm, so very much alive. It must have come as. . .as such a terrible shock! I know how close you were.'

'I'd rather not talk about it.' (Again, not quite true. I was torn between wanting to and not wanting to.) 'Possibly later; perhaps in a day or so. Where shall we have lunch? Here or on the way?'

Questions of importance.

We left the town; were soon going fast – speedometer showing eighty. Impossible to escape him, though, when everything was a reminder. Apart from his having chosen this car in the first place – and no doubt having spent hours of thought on such a purchase – hadn't Oliver sat in the very seat where I now sat, held the very steering wheel which I now held?

*

Yes, impossible to escape him. Yet Scotland helped, a little. Scotland and Elizabeth together. Not to escape him – he was always there – there was never an hour, hardly a minute, when he wasn't at my side, causing me to imagine the comments he might have made, the comments and the judgments, causing me to feel I might be seeing the world through *his* eyes as much as through my own. But the hills, the glens, the lochs, the wild romantic landscapes – the charm, the beauty, the tranquillity (even at a time when I'd have said the very last thing I wanted was tranquillity) – all these things did help. And the need to keep up a façade before Elizabeth. And Elizabeth's natural kindness and good sense and easy companionship. All these things, as well.

In any case – somehow I got through.

25

We were in Edinburgh for Elizabeth's birthday. It was a Sunday but the previous day we'd gone shopping in Princes Street and had chosen an antique ring which was part engagement ring and part birthday present: the jeweller said it was Georgian – turquoises surrounded by tiny pearls. Pretty. It cost eighteen pounds. (Oliver's money.)

Perhaps it was a sign of my getting better that I felt sorry for her on her birthday. Although we'd been in Edinburgh for several days and her parents actually knew where we were staying, she had received nothing in the post, not even a card. I thought about the way it would have been in the States. Dozens of expensive presents – a magnificent party – anticipation – festivity. And despite the fact she didn't seem in the least self-pitying I couldn't believe she didn't feel it. A twenty-first birthday occurred only once in a lifetime.

Therefore I tried to give her a good day. But my desire to take her to a smart restaurant for a dinner-and-champagne celebration was frustrated: even in early spring there weren't many places open in Edinburgh on a Sunday evening.

So we had an adequate but unexciting meal at the guest house; afraid of our money running out we'd made it a rule only to stop at modest places. I suppose we could have gone to one of the big hotels for dinner but I didn't think of it in time. However, we smuggled a bottle of good wine up to Elizabeth's bedroom to supplement the one we'd had with our supper – luckily, since it was a Sunday and Woollies was closed, I'd been able to cadge a corkscrew off the waitress; and the tooth mug in each of our rooms was made of glass, not plastic.

'I'm afraid you haven't had much of a birthday,' I said, whilst drawing out the cork. 'I am sorry.'

'What in heaven's name do you mean?' Her indignation seemed so genuine she sounded angry. 'I've had a lovely time!'

'Not even a proper present. An engagement ring shouldn't have to double as a twenty-first birthday gift. I'll make it up to you.'

Why in fact *hadn't* I bought her something? A dress, perhaps, from Marks & Spencer? I could at least have found the money for that. I could have done it up in fancy paper and bought her other, smaller things – a collection of gaily wrapped surprises – and really made an occasion of it.

No, I couldn't.

But, the dress at least.

'Johnny Wilmot,' she said. 'Come here.'

She'd been sitting on the bed but now she stood up and walked over to me. She took the corkscrew from my hand – I'd been untwisting the cork from it – and placed it on the dressing table, by the bottle. 'Don't you ever again *dare* apologize for the birthday you've just given me. I wouldn't have wanted it any other way.' Her arms were about me and she kissed me. . .again, almost angrily, it seemed. One of her hands went underneath my jumper and moved slowly up my spine. I wasn't wearing any undervest or shirt.

She had never done that before.

Throughout the time we'd spent in Scotland it had never seriously occurred to me to anticipate our marriage. Our kisses had been chaste – on my side, almost mechanical. (She had viewed this as consideration!) But now, of course, I recognized the signs; and within five minutes we were both undressed and in the bed.

It was disastrous. Perhaps I seized on it as an opportunity for losing myself in a vast, mind-shattering explosion; I was too frenzied and too quick; humiliatingly quick; and the explosion, such as it was, would scarcely have rocked a teacup.

So – added to everything else – I now had an extra shame and an extra guilt to contend with: one that in the darkness brought hot, silent tears running across the bridge of my nose and down onto her pillow.

But that was the nadir. On successive occasions I was more thoughtful, and the situation improved, for both of us.

In the end, however, we didn't get married in Scotland; there seemed no point. We came back to London and on the thirteenth of May were wed at the Marylebone Registry Office. My mother was there (spared, I couldn't imagine how, by Mrs Watson) and Aunt Clara and a great-aunt on my mother's side, whom neither she nor Clara had ever much liked. A schoolfriend of mine, down from Cambridge for the day, also attended. But he was the only male apart from me, for neither of the Sheldons was present. They had finally returned to America three weeks before – having paid us a surprise, abortive, upsetting visit in Edinburgh, on the day after Elizabeth's birthday.

What a farce! Amongst other things, Theodore Sheldon had declared he couldn't think why he didn't knock me down. Sturdy though he was, I could have given him a hint. But I refrained – throughout, I was remarkably controlled. It was he who did most of the talking, while his wife – tired, resigned – continually put me in mind of my mother. With one major addition, what he said was merely a repetition of all he'd said before: I was despicable and Elizabeth was a fool, heedless of her obligations, little knowing what she was throwing away – the love of her family, the respect of her friends, the place in Bostonian society regarded as her due. 'Have an affair with him if you must,' he told her. 'Thresh about in a bed. Get it out of your system in that way if you can't in any other. . .' I was thankful at least that the previous evening had been succeeded by the following morning, *that* morning, otherwise I should no doubt have felt quite as small as he'd intended me to. He forecast dire results for the marriage and was convinced we'd live to regret it. He gave it less than a year. He appealed to my better nature and – here was the addition – tried to buy me off. One day, I thought, they might open a club for those who had tried to buy me off. Elizabeth later informed me that at the mere suggestion I'd turned pale. Not unnaturally she ascribed this to righteous indignation but in fact I was suddenly remembering Mrs Cambourne's cry: 'I am not prepared to stand by and watch him suffer. I am not! I protect my son, Mr Wilmot, I do everything in my power to protect him!'

But after a tense two-hour interview the Sheldons eventually left. The short taxi-ride to Waverley Station was accomplished in almost total silence, presumably meant to shock Elizabeth, even at this late stage, into a proper sense of what she was doing; into a full knowledge of the awful remorselessness of parental renunciation. There had, of course, been no suggestion of a present, although there'd been an intimation of the ones she might have received if she had only proved herself worthy – if she had only displayed that grit which, heaven knew, was never easily acquired but which became all the more laudable for that very reason and had always been an integral part of the true Sheldon heritage. 'Elizabeth, there was never a time when we thought it possible we could one day regret. . .' And *he* had called *me* despicable, I murmured contemptuously – at the moment when my restraint came nearest to giving way.

Neither of them mentioned Oliver's death; I had no idea whether or not they knew about it. But at no time had *I* felt like introducing the subject. At best, in such an atmosphere of ill will, they would have viewed it as subsidiary; at worst, they might have seen it as a form of special pleading, calculated to tone down their attitude.

So I had no idea whether or not they had written to Mrs Cambourne.

Clearly – now on our wedding day – they had not written to us.

Not officially, that is. And not the two of them together. But nevertheless, in her handbag, Elizabeth carried a letter posted by her mother immediately before departing London. The package containing it had been forwarded by the guest house.

'My darling, your father doesn't know I'm writing this but I absolutely cannot leave England without wishing you all the happiness in the world and telling you how much I love you and am prepared to love John, for your sake. Enclosed is the necklace I always planned for you to wear at your wedding and a very small amount of money (but as much as I can lay my hands on) to help tide you over until your own stalls coming through. . . Please write to me as often as you can, letting me know how things are going for you both. . .'

Elizabeth kept it in the same wallet as the letters she'd received from myself whilst she had been in Europe.

A change of heart – or, rather, a belated surrender to it. Not so startling as it would have been in her husband, but, because we knew there could have been no coercion involved, far more welcome.

And it was mirrored by my mother's.

Not simply had my mother bought a new outfit for the occasion, a light-blue linen costume with a matching hat and gloves, so smart and up-to-date it could only have been chosen with Aunt Clara's assistance, but her manner seemed wholly back to what it had been, prior to the revelation of the car; as far removed from the grotesquery of her performance in the restaurant as from the frank coolness which – since January – she had been showing me at home. The reason for this, I knew, wasn't *only* Elizabeth and the wedding. When I had written to tell her of the date, I had also apprised her, on a separate sheet, of what had befallen Oliver, requesting she should never refer to him again.

Well, she hadn't. . .not verbally. But I knew that I still read – in her eyes, in her kiss, in the pressure of her hand – a gravely meaningful allusion to his death; and I should almost have preferred to witness honest pleasure than be subject to such basically insincere, such very woolly, sympathy.

Still, she was changed – and in every other way, naturally, this was something to be grateful for. As a wedding present she gave us a dinner service which came from Harrods and for which she and Aunt Clara had made a special trip to town, two Mondays earlier.

After Harrods, they'd come to Gloucester Place, to meet Elizabeth in person. They had liked her; taken it for granted she should be living at the flat; complimented her fulsomely on her cooking.

But although on one level it had been a success – Elizabeth had judged it so in any case, and in all likelihood my mother and aunt had too – for me it had been impossible not to draw comparisons. No waltz-time for Anna and Michael, no evening birthday treat to anticipate, no meaning any longer to that happy, frightful pun. *For all time* had dwindled down to just three months, and then had stopped, irreversibly.

When we left the registry office we all went to a restaurant in Baker Street – that was part of Aunt Clara's wedding gift. Elizabeth and I weren't going on honeymoon; for the time being we felt we had done enough travelling. (Or, to be more accurate, it could hardly have mattered less to me whether we honeymooned or not.) There was another reason, however: some small delay with regard to the inheritance. So, on a temporary basis, I went to work at Selfridge's. Elizabeth, who – married – now had no further problems concerning visas and work permits, also considered taking a job there. But in the end she thought better of it. We could get by on my wages and commission. . . especially when these were bolstered by the little I still had in the bank and by the money Mrs Sheldon had sent us. So Elizabeth stayed in the flat, made new curtains, did tapestry work, bought dress patterns and recipe books – and told me she was happy.

It was only after I had started at Selfridge's, in their luggage department, that I remembered this was the very place where Oliver had come to buy my pigskin suitcase, on the morning we had flown to Biarritz. They still had several others of that size in stock.

But what the hell. I was having to get used to the idea that, almost anywhere I set foot, he had probably been there before me.

26

I should have written to Mrs Cambourne sooner. Of course I should. If I'd written to her from Scotland – if I'd gone straight down to see her – or if, at the very least, I had telephoned – then perhaps I could have salvaged something. In spite of whatever evidence James might have given to the contrary – the brusque departure he had witnessed, my missing clothes, maybe even something Oliver had said – I could have claimed that we had had a lover's tiff and that I'd driven north for a few days to cool down. Yes, it *might* have been possible. . .if only I had acted promptly and had met with a vast amount of luck.

She wouldn't have needed to know about my relationship with Elizabeth. Not until such time as a conveniently postdated marriage might have been acceptable.

With a *vast* amount of luck.

(Though, in truth, the whole concept of 'luck' now seemed superfluous. More than that – it seemed repugnant.)

But I'd been too stunned: I hadn't been thinking. And when I finally wrote to her, early in June, it was an act of idiocy. For how did you explain the inexplicable: that matter of a ten-week gap?

Up until then, indeed, I must have recognized the utter futility of sending any form of condolence; especially the full and frank confession which I sometimes felt tempted to make, in the hope of partial absolution. But on the particular evening I composed and posted my short message Elizabeth had gone to bed early and I was slightly drunk.

'Dear Mrs Cambourne,' I wrote.

'I have only just heard what happened and I can't find words to tell you of my sorrow. Your sense of loss must be infinite. Anyone who knew Oliver must surely miss him dreadfully and I know I don't need to tell you how great the void in my own life. He was the best friend a man could ever have, just as I am sure he was also the best son. Perhaps I could come to visit you sometime in the near future?

'Yours very sincerely,
'John Wilmot.'

But three days later I received these few words in reply:

'Mr John Wilmot.

'Were *you* the best friend a man could ever have? I think a visitor from hell would be more welcome.

'Sarah Cambourne.'

Yet didn't she understand? That's exactly what I would be.

*

Her letter was brutal. . .although neither surprising nor unreasonable. But I remembered our time of closeness during Oliver's depression on Boxing Day. We had been similarly close on many other occasions – in fact, a great deal closer than, over that same period, I had been with my own mother – but as members of a trio, not a duo. I particularly recalled a Sunday when the three of us had driven to Forest Green to have lunch at a small hotel, and how we'd afterwards sat in the lounge to drink our coffee. A small, genially fussy old gentleman had played a recording of the Queen's Christmas broadcast, which his son-in-law had taped for him and which by now he probably knew word for word. He had begun by playing it quite softly, to another old gentleman sitting in the same corner, but when it seemed that the remaining seven or eight of us were also listening, he had given several tentative though hopeful nods – and had obligingly turned up the volume; had obviously mistaken the silence of surprise for the silence of respect.

At least, on the part of some of us. With others, evidently, it *had* been the silence of respect.

For when, following the speech, the National Anthem had been put on, a retired army officer had at once sprang to his feet and stood stiffly to attention. His wife followed suit and so did the two old gentlemen. Hesitantly, sheepishly, the rest of us joined in. But the anthem seemed to last forever and there was something so absurd in the spectacle of all of us caught there in this unnatural attitude – self-consciously reverential – that Oliver and I were sufficiently ill-advised as to look at one another.

Oliver instantly transferred his attention to the floor; I reached for my handkerchief; but still I saw his shoulders shake and I couldn't suppress a muffled sob.

His mother, standing between us, stared straight ahead, admirably solemn and aloof – until, almost at the end, when that magnificent composure started to crack and, after a brief but hopeless struggle, she too succumbed.

The three of us sat down some twenty seconds later dabbing at our eyes and feeling like naughty ten-year-olds. Under such conditions it was hard to take part with any sincerity in the grateful murmurings that ensued.

'You wicked reprehensible pair!' she said, as we drove away. 'Shall we ever dare show our faces there again?'

And now, unforeseeably, it was our giggling together that I chiefly remembered as I stared down disconsolate at the curt note in my hand. I had saved it until I'd found a good time to read it: away from Elizabeth, the driving rain, the hurrying pedestrians: and until, also, I had managed to summon up the courage.

'Not bad news, I trust?'

It was Mr Chauncey the under-buyer: a kindly if somewhat colourless man, fifty-odd with small children.

'What?'

'I was wondering if you felt ill? Are you going to be all right?'

'No. Yes. I'm sorry?' I scarcely knew what I was saying. 'Oh. . . *ill*? Yes! I'm not sure.'

'Then why don't you take your coffee break a bit early? You don't have to hurry back. It's not busy, we can manage.'

'Thank you,' I mumbled.

It struck me for the first time, standing on, of all places, the down-escalator in Selfridge's and thinking about being ill, that not so long ago in this world there had lived a man who had once cleaned up my vomit. . .and still gone on loving me.

*

Elizabeth had read my book. 'I mean to read it again, Johnny. It was good – and very funny in places. Oliver thought it was outstanding, didn't he? And maybe he's the one who knew.

But. . .well, I want to be as truthful as I can. I just feel you could do better.'

I nodded, in unconcerned agreement. 'It gave me some valuable practice – that's really all.'

She relaxed, perceptibly.

'But, darling, you seemed so pleased with it. And Oliver did too,' she repeated – more anxiously again.

'No, Oliver hadn't read it when he spoke as he did to your father. And when he did read it. . .well, he didn't like it, either.'

In one way I could talk about it easily: the book was dead for me, had been since March; it was she who'd brought it up again. In every other way it was an ordeal. Why hadn't I been able to let him know that I agreed with his verdict? In my heart I must have appreciated its soundness, nearly as soon as I had heard it. (Oh God – and why hadn't I accepted that offer of working with him on a new synopsis?) Now the only thing to prevent me from throwing the typescript in the dustbin was the knowledge that he had handled it, had looked with care at every page, and by doing so had made of it a relic.

'Honey, I never knew anyone take criticism in such good part.'

I shrugged. 'That isn't what Oliver would have said.' But I wanted to forget the novel. 'Elizabeth, tell me something. Do you think it's possible that, somehow, your parents didn't hear about what happened to him?'

She hesitated.

'That's funny, I really don't know. Why?'

'I'm puzzled, that's all. They certainly didn't mention it in Edinburgh. But, on the other hand, they didn't think of asking him to use his influence, either.'

'Perhaps,' she said, speaking rather slowly, 'they didn't realize that his influence would be so strong.'

'And something else. Do you suppose Oliver's mother knows about us?'

'Heavens. That's anybody's guess.' She smiled. 'But in any case – why don't you write to tell her?'

27

One lunch hour, when Elizabeth was at the dentist's and I had said I'd eat in the canteen, I took a taxi to Gerald Road in SW1. It had been on my mind to do so for weeks – yet I now felt I was acting almost on impulse. And I didn't really know why I was going. In the taxi I experienced a dryness in my mouth which had little to do with the heat of the day – and, in fact, I leant forward at one point, about to tell the driver to turn back.

The dryness lasted until I was actually inside the police station and talking to the sergeant on the desk.

'Yes, sir?'

He had a neat, bristling moustache and thinning grey hair. Before he'd spoken I had thought he had a formidable expression. I'd been waiting well over a minute for him to finish off the paperwork currently engaging him; and I had dreaded that at any instant the swing doors might be pushed open and I would find some harassed, bad-tempered or – possibly worse – patently inquisitive individual then standing right behind me. Perhaps more than merely one. Even the forming of a small queue.

But I seemed to have chosen a good moment.

'I want to ask about something that happened last March. The twenty-fourth of March. That night a body was. . .' Yet even with the opportunity for rehearsal it wasn't easy to get the words out. '. . .taken from the river,' I said.

Then I began practically to gabble.

'The name was Cambourne. I'm not sure which bridge he actually fell from, but I've assumed. . . I think it was probably Chelsea Bridge and that's why I've come here, this being the nearest station. . .'

Yet at least the dryness was gone.

'And what exactly, sir, is your particular interest in this affair?'

'I was a friend of his.'

'I see. Well, yes, as it happens, it was Chelsea Bridge. And yes, as it happens too, I was on duty. I remember it.'

This was what I'd been hoping for – both hoping for and fearing.

'You mean. . . Was the body brought in here, then?'

He seemed surprised. 'No, sir. It was taken to a mortuary.'

'But you said you remember. . .?'

'There was a witness to the incident. An oldish chap – though he came rushing through that door like a four-minute miler! And I was the one who telephoned the Yard.'

'Why the Yard?'

'Well, that's the way it works. We notify them and *they* get in touch with the river police – whichever boat is nearest. I mean, nearest the scene of the accident.'

He was being patient with me. I appreciated that. And I also appreciated that word he'd just used. 'Accident'.

'If you'll wait here a moment I'll go and look out our copy of the file.'

Although he wasn't gone for long, I began to worry again about newcomers.

'Naturally, sir, you understand that all police reports are confidential. . .yet so long as your inquiry isn't too specialized there shouldn't be much problem.'

He had already started looking through the sheet he held.

'Well, then. Cambourne. Oliver Thornton. Admitted to mortuary 11.15 p.m. Driving licence in pocket. Formal identification made by a Mr James Furness, manservant. Autopsy carried out by Dr Mangrove. Corpse had been in the water some thirty minutes, sir – I'm paraphrasing – high alcohol content discovered in blood stream. . .' The sergeant paused, scanning the entry for salient details. 'What kind of thing were you wanting to find out, specifically?'

'That old chap you mentioned. The witness. Would it be possible to have his name?'

'Why would you want that, sir?'

'Well, if he was the only one who saw. . .what happened. . .' I suddenly felt the full absurdity of what I was asking. 'But that's the whole point,' I urged. 'Did he actually see Mr Cambourne jump or did he – ?'

'Yes, he said he saw him jump.'

'Yes, but I was wondering whether. . .'

'Wondering what, sir?'

'Whether he might only have imagined it. After all, at half-past-ten or whatever the exact time was, it can be very dark. And there's a lot of distance between each of those lamps on Chelsea Bridge. So I was wondering if he might merely have seen some movement – for instance, it's possible that Oliver might have been leaning out too far over the parapet – and then only *assumed* he saw. . .'

'You're asking, in fact, whether the gentleman's fall could have been unintentional?'

'Yes,' I answered – eagerly. Something in the way he'd said it seemed to offer hope.

'No, sir.' He shook his head. 'Not a chance. You could leave the evidence of the witness out of it altogether. I'm afraid there'd still be something else.'

But I too shook my head – and far more vehemently. 'Yet don't you *see?* Even if there was a note he could still have changed his mind. Between the time he wrote it and the time he was out there standing on the bridge. . .'

I stopped. Again and again and again: splitting hairs! What possible difference could it make? Oliver was dead.

And if he'd drunk glass after glass of whisky when I hadn't been there to stop him – *because* I hadn't been there to stop him – then I had killed him just as surely as if I had shot him in the back.

The sergeant looked down at the paper only briefly. He said: 'No, there wasn't any note. What there was, though, was a couple of heavy bronze things. Apparently meant for paperweights. Found in the gentleman's overcoat pockets. I'm very sorry, sir.' He paused. 'I only wish I *could* have said it was an accident.'

*

That someone could be snuffed out like that! A leap into deep water in a weighty overcoat; then a minute or so later – or, dear God, *three* minutes or so later – nothing! I lay in bed that same night with a different kind of anger burning inside me: not an anger directed against Oliver any longer (how long, indeed, had *that* lasted?) but an anger directed against life itself. Oh, the waste! What appalling waste! All the thoughts, feelings, knowledge of a man, everything that went to make him what he was – eradicated! Gone; totally wiped out! As though they had never existed. So the world lost forever one unique record of experience; lost it and hardly noticed. What a joke! What a pointless, horrifying joke.

And yet did nothing count? Certainly not that poor sodden body cut about by Dr Mangrove and now finally rotting down beneath the ground – or sitting perhaps on Sarah Cambourne's mantelpiece: a jarful of what had once been skin and bone and blood and muscle and hair and chest and penis and that funny little strawberry mark on the left thigh. . . Did nothing count? Not even the soul?

(Though what did one mean by 'soul'? And what did I mean by 'count'?)

I remembered what he had said about reincarnation.

If *only* I could have believed it.

28

The letter from Robertson and Keyes (Solicitors, Notaries Public and Commissioners for Oaths) had asked me to be good enough to contact their Mr Blackmore, adding that when I did so I should hear of certain matters that might be to my advantage.

'It's about Oliver, isn't it?' said Elizabeth. 'He must have left you something.'

I nodded, slowly.

She said: 'That was kind of him. Are you surprised?'

'Very.'

Their office was in Curzon Street. I phoned and made an appointment. I had given up the job at Selfridge's.

'May I come too?'

I shrugged. 'If you want to.'

We arrived early and sat in a plush waiting room with Regency chairs and old prints of Hampstead and Highgate. I leafed through the current *Punch* but didn't find it either funny or absorbing. Elizabeth, on the other hand, had picked up a *Country Life*. 'Oh, honey,' she kept saying, 'just look at this one!' or, 'How would you like a place like this?' She had often spoken about buying a cottage in the country. 'Something old, with brick paths and wild flowers under the apple trees. And a seat in the herb garden. Doesn't that sound lovely?'. . . She was almost disappointed when someone came to get us.

Mr Blackmore was a young man, spruce, friendly. He had a firm handshake and wore what I took to be a public school tie.

'Thank you for coming, Mr Wilmot. How nice you brought your wife.'

'Thank you,' said Elizabeth. We sat down.

'I doubt it will surprise you to learn the reason that you're here is to do with the will of our late client, Mr Oliver Cambourne. I believe he was a close friend of yours, Mr Wilmot?'

I answered yes. My eyes didn't leave his face.

He went on after an instant: 'I hardly know whether my duty is, or is not, a pleasant one. You see, Mr Cambourne has bequeathed you a quite considerable legacy. But at the same time, unhappily, I have to inform you that the will is being contested.'

'I see.'

'On what grounds?' asked Elizabeth.

The solicitor spoke carefully.

'Shall we say. . .certain members of his family feel Mr Cambourne's first obligation lay towards themselves, rather than towards someone he hadn't known for very long?'

'Members of his family,' I repeated. 'Mrs Cambourne?'

'She principally, of course.'

'But surely Oliver would have taken good care of his mother?'

'Oh, yes; he left her Merriot Park – in the event of her happening to survive him, that is – together with a substantial income. She's more than adequately provided for.'

'Then it sounds to me as though his first obligation was well and truly fulfilled.'

'You haven't inquired yet what Mr Cambourne left yourself.'

I supposed I had to do so. I still looked him in the eye.

'All right.'

'Well, to begin with. . .after his mother's death, Merriot Park will come to you.'

'My God,' whispered Elizabeth.

'To begin with!' I said.

'He also left you his flat in London, along with all its contents . . .and his yacht. . .and a whole list of smaller personal effects – and close on ninety-three thousand pounds. It was more than half his fortune.'

'Darling! *Darling*!' exclaimed Elizabeth.

I said nothing.

'So you see, Mr Wilmot, even when death duties have been taken into account, it's still a sizeable estate we're speaking of.'

I remained silent. Elizabeth leaned over and clutched my hand.

'Sweetie, shouldn't we be going wild or something: hanging from the window and shouting out the good news?'

Mr Blackmore smiled indulgently. 'I understand exactly how you feel, Mrs Wilmot.'

But I could neither respond as she desired nor even be bothered to pretend.

'When,' I asked, 'was the will made?'

'Finalized in February. To be precise – on the twentieth of February.'

'The day before the Lakes.'

'Excuse me?'

'Nothing.' We had spent nearly a week in Grasmere, walking and climbing during the days (but not very high) and in the evenings sitting by a large fire, either reading or writing or playing Scrabble. It had been an almost perfect holiday. Oliver had said we should return there later in the year so that I could see the place in summer. 'Tell me, Mr Blackmore: what chance do his relatives have of winning?'

The solicitor unscrewed the cap of his fountain pen; then screwed it back on. 'It's hard to say. Naturally I don't know all the circumstances. Yet, even so, I'd think their chances small.'

That answered a further question: obviously Robertson and Keyes weren't acting for the family.

'You would?' confirmed Elizabeth.

'The trouble is, proceedings of this sort are invariably time-consuming and unpleasant. It's a truism, of course, yet wrangles over money unfailingly bring out the worst in people. Most people.' He gave a grave but gallant smile in the direction of Elizabeth. 'And forgive me but in this instance one gets the impression of – how can I put it? – not so much concern over the actual money or even over the property – as – as. . .' He sought for the right way to express it.

We waited.

'A feeling, perhaps, of vendetta?'

'Oh, no, that couldn't be,' exclaimed Elizabeth. 'That would be ridiculous.'

'I'm sorry. Maybe I shouldn't have said it. Strictly off the record. But all I mean is – I'm afraid it won't be pleasant.'

I didn't think it ridiculous at all; and was well aware that Mr Blackmore had known I wouldn't. More. . .I recognized his statement as being in the nature of a warning and wondered how usual it was, or even ethical, for a solicitor to pass on such impressions: impressions which could only have been gleaned from the confidences of opposite numbers. Nevertheless, I felt a grudging gratitude.

'Tell me,' I said. 'It's slightly off the point but did Oliver – Mr Cambourne – leave anything to his manservant?'

'Oh, yes. He made Mr Furness a most generous legacy.'

I nodded.

He went on: 'I didn't know Mr Cambourne well, but what little I did know of him. . .this would certainly have led me to expect he would take care of everyone.'

'Yes. . . I put the question badly.'

'And, in fact, I can tell you that not a single member of the staff at Merriot Park has been overlooked.'

'Like you, I didn't know him well,' said Elizabeth, 'even though we were distantly related. But he struck me, too, as a very sweet person. A very gentle man.'

'Yes.'

There was a further silence,

'Well, now, there are a couple of other points I should be bringing to your attention. . .'

Mr Blackmore went on to talk of procedure: chiefly how long the litigation might take and about the possibility of an out-of-court settlement. When he had finished and we had run out of questions (though it was mainly Elizabeth who'd been asking those) he said: 'I think, then, we might leave it there? I don't want to take up more of your time than necessary. Naturally, Mr Wilmot, I shall be putting it in writing.'

He asked for the name of my solicitor and made a note of the firm in Baker Street which – about ten months ago – had drawn up my tenancy agreement.

'Or perhaps, honey, Mr Blackmore would be willing to represent you?' suggested Elizabeth.

He smiled. 'Yes, of course. We'd be happy to do that, Mrs Wilmot.'

'Fine,' I said. 'Thank you.' We shook hands at the door of his office.

29

A minute later we were in the street.

'Well, darling,' said Elizabeth. 'Well!' She took my arm and gave it an excited squeeze. 'Good old Oliver!'

Outwardly, I could smile.

Inwardly, I was feeling sick all over again, much as I had felt during the last days of March, and all through April, and still to some degree in May and June.

Even now in July a wave of remembrance swept over me at times: *Oliver is dead.*

Even now in July I woke up most mornings and lay there contentedly for a second or two before receiving the blow afresh: *Oliver is dead.*

Quite frequently I had thought at various points in the day: *That will be something to tell Oliver.* Some silly joke I'd heard; some trivial incident I'd seen.

Or:

I must ask Oliver about that.

And standing now in Curzon Street, with Elizabeth holding my arm and gazing up at me excitedly, it was almost second nature by this time to be able to return her smile, listen to her comments – and yet, essentially, to be somewhere else.

He was prepared to do all that for me. What, in return, did I do for him?

What did I do *to* him?

'Such a marvellous, marvellous thing!' she said.

I know what I did to him. I knocked him so off-balance he forgot to phone his solicitor before jumping in the river. That's what I did to him.

'Honey, I need a glass of tea. A nice cool glass of tea. With mint in it.'

Or so off-balance he couldn't be bothered. Had he reached such a point of apathy that even retaliation became a matter of indifference?

'Tea?' I said. '*I* need something a lot stronger!'

For he could scarcely have guessed, could he – even complex, unpredictable Oliver – scarcely have guessed that he had stumbled on the one quite perfect form of retaliation?

'Stronger than tea?' laughed Elizabeth. 'At three-thirty on a Wednesday afternoon in England! Fat chance! But come on, darling, there's a nice place over there. We can go and dance on all their tables, the more they have the better!'

Yet how in heaven's name could he ever have been that naive?

I put the question direct. How *could* you? Did you really think. . .?

Oliver – oh, come on! – you'd had plenty of lovers. You must have known! You can't have changed your will each time you fell in love.

Or – *this* time – did you really think – really think – *this* time it was going to be for keeps?

Oh, for God's sake, man!

You were twenty years older than me. How could you have thought such a stupid thing? How could you have *done* such a stupid thing? Your mother was just so right when she said – when she told me –

I remembered an incident in San Sebastian. We had eaten our lunch there: just plain fish fried in a light batter but the freshest, most delicious fish I had ever tasted. We sat on a long wooden bench in a crowded tavern, shoulder-to-shoulder with rowdy, gesticulating office-workers; and Oliver had said that, on account of my blond hair, quite unusual in Spain, the custom of the country demanded I should kiss any redhead who sat near me on a tavern bench.

'Oh, don't you *ever* learn?' I had cried.

And he had immediately, of course, been obliged to shoot out a restraining hand to prevent my leaping up to obey the custom of the country.

'Johnny, do you *realize?*'

It was odd to find that, somehow, we were now seated. At a table by the window,

'This ought to make such a world of difference to my father!'

I stared at her, blankly. 'I'm sorry?'

'Because – don't you see? I've married a rich man, after all.'

'Oh, Angel Face.'

'Yes, darling?' She laughed and laid her hand upon my sleeve. 'Don't look at me like that. I can't help it if I prefer a rich husband to a poor one. It isn't so unforgivable, is it?'

I shook my head and smiled,

'And surely it *is* preferable? For one thing, people won't be so quick to say you married me for my money.'

'Who cares what people say?'

'I do, on the whole. But there's something else. Now, you'll never need to feel financially dependent. You'll never need to grow resentful. Oh, yes, Johnny, that could have happened!

But Oliver has saved us from it – and therefore I, for one, think it's a *lovely* inheritance!'

That old insidious argument. For a minute or so, while we sat in silence, her hand still on my sleeve, I thought about being rich. Rich in my own right. Something I'd probably always hankered for since I had first been exposed to all those bright romantic comedies, all those bright glossy musicals, in which life was endlessly civilized and full of exciting opportunity: a far cry from Folkestone High Street in the rain after the four o'clock performance. During the short walk home I hadn't invariably been at my nicest.

A rich man. A man of property.

And what a property! Paradise. If that was a word which had occurred to me at the beginning of November when I'd had no more idea of the place ever being mine than I might have had of becoming king – less, as it happened, because I'd sometimes had fantasies of marrying Princess Anne – if it had seemed to me *then* very nearly a paradise, how would it appear in full summer, with the rose gardens ablaze, the lily pond sparkling in the sunshine, the doors of the summerhouse thrown open... the freshly mown lawns, the fruit orchards, the swimming pool...?

But put aside all that. Merriot Park was the home in which Oliver had grown up; where he must have been familiar with every corner of the house and garden – played on the tennis court, slid down the banisters, explored the clock tower, placed his hand on every doorknob. If I were to own Merriot Park – oh my God, *if* I were to own Merriot Park! – only imagine the sense of sharing; the sense of connection. The sense of continuity.

And yet... And yet...

And yet it was during this minute of silence, with Elizabeth's hand still resting on my sleeve, that I was finally able – no, not to make up my mind (for I was sure I had done that already) –

but to find the courage, the resolution, to put my decision into words.

I said: 'I can't accept it.'

'Can't accept what, honey?' (Such a quantity of good luck? Such unforeseen benevolence on the part of providence?)

'I can't accept the legacy. Either the money *or* the house.'

After a moment, she removed her hand, slowly.

'But Johnny – why ever not?'

'I just can't, that's all.'

'You mean. . .because of the family? All the nastiness there'll be?'

'Partly.'

'But Oliver wanted you to have that money. The money *and* the house. You, not them. He left those things to you, Johnny.'

'No, Elizabeth. You don't understand. And in any case. . .'

'What?'

'We already have enough money.'

'Forget the money, then. The house.'

'No.'

'Why not?'

I shrugged.

She said, coolly: 'Merriot Park is the kind of house I've always dreamed of. And now it's being offered to us as a gift – as a *gift*, mind! But when I ask why we can't accept it, all you do is shrug and turn away. Well, I'm not satisfied with that. I happen to be thinking not only of our own futures but those of our children. Have you thought yet what an incredible place it'd be to bring up children?'

'Yes, but have *you* thought yet that Mrs Cambourne could easily live for another ten years? Twenty years? Our children might grow a bit long in the tooth while waiting to be brought up there.'

'I doubt she'll live for another twenty years.'

'Then will you be hoping for her to die?'

'No, but. . .honey, couldn't we maybe move in with her? Perhaps she'd be glad of the company. Our oldest son: we'd call him Oliver! Young Oliver! Wouldn't it be like – practically be like – having her own grandchild running all about the place?'

Had she but known it, she had picked on the most seductive argument she could possibly have found.

'And supposing we don't have a son?'

'Why, we'd call our first daughter Sarah. But, anyway, we *shall* have a son.'

'You might change your mind and want to call him Theodore?'

'No. I promise you.'

'Not even if by then he's come around, is playing the devoted dad again?'

'Don't you trust me? I've given you my word.'

There followed another long silence.

'Sometimes,' I said, 'I feel that you view life in very simple terms.'

'Sometimes I feel the same about you.'

'But I'm not the one who said it would be just like having her own grandchild running about. Why would it?'

'Because she's a lonely old woman – and probably all mothers want to be grandmothers.'

It was hardly worth discussing.

'Yet listen, Angel Face. If you've truly set your heart on Merriot Park – you know what? – possibly we could buy it one of these days? *I'd* like that. I really would.'

The idea began to excite me – in a way that nothing else had excited me for months – although to her it must have appeared crazy.

The next moment, however, there was a waitress standing beside us. The suggestion disappeared. I wasn't sure if this was the right time to revive it.

'Sorry to keep you waiting. We're that busy! What would you both like?'

Merriot Park, please.

'Just tea,' I answered, absently.

'Pot of tea for two? Cakes?'

'No, thank you.'

The girl moved off. Elizabeth said quietly, 'Honey, simple my view of life most likely is – but, even so, I wasn't born yesterday! I know why Oliver left you Merriot Park. I don't mind. Honestly I don't. It doesn't make me love you one jot the less. Nor him, either.'

'Oh, come off it, Elizabeth – you didn't love him at all. You simply thought he was sweet. . .*very* sweet. Very gentle. Have I quoted you correctly?'

'Johnny. Don't fight me. This is much too important to get swallowed up in some fight.'

I cupped my chin and stared out of the window.

'Honey. . .'

'How long have you known?'

'Oh, for ages – just ages! But let's make a pact. If *I* don't find it traumatic, *you* mustn't, either. Deal?'

I turned back to face her. Knowing she had guessed didn't seem to have affected me.

'Okay,' I said. 'Deal.'

The waitress brought cakes. When she had left, I offered the plate to Elizabeth. She smiled at it, too. . .and accepted a brandy snap.

'But only if you do – there's one for you, as well.'

'You didn't get your iced tea.'

'Sweetie. Going back to what we were saying.' She handed me my cup.

'Must we?'

'Oliver wanted you to have that house. Obviously he did.'

I felt a chill run through me; gave a shudder. 'Yes, I'm sure he did. While he was making out his will.'

She looked at me, bewilderedly.

'Darling, do I really need to spell it out?'

'Spell what out?'

But in her tone I caught the glimmers of awareness.

I said it nonetheless. I felt a certain release in saying it – saying it out loud for the first time. Heaven help me, perhaps I felt a certain pride.

'It was because of me he killed himself.'

She continued to gaze at me.

'But you said...' Her voice was practically a whisper. 'You said that...'

'His death was accidental?'

She nodded.

'Well, naturally I did! What else would you have expected me to say?'

I added – and with a distinct touch of cruelty which I probably intended:

'Does that throw a different light on things?' (Have another cake, Elizabeth.)

'Of course it does.' And after a moment: 'Yes, of course it does!'

For a long time we stayed immersed in our thoughts. Now it was she, principally, who gazed through the window.

'Well, then, that's it,' she said, turning back at last. 'That's it, isn't it? At least it made a nice dream. While it lasted.'

'Yes.'

I paused.

'There was another reason we couldn't have accepted it, though.'

'Was there?' She sounded indifferent.

'If the will were contested, imagine the muckraking that would follow. The media would have a field day.'

'They didn't have much of a field day over his suicide.'

'How do we know? Apart from those few lines in the Stop Press we didn't even see the papers. We didn't listen to the radio. Didn't watch TV.'

I picked up a fragment of brandy snap, transferred it to my mouth.

'And, anyway, we'd never want to run the risk – surely? Bearing in mind what damage it could do to Oliver's reputation.'

'Not to mention yours.'

'No. . .but, oddly enough, I wasn't thinking of that.'

'I know you weren't. But I suppose you can't blame *me* for doing so?' The warmth had started to edge back into her voice; she seldom stayed cross for long. 'In any case, Johnny. . .how do you know that Oliver's mother isn't bluffing? Wouldn't she be the very last to want to cause damage to his reputation?'

'Well, I'm not so sure,' I said, after I had briefly mulled this over. 'I can imagine Sarah Cambourne forgetting everything in her desire to get even.' (No, she could never get even; the Furies themselves wouldn't have been able to find the eye or the tooth matching those which she had lost.) 'Right from the start she gave me to understand she was ruthless. Pitiless in the protection of her young.'

'A slightly *unusual* style of protecting your young?'

'Maybe. But she evidently accepted the way that he was. Perhaps that side of things isn't important to her. And, clearly, she'd have gone all out to show how he was put upon – would possibly have won much sympathy in the process.' I didn't add *And rightly so!* but I came close to it.

'Oh, darling, how can you say that? 'Put upon', indeed! What nonsense.'

'Shall we leave?' I tried to catch the eye of the waitress.

'All right. But first let me say one thing which I consider needs to be said. I think you're rather a nice person, Mr John Wilmot. Yes, I do – no, don't scowl at me like that. I may not have married Mr John D Rockefeller but I think I did okay for myself, just the same. So there you are. *Now* you can try to attract that poor girl's attention.'

30

I spent some drink-dulled hours in Fleet Street. The fullest obituary was in *The Daily Telegraph*, although the art critics of *The Times* and *The Manchester Guardian* had also written appreciations. There was little that was personal in any of these accounts. 'Oliver Cambourne, who died so tragically on Tuesday night. . .' 'His last exhibition, which was held in September at the Millwood Gallery. . .' 'It is interesting to speculate on how, had he lived, his art might have developed. . .' 'The 39-year-old artist, who was unmarried, will be sadly missed by anyone who cared at all about the state of contemporary painting. . .' Et cetera. There was also a report on his death in all the other papers I looked at; but in none of them was it a detailed coverage; I learned nothing new. Both *The Times* and *The Telegraph* carried a photograph: one that I hadn't seen before: and I wondered where they had found it. I felt angry about it – that this last picture should be so very unflattering – why hadn't they re-used others which I had seen in his book of press cuttings? But in fact I soon discovered it wasn't the last: I came across a far better one in the *Illustrated London News*. ('Sadly, since this interview took place, the art world has lost one of its warmest, most ferocious, gentle, uncompromising denizens and not only the art world will be a poorer place for that. Perhaps his own words comprise his best obituary.') Certainly his own words – in so far as they were his own words – made more interesting reading than anything else I had seen that morning; but either the hilarious replay he had given me straight after the interview had been more exaggerated than he'd let on, or the piece had been skilfully edited, for remarkably little of it seemed familiar. But it had immediacy. And this, despite the two strong gins I'd drunk beforehand.

Thank God I had had those. Reading through the obituaries I hadn't felt particularly melancholy but I did so later, standing alone in the churchyard about a mile from Merriot Park. Yet this state of melancholy wasn't due to my discovery of Oliver's tombstone; my first reaction on finding his grave had been practically of gratitude. No, it was due more to the fact of being surrounded by people whose lives had once meant so very much to them. *That* was depressing. While I stood there I felt I wanted to revolutionize my own life, turn over immense new leaves, be kind and wise and loving, invest every hour of every day with goodness and tranquillity, beauty and significance. But it was too late. After barely three minutes I realized this. The second date on Oliver's tombstone informed me it was too late. 'March 24th, 1959.' The lettering was harshly new beside the weathered anonymity of most of the other stones.

The lettering gave the name, the dates and the following not very original epitaph: 'To live in the hearts of those we love is not to die.'

I looked for other Cambourne graves. There weren't any. I had never asked Oliver much about his father but I remembered he had died in the States, less than a year after his divorce.

'To live in the hearts of those we love is not to die.'

But hadn't they made some mistake? I began to feel resentful. To live in the hearts of those *who love us* would surely make the better sense. And – damn it – why the present tense and not the past? It was ridiculous to think the dead could go on loving and even 'those we *loved*' in some way would have drawn me in. I felt resentful even though I knew of course that mere words altered nothing. But at least – as I'd found out before – anger was an easier thing to cope with than awareness: awareness in this case that I was standing a few feet over a decomposing (decomposed?) body which I had once lain close to, held and been held by, kissed and fondled; a body which was now grotesque, ugly, revolting; which might one day become, if it hadn't already, a home for beetles, woodlice, maggots and the like. Oliver – revolting? I unexpectedly felt sorry he *wasn't* just a jarful of ashes on Mrs Cambourne's mantelpiece. And yet, for myself, the notion of lying beneath the hummocky grass in some quiet and bird-filled setting such as this was still more appealing than the tidier and cleaner efficiency of the crematorium.

Because I was lost in this sort of contemplation I didn't hear the footsteps behind me and I was startled when a plummy voice addressed me. 'Good afternoon, what a perfectly splendid day we're having!'

Naturally, I returned the greeting, though with none too good a grace.

'No more peaceful place on earth,' the vicar said, 'than a country churchyard in the fullness of summer.'

I nodded.

'Passing through? That's a very fine car you have, if I may say so. I noticed it on my way in.'

'I'm *en route* to Merriot Park.' I hadn't meant to say that and couldn't think why I had.

'Ah. . . You know the Cambournes, then?'

Inaccurate, I thought. The Cambourne. Singular.

'Yes.'

He gestured towards the gravestone. 'Tragic! What a tragic accident! Cut off in his prime. A man with such a gift.'

'Yes,' I repeated, rather more graciously. There were times when talking about Oliver with anyone was better than not talking about him at all.

But he only shook his head and said slowly, 'Still. . . Do you know the words of that fine hymn by William Cowper: 'God moves in a mysterious way his wonders to perform'?'

No, I didn't know the words of that fine hymn by William Cowper, and there was no 'Still. . .' about it whatsoever, not in my opinion.

'I especially like the fourth verse,' he told me. 'The one that goes like this:

> 'Judge not the Lord by feeble sense
> But trust him for his grace;
> Behind a frowning providence
> He hides a smiling face.'

So true; so absolutely true; something we should always strive to bear in mind.'

Oh, yes? Try telling that to the Jews in the concentration camps – or to the victims of a violent earthquake. To the man on the gibbet; the witch at the stake. To the people of Hiroshima; the soldiers on the Somme. Try telling it to all those starving masses in Africa and Asia.

Try telling it to Oliver.

'Behind a frowning providence he hides a smiling face. . .'

He added then, with a little more insight than I might have given him credit for, 'But it's a bit difficult to believe it sometimes – eh?' He smiled and began to take his leave. 'Heigh-ho, on such a lovely day, duty has no right to call. Good afternoon to you, young man; this was a very pleasant meeting. Tell Sarah Cambourne that Martin Hanbury sends his love and hopes to pop in to see her pretty soon. God bless you and keep you and cause you to thrive.' I watched his portly figure make its way comfortably towards the front of the church. Before it finally disappeared, he stooped to sniff a rose bush.

31

James opened the door.

'You!' he said. It was involuntary. In all his days in service he had probably never betrayed himself in such a manner.

So why did I need to recall that current of sympathy which had passed between us, in the study, on the morning of – ? Need to recall it with a pang?

But then I'd expected this to be that sort of visit – pilgrimage almost: a whole succession of pangs. On the way down I had tried to protect myself against them, yet didn't know how well I'd succeeded, when nearly every mile in the road had furnished some small insidious recollection. Once, I had actually been on the point of turning back. If the mere journey could be that bad, what of the arrival? The house, the garden, the garage; each familiar room? Especially knowing that all of these things might one day have been mine. But I'd pressed down on the accelerator and – by and large – had maintained a good speed.

'James! I had no idea *you*'d be here!'

(Well, obviously.)

'Yes, sir.' Mask back in place.

'What happened to Tranch?'

'Retired.'

'And you? How are you, James?'

'Quite well, thank you, sir.'

But he still had the knack of rendering me uncomfortable – now more than ever, of course. He made me feel acutely the banality of the question I had just asked and the equal banality of the reply I had received.

'Is Mrs Cambourne at home?'

'I'll have to find out, sir.'

'Please tell her it's important.'

'But why have you come here?' That wasn't any inquiry on behalf of his mistress. Patently, the mask had slipped again.

'I hardly think that's much concern of yours. But, if you must know, it's about the will.'

Then I instantly softened my tone.

'Listen, James. I'm sorry for what happened. Words cannot *begin* to say how much. Now please go and tell Mrs Cambourne I'm here; and in the meantime do you think I might come in?'

Reluctantly he let me pass into the hall. The smell of it, as much as anything (which previously I hadn't even been aware of), hit me squarely on the heart.

But I was not, I was positively *not,* going to allow myself to wallow in nostalgia.

'I knew you were trouble the first time I saw you,' he said, 'I've hated you right from the beginning.'

Yes, well, that figures. It wasn't any secret. That's how we came to call you Mrs Danvers.

'I'm sorry about that, James. I'm aware of how you felt about Mr Cambourne and I certainly don't want to quarrel with you – firstly because it wouldn't do either of us any good and secondly because I know he wouldn't wish it – wouldn't have wished it. I remember he once told me he was very fond of you. But I should, please, like to see Mrs Cambourne.'

Yet, as it happened, I had scarcely finished speaking when there was a movement at the top of the stairs and we saw Mrs Cambourne starting to descend. She came very slowly, holding onto the banister with one hand and carefully setting her stick on each succeeding stair before entrusting her full, slight weight to it. She looked older and frailer; much as she had done from the doorway of her bedroom after my refusal to step out of her son's life.

I would have liked to rush up and help her, but the shock would most likely have overturned her balance. Besides, I imagined she might well resent receiving aid from anyone. Let alone from me.

She didn't notice us until she had reached the hall.

'Madam,' James said, now moving swiftly to the foot of the stairs, 'he insisted I admit him.'

'Who?' she asked, peering past him. 'Who did?'

'Mr Wilmot, Madam.'

Her reaction was practically the same as his – but more deliberate.

'You!' she said, as she walked towards me. 'What fresh piece of cruelty and impertinence has brought *you* here? How dare you return to Merriot Park? After what you did. Don't you know how much you're hated in this house and how your name is cursed all round the clock?'

Her body might have been frailer; but her carriage was as upright and her spirit didn't seem impaired.

'Yes, Mrs Cambourne. I do know how much I'm hated in this house. And rightly so.' I hadn't said it in the café but I said it now.

'I'd hoped I should never have to set eyes on you again.'

'But I hear you're contesting Oliver's will. Then you must have known such a hope wasn't realistic.'

'Never again at Merriot Park, anyway. Amongst the things I love, amongst my memories. Contaminating them all by your presence. As I told you, Mr Wilmot, I should sooner invite Satan into my home than *you*.'

'Mrs Cambourne, I really don't wish to quarrel with you.' I used the same argument I'd used with James. 'Oliver loved you very much and I know it would only grieve him.'

I held out my hand to her.

My argument at least seemed partially effective – insomuch as she said, 'After what I've just told you, I find it totally incomprehensible that you'd expect me to take your hand!'

She stared at it disdainfully.

I let it drop.

'Then why is it you *have* come? Not, I trust, to pour out more of those easy sentiments you so recently – and so belatedly – committed to paper?'

'They weren't in the least degree easy. But no. Couldn't we perhaps go and sit down?'

'He said it was about the will, madam,' put in James.

'Indeed I thought as much,' answered Mrs Cambourne. 'A clever beginning you must think it: our quarrelling would only grieve my son. You expect, of course, to go on from there; to persuade me, no doubt, to drop the whole lawsuit. Is that the purpose of your visit?'

'On the contrary.' But that *was* the purpose of my visit, it suddenly struck me. Just not in the manner she expected.

'On the contrary?' she said, with a brittle laugh. 'I can hardly believe *that*.'

'On the contrary,' I repeated, with emphasis. I knew I had aroused her interest.

There was a silence.

'Oh, very well, then. I suppose that we had better go and talk.'

When we arrived in the drawing room, with the French windows open on to a broad terrace and, beyond that, vast expanses of smooth lawn (I turned my eyes from it: I couldn't bear to see the garden, couldn't bear to see the tennis court), she said, 'The laws of hospitality dictate I should offer you refreshment. But if you want a drink you must help yourself. You know where it's kept.'

I poured a whisky. Mrs Cambourne declined to take anything.

I sat facing her, though at a distance.

'Please explain,' she said.

'I want to bypass the solicitors,' I told her. 'I want to get this whole thing finished with – and fast.'

She waited.

'I want to settle out of court.'

'Go on, Mr Wilmot,' she said drily. 'I'm curious. This settlement you have in mind? Will you settle for nothing? Nothing is what you deserve.' With sudden venom she rapped her stick on the stone hearth. 'And if I really had my way I'd even get back that handsome car you've no doubt driven here this afternoon. My son was a fool. But for a short time, I admit, even I. . .'

She didn't continue.

'Your son was not a fool.' I shook my head. 'You've no right to say that.'

'Is that so? Mr Wilmot, please don't drag me down to your own level of cheapness. *I* loved Oliver while he was alive. I see no need to glorify him now that he is dead. My son was very often a fool.'

She paused.

'But perhaps no more of a fool than I was. As I say, for a period you even managed to pull the wool over *my* eyes. When I saw. . .'

Again her voice trailed off.

'When you saw what, Mrs Cambourne?'

'It doesn't matter,' she said.

'When you saw what?'

'When I saw how happy Oliver was and heard everything he said about you I thought that perhaps, against all expectation, you might actually be the sort of person he made out. I observed you narrowly at Christmas and on every other occasion you came. I even grew quite fond of you – do you know that, Mr Wilmot? I could have grown to love you, I believe. In fact, for a while, I very nearly did. Almost like a second son. . .almost like a second son. And that, I can assure you, was something which had never happened to me before. . .'

Then she gave a short laugh.

'But now, I'm afraid, I feel differently. Now, I am impelled to ask, is there no justice in this world. How can it be right you should go free, after the sheer enormity of the crime which you committed? Is there no punishment – is there no prison sentence – is there no brand of Cain to leave upon your brow?'

Did she know about Elizabeth? Did she know that I had married an heiress? It sounded very much as though she did.

She wasn't hysterical. It might have been less awful if she *had* been.

It seemed pointless to search for a defence. In any case, where could I have found one? I stared down at the carpet and waited for her exasperation to pass.

She went on coldly:

'Now I repeat: what is this settlement you have in mind? I, too, would wish to end the matter quickly.'

'I'll give up the money and the house and the yacht,' I said; and then paused while she stared at me.

'Why?' she asked, in a cracked voice.

'Because I – like you – don't consider I have any right to them. And even if I had. . .I'm not sure I'd be prepared to fight for them in court.'

'There's a catch to all this, plainly.'

'No catch. However, I've a list here of some of Oliver's things I would like to hold onto.' As I spoke I drew a piece of paper from my trouser pocket.

'To which you think you *do* have some right?'

'No right, but a desire so strong that, if you won't agree to let me have them, I'll fight you tooth and nail for the entire legacy. Despite what I've just said.'

She hesitated, but not for long. 'Then let me hear your list.'

'I want some of Oliver's books, records and pictures: I mean the pictures painted by him – especially 'Young Men Reading the Paper'. I want the electric train set he bought the day before he died. I want some of his clothes. And I want – perhaps above all – the medallion he used to wear about his neck.' I suddenly had a terrible fear he might have been buried in it. I added rather sharply, 'I think you have to acknowledge none of that's unreasonable.'

'Why the medallion 'above all'?' she asked. I felt the most wonderful relief.

I answered simply, 'Because he always wore it. I don't think I ever once saw him without it. I. . .'

'Yes? You what?'

I shrugged. 'No. Nothing else to explain. He always wore it. That's all.'

For a full minute neither of us spoke. I looked around the room; I allowed myself to remember things. I looked out at the garden, too.

'Mr Wilmot,' she said eventually. 'Why do you love my son, now that he's dead, so much more than you ever did while he was alive?'

'I think that, while he was alive, I loved him just as much. But – unhappily – I didn't know it.'

'And had you known it. . .would you still have married that American girl?'

'No.'

'It's extremely tragic,' she said, 'that it should take a death and the workings of a guilty conscience to make you understand your own mind. At least you do appear to have a conscience. I suppose that's something.'

'It is tragic,' I agreed. And as I said it I felt my eyes begin to smart.

'But I don't think you were even capable of love,' she added. 'Not then, at any rate.'

I looked at her a moment. 'And would you think that I am now?'

'If you are, then it only heightens the tragedy.'

She spoke briskly and with a look of impatience. I gazed down into my glass and remained silent.

'Mr Wilmot. Let us get something straight. I despise you. I think I always shall. Your selfishness and your greed took away from me the only part of life that was truly worth having. In him I could forgive weakness and self-pity. In you, now, those same qualities disgust me. Even so, I'm prepared to admit you may be less wilfully evil than I supposed; though that's a matter for you and your Maker to decide between you and of little or no interest to myself. You may have the articles you ask for; you may take them away with you this afternoon. But unless it is absolutely necessary, I hope you will never feel impelled to try to get in touch with me again. There is nothing more, I believe, that you and I can ever have to say to one another. I have perhaps a further five years to live. Let me live them out in total ignorance of you.'

'If that's what you want.' I stood up. 'But I would like to have...'

'What?'

'Made our peace, I suppose.'

I added: 'The truth is – again, quite contrary to expectation – that I grew fond of you as well.'

She snorted but then said after a moment, 'Well, if it pleases you, you may consider our peace as having been made. It's all the same to me, I can assure you.'

She held out her frail hand.

'Goodbye, Mr Wilmot. James will help you collect the items you have asked for. Perhaps you'd be good enough to send him to me first?'

She could have rung for him.

'Goodbye, Mrs Cambourne.' We shook hands. 'I suppose it's stupid but I'd have liked to hear you call me John again.'

'Never,' she replied.

32

'Young Men Reading the Paper' had been the second picture Oliver painted using me as his model. The paper in question is *The Manchester Guardian* of November 27th 1958 and the fact that it happens to be folded over at the following item, some of which is clearly legible in the painting, is patently coincidental.

'Mr Butler's proposals on homosexuality were much as expected when the Wolfenden Report came before the House of Commons yesterday. He gave no prospect of any early change in the law, a change which many people would misunderstand and regard as condonation. . .'

The young men reading the paper – I played both roles – are seated together on a bench at the breakfast table, one dressed, the other in his pyjama bottoms, each with an arm thrown around the other's shoulder. We only get a back view but the partial profile of their faces and the very posture of their bodies are a brilliant and haunting evocation of tenderness, defiance, insecurity, dismay. Even the furnishings of the room, the geraniums on the windowsill, the unfinished chess game in one corner, the photos on the mantelpiece, are in themselves a feature of the argument. I thought it was a marvellous picture and I was proud to be a part of it.

Now, following my afternoon in Surrey, I had hung it on the wall facing the bed. It was really too large for the room but that didn't matter. I had gone to bed early, while Elizabeth was still taking her bath, and for the first time since March, gazing up at Oliver's picture and wearing his medallion, I felt. . .no, not happy, exactly, but as though happiness was something which one day – one day – I might conceivably get to rediscover.

The medallion was of silver: a St Christopher: and it linked me to its previous owner just as surely as possessing the whole of Merriot Park would have.

Maybe even more so.

And suddenly I came close to making a promise.

I remembered how I had felt that afternoon in the churchyard: the wish – the need – the brief determination – to be so much better than I was. And perhaps, after all, it wouldn't be too late. Couldn't my life from now on be in the nature of a tribute – a dedication – an atonement?

'With each new day, perhaps, I can try to be a little more like you!'

Already this thought was sufficiently potent to give me back a sense of purpose.

'No wonder that I am. . .*almost*. . .happy again.'

The first signs of madness, when you start talking to yourself, or to anybody else who is neither in the room nor at the other end of a phone line. I didn't care. I smiled, cheerfully. *Yes!* Cheerfully.

Wouldn't it be nice, I considered, if he could really be aware of all that I was thinking. (Yes, *all.* Because he'd instinctively know what to discount.) For a few minutes I gave fantasy free rein. I thought of films like 'Sentimental Journey', 'It's a Wonderful Life', 'Wuthering Heights'. If only things could truly be like that. If only when I died, Oliver's spirit *could* come to meet mine, like Cathy's meeting Heathcliff's. I thought about 'The Ghost and Mrs Muir'. It would have been immeasurably reassuring to imagine Oliver watching over me as Rex Harrison had watched over Gene Tierney. Some sort of omnipresent guardian angel, witnessing everything that was happening to me, day after day after day. Everything.

No, merely to *imagine* it was obviously no good. The fantasy dissipated. And not its least ludicrous aspect, of course, was my assumption that Oliver's spirit would even *want* to come to meet my own, or that it could ever be expected to take the smallest degree of interest in watching over me. There were countless occasions when I kept hearing again those desperate and abortive rings at my doorbell; sometimes the very fact I hadn't gone to answer them, had left him standing on the doorstep in despair – this sometimes seemed more awful than any other part of the whole awful business. . .and often the single feature which had the most power to torment me was the idea that Oliver might in some way have known I was there, not simply surmised it but actually have *known*. . .

Yes, it was more than possible that, even had a heaven existed, Oliver would not have wanted to meet me there.

No, it wasn't, I thought. It wasn't more than possible at all. Oliver hadn't been the type to harbour grudges. Despite everything, if I had only had the chance to show him I was sorry, if I had only had the chance to show him how deeply I loved him, how unendingly I railed at my behaviour, then I knew he'd have forgiven me. Wholly; unreservedly. I was sure of it. And if only, I reflected, if only he *could* have realized the extent of the hell I had been going through during these past four months! How terrible that he should never be able to do so; that his final impression must have been one of pretence and ingratitude and rejection. How terrible that he should never learn of all the emptiness and remorse, and of all the devotion, which he had engendered in me.

My brief period of almost-happiness seemed to be over. I looked down at the medallion and across at the picture and struggled to regain it.

I couldn't.

But all the same it *had* left a bit of a residue.

*

And that residue lasted, more or less, throughout the remainder of July. To some extent I lived up to my aim: I was a kinder, more considerate person. I was a better-informed one, too – I made a practice of reading the newspaper every day and of frequently listening to the current affairs programmes on the radio. With a broader knowledge of what was happening in the world there came – more or less inevitably – a greater range and greater depth to my compassion. I was definitely one degree nicer.

But at the start of August I discovered my talisman was far from being foolproof.

I went to bed on the second feeling comparatively at peace with the world; it had been a Sunday and we'd loafed for most of the day in Regent's Park. We'd rowed on the lake and played a game of tennis and later I'd fallen asleep by the water's edge. Afterwards we'd had a meal at *The Volunteer* and gone to the Classic: 'Dial M for Murder' – fairly entertaining (and in which, oddly, the very cinema we sat in had received a mention). Then we'd walked home and drunk hot chocolate and listened to some music, made love, and put the light out a little before twelve. A nice day. Only, as fate would have it, before sleep came I remembered something. Tomorrow, it would have been Oliver's birthday.

His fortieth birthday. A landmark. (Life begins at forty.) I fell to wondering how we'd have celebrated it; the one birthday we *had* celebrated had been mine. Right now maybe, on some alternative time curve, I should have been wrapping up his presents, adding a few last-minute touches, excitedly going over in my mind the arrangements for the following day. I thought (I couldn't help it; I tried not to) of some of the things I might have planned for him. I assumed at first that we'd have been in England rather than abroad, and in London rather than at Merriot Park, but afterwards, the fantasy growing ever more elaborate, I transferred the setting of our celebration to southern Spain (he'd said that in the spring, perhaps, he would take me to Granada and Seville – to the *real* Spain. 'By comparison this northern tip is only made of plastic!'), to the Greek Islands, even to Southern California and Hawaii. To begin with, naturally, such imaginings were at best only bittersweet but there came a point, when I was close to sleep, at which reality and fiction so far merged that the bitterness was siphoned off and merely the sweetness remained. Possibly my sleep was influenced by this all night – I don't know – yet certainly when I awoke next morning it was from a dream so pleasant that I struggled to remain in it, even though it hadn't struck me for an instant that my partner in the dream wouldn't still be lying beside me in the bed, just as, a moment before, he had been lying beside me on the beach.

Still less than half awake and feeling immeasurably contented and secure, I turned over and lovingly reached out towards him.

*

Bank Holiday Monday. Elizabeth had wanted to go to Hampstead Heath to see the pearly king and queen. I couldn't face it. I couldn't face anything. I stayed in bed, with my eyes directed at the wall, and refused to get up. It seemed so pointless. I couldn't be bothered. It required too much energy.

At first Elizabeth was sympathetic.

'What's the matter, darling? What's wrong? I've never known you be like this.'

I continued to say nothing.

'Shall I call a doctor?'

'No.'

She was sitting beside me on the bed stroking the nape of my neck. But she didn't know about the smarting of my eyes. 'What can I do then, honey, that might improve things?'

'Go away,' I said.

Eventually she, too, became depressed.

'Well, if you're not going to speak to me or even attempt to let me help, there doesn't seem much point in my staying in. At least one of us can make some attempt to get a bit of fun out of this dreary day.'

'Good,' I said. 'Go out. Good riddance.'

Three minutes later I heard the front door close.

I hadn't wanted her to go.

Then I tried to shed tears in earnest. I couldn't. I could manage nothing more than a series of dry, frustrated howls.

For a long time I lay there almost without thought: a vegetable, a zombie: only believing I should never be able to cope with anything ever again, no matter how small. For instance, the very thought of having, even once more, to smile at the woman in the baker's while answering her inane comments on the weather filled me with sheer dread. I had no idea what I was going to do. About that or about anything. 'I wish – I were – dead,' I whispered. . .and then louder and with more emphasis: 'I wish – I were – dead!' A childish cry. But I thought I almost meant it.

At about one Elizabeth returned. She appeared more her usual self. She came and sat on the bed again and put her hand on my arm. 'How are you feeling, hon?'

I grunted.

'What's that, my love?'

'Nothing.'

'Poor Johnny,' she said. 'Whatever are we going to do with you? I hate to see you feel like this.'

She laid her head on my shoulder and her soft hair spilled across my back. After a while she straightened up.

'It's just so lovely out,' she said. 'I went into the park again and watched people feed the ducks. And then two boys started messing about in a canoe and it capsized. They had the time of their lives. I was only sorry you weren't there with me to share in all the fun.'

'How could I have been? We'd have been on bloody Hampstead Heath. In all this bloody heat.'

'Oh, darling, is that why you've been feeling miserable? I wouldn't have cared about not going to the Heath. The only thing I care about is seeing you happy.'

'Oh, don't be so *goddamned* thick!'

'Look,' she said, 'I'll go and make some lunch – why don't you have a quick bath and a shave while I'm doing it? Or if you're really not up to that, I'll bring things on a tray, and we can eat in here. I think that's maybe what you need: food. After all, you had no breakfast. And perhaps later you'll feel a little more like doing something.'

'I don't want any lunch,' I said.

'Oh, yes, you do,' she answered gaily. 'And no arguments, either! I just won't stand for them.'

She turned back briefly at the door. 'I'm sorry I was snappy earlier on. Poor Johnny. I love you very much.'

Before she went into the kitchen she put some records on. Recently we'd been listening almost exclusively to classical music but today she chose Gershwin and Loesser and Coward.

'There's a somebody
I'm longing to see;
I hope that he
Turns out to be
Someone who'll watch over me...'

In spite of everything, I found that I was listening; almost automatically filling in the familiar and well-loved lyric in my mind when I couldn't quite hear it on the record.

As usual it struck me as immensely poignant.

'So...
Won't you tell him please
To put on some speed,
Follow my lead,
Oh – how I need
Someone to watch over me!'

The next record was also one I liked; she had clearly been picking out my favourites. It wasn't possible to stay impervious.

'I've never been in love before;
Now all at once it's you,
It's you forevermore...'

I turned on to my other side. I caught sight of my arm lying on the blanket, smooth and tanned and well-muscled, and the line of it was pleasing.

And suddenly – almost as though it were a veil being lifted – I felt the weight of my depression rise. Evidently there remained *some* good things in life. (It might even be feasible again to smile at that woman in the baker's, while answering her inane comments on the weather!)

I moved onto my back and put my hands behind my head.

I had never known anything like it – never. Was this, to some degree, what manic depressives felt? Was it what Oliver had felt? Felt on Boxing Day? Felt on – ?

But I called a halt. . .and maybe only just in time: that line of inquiry could only lead right back into it, especially when I remembered my lack of genuine concern both on Boxing Day and on one other occasion, similarly short-lived, towards the end of January – and also during that more protracted period following his reading of my book. Poor Johnny, Angel Face had said. Well, poor, poor Oliver! I pushed back the blanket and leapt out of bed. I pulled on my underpants. I ran into the kitchen and embraced a smilingly surprised Elizabeth who had a fish slice in her hand. 'God,' I said, 'do I need to pee! 'But we'll fight for the stately homes of England. . .''

*

I discovered 'In Memoriam'. In the past I had never much cared for poetry but I became enraptured over this. I carried the slim volume almost everywhere and read out lengthy excerpts to Elizabeth. At my insistence she also read the poem and – though not as swept away by it as me – seemed happy enough to listen to my observations.

'Tennyson called his son Hallam. And there's a Hallam Tennyson living today: great-grandson or something.'

'I think that's nice,' she said. 'But what did Arthur Hallam actually die of?'

'Cerebral haemorrhage.'

'At twenty-two?'

'Even at twenty-two.'

Yet somehow I found that reassuring. I may not any longer have positively wished to die but I often felt I wouldn't mind.

After all, I'd had some good times. I'd travelled a bit, had enjoyable experiences, been to dances, read books, seen films, met many interesting and/or congenial people. I had known Oliver. *I had known Oliver!* Growing old, I thought now, seemed virtually aimless: a state which had to be survived with the minimum of grief and catastrophe. (That depression, though it had passed, appeared to have robbed me again of any true sense of purpose.) A fatal haemorrhage or a heart attack at twenty-two was no more to be feared than an all-out nuclear war; and I didn't give a damn these days about that. Even success as a writer – and by 'success' I meant widespread recognition – would no longer interest me. That had been a phase: since March, I hadn't given the least consideration to any further writing, other than (who knew – one day, perhaps) a faithful account of the events set going last November. Besides. . .afraid of death?. . .when there was always that faint, faint possibility that. . .

No, there wasn't. There wasn't at all. Cathy had become reunited with Heathcliff only in the pages of a novel, in the flickerings of a film. Each time one forgot that, even for an instant, one further let go of one's saving grasp on reality, one shed a little more of one's dignity as a self-reliant human being. There were degrees of letting go; of fooling oneself. There were degrees of insanity.

'Imagine it,' Elizabeth said, on another occasion. 'His father. Coming back to their rooms in the hotel, after a pleasant day out, and finding him dead in his chair!'

Yes, dreadful for the parents too, of course – *devastating*! – but, as always, it was Tennyson of whom I was thinking. The utter shock of it all, the incredulity, the anguish. The depression, the despair. The 'why, why, why?' The eventual dulled acceptance. The frequent, oh-so-frequent, resurgence of sharp pain.

Lasting for how long?

'Did you know,' I asked, 'that it took seventeen years to write those eighty pages?'

'Yes, you told me.'

'Tennyson had just turned twenty-four when Arthur Hallam died.'

'*We* were in Vienna,' said Elizabeth. She meant herself and her parents. 'We might even have stayed at the same hotel. It's possible.'

'Seventeen years,' I repeated. 'That feeling of sustained grief you get whilst reading it. . .'

'Though Tennyson can't have felt it all that time.'

'Why not?'

'He just can't.'

'Oh, for heaven's sake! Are you suggesting a person can't go on missing somebody for as long as seventeen years?'

'No, that's not what I'm suggesting *at all*! Naturally he can. And longer, much longer – a whole lifetime. But a quiet miss. Without the desperation.'

I apologized. 'I misunderstood you. Yes, a whole lifetime. . . Without the desperation. . .'

'But you know the person my heart *really* goes out to? Tennyson's sister. All that opposition to the match from Arthur Hallam's parents; and then the way they softened when they finally met her. It all sounds very romantic but oh, Johnny, wasn't the timing rotten! Just before that Continental Tour.'

'Do you feel sorrier for her than for Tennyson?'

'Well, obviously I do.' She sounded impatient. 'At least Tennyson married. Did she? And at least Tennyson had the poem to think about – other poems, as well. Besides. I know they say that the love between two men can sometimes be as. . .'

She broke off.

I said nothing.

'Also, of course, he had his religion to fall back on.' She was talking now more rapidly. 'Although, I suppose, Emily did too. One could envy them both that. A belief in God must make things so much easier.'

But I felt angry and I turned away abruptly. It was the last time we spoke about the poem.

33

In September we flew to Biarritz. I'd been speaking of it one evening and Elizabeth, on the sort of rich girl's whim she didn't indulge in very often, had suddenly said it would be great to see it together. . .and preferably as soon as possible, while we still had the tail end of the summer. So it was as well that nowadays I was going out to meet ghosts rather than to lay them – although I sometimes worried that the former might even be the prescribed way of achieving the latter. But we stayed in a far less magnificent hotel than the Empress Eugenie's palace; and in lieu of a suite we had only an ordinary room with shower.

Naturally the resort was more crowded than it had been in November, yet on the other hand it was good to be able to swim and to lie on the beach. This made us lazy. I showed her St Jean de Luz and Bayonne and San Sebastian but otherwise we didn't do a lot of sightseeing.

What's more, we nearly didn't visit Marnie Stark; for I neither knew whether she had liked me at the time of our first meeting – nor how pleased she'd be at the prospect of a second. But unthinkingly I'd mentioned her in London and Elizabeth had at once been interested. 'Oh, Marnie Stark has quite a following in the States!'

Now one afternoon she urged me: 'Honey, do let's go and see her.'

I wasn't sure.

'Oh, yes, Johnny! It will be fun.'

And I did have to admit – privately – that there *was* a certain pull. I'd made a point of not looking up old friends of Oliver's, yet in a way old friends of Oliver's, particularly his women friends, were the very company I craved.

We went.

'Oughtn't we,' asked Elizabeth, 'to telephone first?'

'No, we'll take her by surprise.'

Mrs Stark was just as I remembered: she was wearing either the selfsame smock or else its counterpart; a faded denim skirt in place of a slightly less faded corduroy one; and again a pair of chunky sandals over large and unbeautiful bare feet. November or September. . .apparently the weather made very little difference.

'My God, the honeypot!' she cried. 'By all that's wonderful!'

'Marnie, this is my wife, Elizabeth. Elizabeth – Mrs Stark.'

'Your wife?' repeated Marnie Stark – as she vigorously, if somewhat automatically, pumped Elizabeth's hand. Her surprise was clearly enormous but her manner remained cordial.

'Why did you call him the honeypot?' laughed Elizabeth, on our way into the living room.

'Why not, my dear? Isn't he something, then, to smack your lips over? *I* always thought so.'

She looked around her vaguely.

'Now where are we going to find some space? You'd better sit over there, I think – don't mind Pooh Bah! What will you have to drink? My martinis are rather famous. . .I expect your husband told you.'

The state of everything appeared unchanged. When I had to remove a tilting pile of books from my own chair I would scarcely have been surprised to find it the same pile as before; it was certainly the same chair, although I would have liked the one where Oliver had sat. Marnie handed us our drinks, offered us cigarettes, proposed a toast. 'Cheers!' she said. 'To absent friends!' Her eyes met mine, briefly, as she raised her glass. I felt a tremor of unease.

'Yes, absent friends!' echoed Elizabeth, cheerfully.

'By the way, Honeypot – you don't mind my calling you Honeypot? How *is* Oliver? I haven't heard from him for ages.'

I stared at her.

Elizabeth caught her breath.

'Oh dear,' said Marnie Stark. 'I do apologize. I seem to have been tactless.' She took a long swig at her drink. 'I'm just a stupid old cow who was never too good at diplomacy.'

'But don't you *know* about Oliver?' Elizabeth exclaimed.

'None better. I'm only a little surprised, my dear, that you do.' She gave her raucous laugh.

'Or have I been too previous? Know *what* about Oliver? Come on – you'd better fill me in. All I do know is, the dirty dog hasn't written to me since Christmas; didn't remember my birthday for the first time since we met; and when I rang to ask why the bloody hell not, there seemed something wrong with his number – I couldn't get through. Also – I admit it freely – I was pissed.' Again the rasp of husky laughter. 'Anyway, what's he gone and done, the big sap? Been shoved into some prison?'

But suddenly her voice rose sharply as she evidently took in, at last, the looks on both our faces.

'What's happened to him?'

'Oliver is dead, Marnie,' I told her. 'He died last March.'

'What?'

Elizabeth got up quickly and went to put an arm around her. 'I'm afraid it's true, Mrs Stark. It never occurred to us you wouldn't know. Otherwise, we'd have tried to break it far more gently.'

'Dead?'

The glass fell from her stubby fingers, a spreading pool of liquid soaking into the carpet.

'How?' she demanded. 'Dead? I don't believe it! *How?*'

Elizabeth sent me a swift glance; then turned her attention back to Marnie.

'He had a heart attack,' she said.

'A heart attack! Dear God. He wasn't even forty.' Already tears were running down her face and she looked ugly; she was a messy crier.

Elizabeth mouthed to me the word 'handkerchief' – her own was in her handbag. I gave her mine, then went to stand by the window, with my back to them. My legs were shaking.

'Was it quick?' asked Marnie, having blown her nose – done so repeatedly. 'Did he suffer?'

'Oh Christ!' I said.

'Yes, it *was* quick,' put in Elizabeth.

'At home? In hospital?'

'At home.'

Marnie had obviously started to cry again. 'Oh God,' she said, 'I loved that man. He was the truest friend I ever had.' She sobbed brokenly, for what seemed like a very long time. I couldn't even turn my head. 'Was your husband there. . .when it happened?'

Elizabeth hesitated. 'No.'

'How do you know, then, it was quick? It might have lasted minutes. *Minutes*!'

'Because Johnny was told it was. Instantaneous.'

'Who by?'

'The doctor. Oliver had a manservant. The manservant called the doctor.'

But Marnie refused to be comforted. 'To have nobody with you!' She blew her nose again, as loudly as before. 'How terrible to die alone! A man as outgoing as that. With such a gift for friendship. To die alone. To die alone – after the sort of life which *he* had always led!'

I spun round, impulsively.

'Shut up!' I cried. 'Stop it! Shut up, the pair of you!'

'Johnny!' exclaimed Elizabeth.

'Well, he's dead, isn't he? Oliver's dead. Does she have to go on about it?'

And with that I turned on my heel and left the room. I went out of the front door, round the house and into the back garden. The cicadas were chirruping and the scent of bougainvillea filled my nostrils. The evening air felt refreshingly cool. I began slowly to recover.

Ten minutes later Elizabeth came out as well. She had seen me from the window.

'Sweetie? Are you all right?'

'How's Marnie?'

'A little better. Perhaps we ought to go?'

'Elizabeth,' I said. 'I thought you were pretty good in there.'

'Oh! I wish that were true. I felt so inadequate.'

We returned inside.

Marnie looked both wild-haired and puffy-eyed but she had stopped crying. She had even powdered her face. The effect was incongruous; you felt she rarely used cosmetics. She seemed to have put the powder on in patches, with defiance, as a child might. She was pouring more martinis.

I said: 'I'm sorry I blew my top.'

But she waved away apology. 'No, no. My fault. I respect you for it. Have another drink. You, too, Elizabeth.'

'Wouldn't you rather we went?'

'No, no,' she said again. 'Oh, please – not yet! I'd hate to be alone.'

We sat down. Took up our glasses. Marnie began to sound like a hostess with a party that was flagging. It wasn't a role which came naturally. It was dreadful to listen to.

'Tell me more about yourselves. Married! How marvellous! Do you realize I've neither congratulated you nor drunk a toast to your happiness?'

'Thank you, Mrs Stark.'

'Marnie! *Marnie!* Haven't I been calling you Elizabeth?'

She raised her glass again.

'I hope you'll both be *exceedingly* happy! May all your troubles be little ones!'

'Thank you. Thank you. . .Marnie.'

We sipped our drinks. I struggled for something to say.

I wasn't fast enough, however. Our hostess was faster.

'But far too soon to be thinking of little ones! I imagine this must be your honeymoon?'

'Yes – but, oh, such a delayed one!' Elizabeth spoke with that same awful brightness. 'We were married in May.'

'May? What – a whole four months ago? And when were you engaged?'

There was suddenly a note of something new. I picked up on it at once and just as quickly recognized the reason for it, but there was nothing I could do. Elizabeth, thinking only of being an easy guest, rushed on without a pause.

Brightly, brightly.

'We became engaged in March,' she said. 'It was all rather romantic. Wasn't it, darling? I mean, in a slightly horrid sort of way. You see, my parents –'

Then at last she stopped; belatedly sensing, I suppose, the change of atmosphere.

'Did Oliver know of your engagement?'

There was a brief but highly tension-filled hush – broken only by the heavy breathing of Pooh Bah.

I said: 'Listen, Marnie. I was going to tell you, anyway. It came to me, out there in the garden: the sort of friendship you enjoyed with Oliver – it was wrong to try to fob you off with just a lie.'

But then I faltered.

'So we finally arrive at the truth, do we?' Her tone may have been sarcastic, but it no longer seemed to threaten tears, even if the powder on her cheeks looked more than ever ludicrous. 'And what *is* the truth the sort of friendship I enjoyed with Oliver would now appear so gloriously to merit?'

'Oliver didn't die of a heart attack,' I said. 'Elizabeth was trying to spare your feelings. He threw himself into the river.'

'Oh, honey, that was blunt,' exclaimed Elizabeth. 'You could've made it softer.'

I turned on her, savagely. 'Softer? Tell me, then – how would you have done it? How would *you* have made it softer?' But after a moment I relented. 'I'm sorry, love,' I said, wearily. 'Yes, you're right. Of course you are.'

Our eyes went back to Marnie.

'My God!' she exclaimed. 'My God! My God! My *God*!'

She then began to laugh.

'Stop it, Marnie!'

'He killed himself because of you?'

I didn't answer.

'And can you guess why I'm laughing? To hear you say, 'I'm sorry, love.' Oh, my God, that's good, that's really good, that's rich, that is. 'I'm sorry, love!' I mustn't forget that one. I must put that in my next book. The trouble is: no one would ever quite believe it.'

'Mrs Stark,' said Elizabeth, ' – please – is there anything we can do for you before we go?'

'You bitch!'

'Marnie! For God's sake! It wasn't Elizabeth's fault.'

'You bitch! You goddamned fucking bitch!'

'*Marnie*!'

'How much are you worth?' Marnie's attention was still firmly fixed on Elizabeth; it seemed as if nothing could tear it from her. 'Tell me that, eh? A million dollars? Two million? Three? How much does it take to buy a honeypot? A homosexual honeypot? And has your money been well spent? Does he fuck all right? Does he satisfy *you* the way he used to satisfy poor Oliver? Yes? Then savour him, my pet. You won't have him very long. There'll be another bee buzzing into sight one day, with a heavier money bag than yours. I tried to point this out to Oliver. But he was too besotted. *He* wouldn't –'

I used the age-old remedy of Hollywood. I slapped her. My slap was highly inefficient. She gave another burst of laughter.

'Strong man! Does that make you feel all grown up? You're becoming such a big boy now. Twenty yet? What a triumph! Imagine – by the time you're twenty – to have had somebody kill himself for you! Only a queer, of course, no one of the top rank. Yet – still – not a bad achievement. Something to notch up. A beginning.'

'Come on,' I said to Elizabeth. 'It won't do any good to stay.'

But Elizabeth seemed incapable of leaving her seat.

Marnie, though, appeared to leave hers with ease.

'Yes – get out of here!' One would almost have expected her to point: *Never darken my doorway again!* 'The two of you – get out of here! You deserve each other. . .my God, how you deserve each other! And what worse thing could ever be said about anyone?'

She spat at us as we drove from the house. She hurried after us and spat. Her spittle ran slowly down the windscreen of the Renault we had hired, and when I set the wipers in motion they only smeared it right across the glass.

'Oh – spit!' I said.

There followed a minute or two of stony silence.

'I'd better phone Robertson and Keyes as soon as we get back to London.'

She didn't ask me why; but I continued as if she had.

'Well, there's clearly been a letter that must have gone astray.' Again I tried to add a lighter touch; I felt we stood in need of one. 'Or you never know – perhaps it's just been buried underneath the clutter! Did you ever see anything like it? Perhaps Pooh Bah was sitting on Mr Blackmore's unopened correspondence!'

I turned to look at her. She was staring straight ahead, along the road lit by the Renault's headlamps. Her face showed not the shadow of a smile. But at least I did receive an answer.

'If you don't shut up,' she said, 'I shall open the door and jump out! I think I really mean that. Why must you *always* talk? Is it because you're so young? Is it because you're only twenty?'

I pulled a face. It was such a small thing at the moment, but she might as well be set right on it, even so – that one last silly detail.

'No,' I said. 'I shan't be twenty, as it happens, until the fifteenth of December.'

34

My only proper row with Elizabeth was more far-reaching than the one I'd had with Oliver.

It chanced that a minute earlier I had mentioned his name. I now went on: 'When did you first realize about him and me?'

'Why?'

'Why not? I'm interested.'

'Like in everything else that relates to you and Oliver! Your main area of interest, bar none.'

I ignored this. 'Was it when I told you about the car?'

'No. Way before that' Did I detect some undercurrent of scorn? 'The night you came to the Savoy together.'

'You knew as early as that?' (*As early as that*? We'd gone to the Savoy on a Monday and she had heard about the car exactly one week later.)

'Not knew. Suspected.'

'My God. Were we so obvious?'

'Not to everybody, I suppose. It was only when Daddy asked what you were living on. You turned the conversation – as usual, of course – with one of those tediously flippant remarks of yours...'

She paused. I thought how all the people who knew me best invariably ended up by growing soured.

'...but I'd caught that look which passed between you.'

'I don't remember any look.'

'Fleeting but unmistakable.'

'And yet – even suspecting it from then on – you still wanted to marry me?'

'I told you,' she said drily. 'By that time I'd fallen in love with you. By that time I'd decided I was going to have you.'

'*Decided*?' I said. 'That's nice.'

'Yes. Why not? *Decided.* Anyway, it's honest.'

'Oh, sure. We can do with some of that. Honesty.'

'I think perhaps we can.'

'Well, weren't you at all. . .dismayed. . .by your suspicions?'

'No. Not particularly. I'm used to overcoming things.'

'You're quite a girl, Elizabeth.'

'You said that once before. Only – I'm not sure – that time you may have said it with a little more affection.'

'This time I may have said it with a little more awe. You're quite a *frightening* girl is maybe what I meant. I begin to see in you the cousin of your cousin: your cousin Sarah, naturally!'

'No more frightening than you, though. Perhaps Mrs Stark was right: we do deserve each other. The two of us are fighters, aren't we? We both believe in getting what we want.'

'I've never especially thought of you as a fighter.'

'That's because you don't know me very well. As a matter of fact, I don't believe you know me at all.'

'I could be starting to agree.'

'I've always been a fighter.' Previously, she might have spoken with contempt. Now she used the word with pride. 'Even at the age of three. I was still in the orphanage then. If you didn't stick up for yourself in the orphanage you went under. It was as simple as that.'

Eighteen years ago. Suddenly I could picture her when she was only three. 'Actually,' I said, 'I don't stand by that word 'frightening'. I'm sorry for using it. I was speaking out of anger.'

All this was happening in the flat one Sunday evening. It was November. We hadn't eaten a proper lunch and now Elizabeth was peeling potatoes at the sink. She kept turning round to emphasize a point. I was seated in one of the armchairs. Up until a short time earlier I had been reading.

'Why were you so withdrawn,' I asked, 'those couple of days after seeing Marnie Stark? *Now* will you tell me?'

'Yes, if you like.' She spoke without expression. 'Two reasons.'

'The first?'

'Well, I finally realized you were just what my father had said you were. A fortune hunter.'

'I see. So you believed in all those ravings of a woman made hysterical by shock? Well – thank you for that, thank you very much!'

'It seemed to me I had no choice but to believe in them. Why did she immediately assume I was rich? She hadn't heard of me. There was nothing in my appearance to suggest it.'

'But she knew that we were staying in Biarritz.'

'So what? You don't need millions of dollars, not even for Biarritz! But perhaps there *was* something in my appearance: the fact that my face could never be regarded as my fortune. Moreover, you're a person who's always been particularly drawn to good-looking people. So. Putting those two things together. . .'

I sighed. 'To me, Elizabeth, you're pretty. And even if you weren't, facial beauty would come a long way down my list of things to look for in a wife. In fact – it's almost a non-starter.'

'Then what comes at the top? Money?'

'No – a kind heart. Courage. Intelligence. A sense of humour. All of which you happen to possess in abundance.'

She gave a sharp, incredulous laugh. But then apologized for it. 'Excuse *me*! That's my sense of humour, no doubt.'

'Not to mention silky black hair and a nice big smile – an almost perfect figure – a flair for just the right clothes to set it off – then grace, charm, common sense, patience – the ability to cook. . .' I grinned. 'If you wanted to know the things I married you for, I think you have to admit I'm not doing badly?

Come on, sweetheart. You can't argue with a fellow who's just drawn up a list like that.'

But even as I was rising from my chair her next words sent me straight back into it.

'No,' she said. 'Stay away from me. There's only one thing which that manages to prove. You have the gift of the gab. And that – on *my* list, I may say – would be a total non-starter.'

I should have stood up, anyway, whilst the impulse was still a recent one, and put my arms about her and tried to hold her close. I realized the gravity of what was happening all right (we'd had enough quarrels of a lesser nature to let me know the difference) but the moment when it might have been possible to do it with the energy, the good humour, the conviction it required – that moment was quickly gone. I told her instead:

'I never knew you suffered from *quite* such an inferiority complex!'

'At the risk of repeating myself – I sometimes wonder how much you do know about me.'

'Meaning?'

'I've felt absolutely wretched for the past six weeks but you haven't seemed to notice a thing. You talked about my being 'withdrawn' for just a couple of days.'

(Yes, well. I felt absolutely wretched for far more than six weeks, and you didn't have the least idea.)

I said: 'Of course I noticed. Even though you certainly managed to disguise it pretty well – something I admired terrifically. There you are, you see. That's the courage I spoke of.'

'We can't all take to our beds,' she responded coldly, 'the first moment life goes a little wrong.'

I made no reply – although she could hardly have said anything more hurtful.

'And even if I did disguise it pretty well,' she added, 'I can't help thinking any man who really loved me would have sensed it.'

I'd already told her that I had. I picked up the book from my lap and pretended to be – as if through utter boredom – reading the blurb on the dust jacket.

'And that's the trouble, Johnny. I don't think any longer that you really do love me. Or maybe ever did. Oh, I can't deny you've been attentive and kind and have possibly done your best. But you've always kept me at a distance; I can see that now. The times when there's been the most real warmth in you – the most animation, the most love – those times have had nothing to do with me at all. They've been the times when you've been talking about Oliver. And you've no idea how often I've said to myself, 'If he mentions that name even once more I shall go crazy!'. . .or how often I've felt so plumb jealous that if Oliver hadn't already been dead I should probably have wished him so. Well, we live and learn, don't we? Six months ago I was just so innocent it would never have occurred to me that I could hate so much.'

She had finished with the potatoes and the carrots and the sprouts. She was holding onto a chair back and sometimes looking at me, sometimes looking at the floor.

'But now I don't feel jealous any more. And now, too, I know it isn't true that I hate Oliver. I've gone past feeling hate – or love – or anything. I just feel tired.'

There was a pause. I answered bitterly: 'If I may say so, you seem to have done an awful lot of living during these past six months – if finding out all about your capacity for jealousy and hate can rightly be termed living. Of course, I know that on the afternoon you believed we were going to inherit Merriot Park you thought that Oliver was dreadfully *sweet*. You did think him *sweet*, didn't you?'

She gave an impatient exclamation and gazed at her knuckles for a moment, white against the chair top. 'Which brings us to the second thing I learned from Marnie Stark. Oh, I suppose I realized it a long time before that, of course – but up till then it had somehow always been possible not to let it crystallize.'

I waited. 'Sounds promising.'

'I fought for you, Johnny,' she repeated. 'From the evening we saw 'Auntie Mame' I knew I stood a fair chance of getting you. And I felt determined to succeed.'

'Which is something, do you realize – since it appears I had so little choice in the matter – that makes nonsense of what you said about your face not being your fortune? A complete irrelevance.'

'No, it doesn't. One still lives in hope. One still clings to the old romantic fairytales. Until somebody comes along and spells it all out for you and the illusion shatters. The admittedly fragile illusion.'

'Very well. You fought for me. Bully for you. What then?'

'What then? It was at Mrs Stark's that I finally faced up to it. *I killed Oliver just as surely as you did.* Except that I was worse than you. Lady Macbeth to your Macbeth. . .knowing that all the perfumes of Arabia couldn't possibly sweeten this little hand. No wonder – as you put it – that maybe (oh, merely for the odd day or two!) I may have seemed a bit withdrawn.'

I stared at her.

For several seconds she stared back. 'Well, say something.'

I said something.

'You bitch. . .'

'Yes. 'The Bitch and the Bugger'. Perhaps she'd like *that* for the title of her next book?'

'She was right about you, wasn't she? You *are* just a fucking goddamned little bitch.'

'Well, apparently. With intelligence, courage, charm, grace and – what else was it? – oh, yes, the ability to cook.'

We were silent. Still standing, she folded her arms; and now she dropped her eyes again.

'I feel so tired,' she said. 'I sometimes think I must be heading for a breakdown. Even almost hoping that I am. Because is this my natural self? I used to think I was a little nicer. So *very* tired,' she repeated.

'Well, that makes two of us.' I remembered Icarus flying too close to the sun. 'The question is: what do you want to do now?'

'Do?'

'Yes. About us. Is this the end of the line?'

'Actually, I feel it may be.' A solitary tear moved slowly down her cheek. She brushed at it impatiently. 'I want to leave you, Johnny.'

I think I'd realized she was going to say that. Half realized it. Yet I felt positive that until I'd put the notion in her head those words hadn't yet formed. I didn't know much about telepathy but I thought that in some way I had willed them.

At length I said:

'You can't.'

'Why not?'

'Because it makes the whole damned thing so meaningless! That's why not!'

I had practically shouted it.

Very briefly, our eyes met.

'You can't.' I'd said it now more gently.

'I don't necessarily mean forever. For a month or two. To think things over. Quietly. We both need a chance to do that.'

'No.' Stubbornly I shook my head. 'I promise you *I* don't.'

'Yes, you do. Before we start a family. I think we're lucky not to have done so already. If we have made a mistake, this is plainly the time to correct it.'

'Okay,' I said, woodenly.

'Okay?'

'Where will you go?'

'Home.'

'Yes. You've never really thought of this as home, have you?'

'Of course I have.'

To neither of us, probably, did her tone sound that convincing.

'Anyhow,' I said, 'I can tell you of someone who'll be pleased. Your father said it wouldn't last a year. He's clearly a whiz kid with the horoscopes!'

'Or maybe just a shrewd judge of human nature. No, I'm sorry,' she added quickly, 'I don't want to start it up again. But – as I said – I'm not even sure it will be permanent.'

'Oh, don't be so naive, babe. As soon as you get back to all those red-blooded, clean-cut, wholesome young Americans, and back to your mommy and daddy, it will be permanent all right.'

There was another silence.

I shrugged. 'Well, never mind. I daresay I can always find someone else to keep me. Third time lucky, don't they say?'

She replied: 'I'll leave you some money – enough to tide you over for a week or two. Obviously I had no intention of clearing out the account. And after that we'll have to see.'

'An allowance! Gracious me, how bountiful! Perhaps I'll even get some alimony. And when do you propose to leave this humble residence, my lady, which you could never look upon as home?'

'Immediately,' she said. 'After I've cooked your supper. There's no purpose to be served in drawing out the agony – not now that we've made up our minds. I shall go to a hotel tonight and catch a flight back to the States tomorrow.'

'Tonight?' I said.

'Yes, Johnny. And please don't try to stop me.'

'I wouldn't think of trying to stop you. How could I – your now being such a woman of action? Only please don't bother to cook me any supper. It would surely choke me.'

'Very well. I'll get my things ready. May I ask you to look after these peelings?'

In another twenty minutes she had packed her suitcase. I remembered the girl who had struggled across the Strand with two of them that size. She had her coat on. In the meantime, I had scarcely moved.

'I'll send for the rest later. There isn't much. It shouldn't be too complicated to have it all shipped out.'

I thought: there speaks the one who's coming back. It wasn't worth putting into words, however.

Nothing was worth putting into words.

As she passed my chair she touched my forehead lightly with the back of one hand. 'Johnny, it is for the best, you know.'

'I ought to warn you,' I said. 'Once you go I may not be prepared to have you back – even should you want to come.'

'Well, I'm afraid that's a risk we'll simply have to take. Isn't it?'

For a moment she stood beside my chair.

'Goodbye, honey. Look after yourself.'

'Oh, I think you can rely on me for that.'

I heard the front door close. It reminded me of the August Bank Holiday, when she'd gone off to Regent's Park and had seen those two lads capsizing their canoe. She had wished I could have been there with her, to share in all the fun.

35

I didn't start looking for work. I went on a round of frenzied entertainment – nightclubs, theatres, cinemas (I saw five films in three days) – always getting up late, usually after midday, and then sitting well into the small hours every morning, always with a glass in my hand, leaving an accumulation of other unwashed glasses and coffee cups and dirty laundry. But mainly glasses. Memories had to be erased.

Yet memories also had to be revived. I had nothing else to live on.

And so one Sunday in January (it couldn't be a weekday; by then I'd started back at Selfridge's) I returned to Merriot Park.

'Oh, no! This is too much! Am I to find *no* sanctuary?'

'I agree that – to use your own phrase – it isn't 'absolutely necessary'. But it's important.'

'Important to *you*, I suppose? To Mr John Wilmot? Well, yes, of course! What else could ever be important?'

I was growing accustomed to the weariness in her tone; the resignation.

'So tell me the worst,' she said, 'and get it over with!'

'I'd like to see some snapshots of Oliver. When he was young. Before the war, during the war, anything you have.'

'You'd like to see them, or you'd like to take them from me? As a further part of your – in quotation marks – settlement?'

'I wouldn't take them from you. Unless, that is, you had copies. Or copies could be made.'

She rang a bell. 'Janet will fetch the album,' she observed, tersely – and for the second time during my visits to Merriot Park I experienced a keen sensation of relief.

I hadn't seen James that day. Janet had opened the front door. When now she brought the album she naturally went towards her mistress.

'No, no. Give it to Mr Wilmot, please.'

Janet did so and then left. Without opening the album I turned to Mrs Cambourne and indicated a sofa in the centre of the room.

'Couldn't we sit on that? Then you could provide me with a commentary. Which I know would double my enjoyment.'

'Your enjoyment? Why should I regard that as any matter for concern?'

'No reason whatsoever.' But I took a chance. I smiled as I said it.

She gave a token grunt of impatience; yet then rose from her chair and, as always now, leaning on her stick, took careful steps towards the sofa. I helped her down onto it – it wasn't very low – and so far from shrugging off my assistance she even acknowledged it. 'Thank you, Mr Wilmot. Perhaps you would hand me my glasses?'

And less than a minute later we were settled. It felt distinctly strange, after the great distance she had recently kept between us – physical as far as she could, as well as metaphorical – now to be so close that our knees were almost touching, with the album resting bridge-like on our laps. I thought that she must be aware of this, also; she appeared more than usually brusque as she commenced her exposition. Indeed, she turned over the first few pages without even giving them a glance. 'Those are photographs my mother left me. Mostly of myself as a child. They won't be of any interest to you. Neither to you nor anybody else.'

'Oh, but I'd like to see them if I may.'

She shrugged. 'As you like.' Her tone implied it was entirely immaterial. 'Then you'd better be the one to turn the pages.'

I went back to the beginning and was taken at once into another world. The eighteen-nineties, early nineteen-hundreds. Beach pictures: bathing machines, donkeys on the sand, moustachioed men in striped swimming apparel, giggling young beauties in frills and flounces. Picnic parties on the river: punts, parasols, straw boaters, white summer dresses. The grounds of a large country house: croquet hoops, delicately trailing willow trees, a young girl crossing the lawn. On closer inspection this young girl turned out to be Sarah Cambourne herself. She had figured a good deal in earlier photos, too – a pretty child with fair curls and a slightly aggressive tilt to her chin; but here she looked for the first time a positive beauty, vivacious, assured, aware of the promise life held out to her and determined to take hold of it. That made me warm to her a lot: I, of course, had once felt much the same. At her side – an almost indistinguishable blur – bounded a small dog. 'A fifteenth birthday present', I read beneath the photo. 'What did you call him?' I asked, smiling.

'Her,' she said. 'Patience. She was two months old.'

'And not precisely living up to her name, by the look of things.'

'No, she was irrepressible. I remember once –' Her voice had taken on a spontaneity I hadn't heard in it since March.

'Once?'

'No, nothing. It wasn't of the least importance. Please turn the page.'

'Did she live on to a ripe old age? Patience.'

'I expect she did. I really don't remember. It was a long time ago, Mr Wilmot.'

I turned the page.

In the top right-hand corner of the next I read: 'First grownup dance. Partnered by Oswald. May 1909.' And this time she was standing next to a very erect and dignified young man in evening clothes. 'Was that your husband?'

'Good gracious, no. It was almost ten years before I married. Oswald was a cousin. I thought him rather dashing.'

'Your dress is very pretty.'

'A seamstress in the village made it. Her name was Mrs Jarvis; we called her Jarvie. A kindly woman, who always took such pains.'

I wondered what had happened to that dress which once must have mattered so much; and – by extension – to all dresses which once must have mattered so much.

'I've sometimes wondered that, as well,' she admitted.

And against all hope it gradually began to feel companionable again, as it had felt companionable two Boxing Days ago. The past exerted its spell. Mrs Cambourne pointed out members of her family – mostly dead – and I gazed at each photograph carefully, noting the backgrounds, drawing her out with questions to which I genuinely wanted to know the answers. My sincerity must have communicated itself.

In some ways it was a bit like sitting in a theatre before the curtain went up. Listening to the overture. But the overture was enjoyable in its own right, besides being valuable, and it also enhanced one's appetite for the play.

She spoke briefly about her mother. . . 'whom nowadays I resemble.' She mentioned that Oliver had been very close to his grandmother, who hadn't died until he was eighteen.

'And this was my husband,' she said. 'On our engagement day.'

The caption was of one word. 'Landed!' I'd have expected there to be other pictures leading up to it.

'And Oliver was very like him,' I remarked at last, after staring at the album for a long time.

'Only in looks. Not in character.'

There followed pictures of the wedding. It had obviously been a huge occasion, with long lines of expensive cars and crowds of wealthy-looking guests and a marquee on the lawn – '*Here*?' I exclaimed.

'Yes, here,' she answered. 'You see, my husband rather took over the wedding – my parents had wanted something smaller, altogether more modest. It was the final summer of the war but Henry had only recently acquired Merriot Park and it seemed he wanted to show both me and the house off together. It was a very grand affair. Someone happened to say it was worthy of Ziegfeld and Henry took that as a great compliment.'

She sighed.

'I'm afraid my husband was in no way an admirable character. Not to put too fine a point on it, he was a malingerer and a profiteer. And his friends were mostly of the same ilk. But I was dazzled and my head was turned. . .I haven't even the excuse of youth. I wasn't particularly young – especially not by the standards of that time. And I'm sure my parents were worried

I'd be left unwed. During that period, of course, so many women were. . .'

She stared at the photographs.

'It was a miserable mistake – and one I very soon regretted. Apart from Oliver, that is. . .and apart from Merriot Park.' I glanced back, on the preceding page, at those two syllables of humorous self-congratulation and of faith in a secure future. 'Landed!'

There then followed a few honeymoon snaps: the newlyweds sitting on camels in the desert, riding ponies along the chasm leading into Petra, Sarah Cambourne leaning elegantly against a rock tomb.

But the next picture was something altogether new.

Now she was wearing a knee-length dress, and a long string of beads, and holding in her arms a baby: 'Oliver at three weeks'. The overture was over.

Yet it wasn't until the child was nearly ten that I could really start to believe this was the person who had so completely changed my life.

And now our progress grew even more leisurely. I heard how Oliver had excelled in theatricals at the day school he'd attended until the age of twelve but how on one occasion, not having properly learned his lines, he'd adlibbed his way through most of the performance; how after the curtain calls he'd been so overcome with remorse that unknown to both his parents he had given away all his favourite toys – one to each member of the cast – in a desperate bid to atone for such flamboyance.

'When his father found out, he was livid,' exclaimed Mrs Cambourne, raising her hands and giving a soft, relishing chuckle. 'Good gracious, how the feathers flew! Just bread and water for a whole day! Or that's how it *would* have been! Practically Dickensian.'

'Did Oliver cry?'

'No. He seldom cried.'

There were other stories of how he had made his father angry: once by removing worms from the path of a public park in case they should be trodden on; once by insisting on picking up shattered glass in the roadway.

I mentioned how my own father had reacted to my throwing my pyjamas into the apple tree beneath my bedroom window.

Now we had reached the thirties. Sarah Cambourne, although she must have been over forty by this time, still looked carefree and frivolous in a series of gay little hats perched saucily over one eye. Oliver on the other hand – at fifteen – was looking surprisingly serious: pale-faced and introspective. But there was a snapshot of him gazing at his mother ('One of my favourites,' she said) – and she was gazing back at him – in which his tender, slightly mocking smile made him look so handsome, so unexpectedly familiar, that my head swam and I thought that I might faint. For a short time my sense of loss returned to fever pitch. But slowly such intensity subsided – and I could take note again of photographs of various tutors and associated activities: '*The Tempest* in the Garden', 'Summerhouse Maths', 'Botanists on the Hog's Back', 'Looking *Affectedly* Academic in the Library'. That adverb had been added, and underlined, above the usual sign to indicate a word left out, in Oliver's own hand.

Afterwards came snapshots of Oxford – mainly records of the days on which his mother had visited. Sometimes he stood chatting in a group of undergraduates and I wished I could have listened to their chat. It was impossible not to speculate a little, looking closely at all those faces, on whether any of them had ever been something more than a friend. There was a picture of Oliver standing alone on a bridge over the Isis which – along with that other, earlier one – I would particularly have liked to have.

There were no photographs of graduation.

But then I realized why. He would only have been twenty – just turned twenty – when war had been declared.

Also, it occurred to me, 'A Yank at Oxford' had been made during the period Oliver was at Oxford. I wondered now if he'd seen any of the filming – whether he could even have taken part in it, as an extra. Surely, at least some of the time, Vivien Leigh and Robert Taylor (those two who'd been in 'Waterloo Bridge') would have been working there on location. . .which might well have caused a certain degree of excitement. But I didn't even know if he had seen the finished product. It was only a little thing. Yet again – for a minute – I felt desolate. There was so much I'd never thought to ask him.

The album was coming to an end.

If only there could have been a second album – equally thick!

Again, it was like being in the theatre or, more particularly perhaps, the cinema: illuminated clock above the exit – merely ten minutes remaining and, oh, how you wanted them to crawl!

The second to last page showed Oliver in uniform.

He still looked youthful but – now – more consistently recognizable. There was a picture of him with two small evacuee children, the little girl sitting on his shoulders, her brother with his arm around his waist and gazing up at him in adoration. There was another picture of the children, this time on their own, and then two of Oliver with Mrs Cambourne, both mother and son striking absurd poses in front of the house – 'My Hero!' read one of them. It was an odd thought that I'd been only nine days old when those attitudes were being struck, on the Christmas Eve of 1939.

The final page was blank except for, in the top left-hand corner, a snapshot of Edmund Marshall.

By then I'd given up all hope he was going to be included.

The caption, of course, supplied the name. The photograph showed a tall and fair-haired man with an attractive face.

I affected ignorance.

'Who was this?'

'A friend of Oliver's,' said Mrs Cambourne. 'It was he who took those pictures there.' Having momentarily turned back the page, she indicated the four preceding photos.

I was frightened she might regard his role with the camera as sufficient clue to his identity. But she added, after a moment, 'Really, I suppose, he wasn't dissimilar to you.'

I didn't know if she meant only a physical resemblance. Oliver had spoken of one. I couldn't really see it, apart from the dark blond hair.

'He was very charming. He seemed kind. I liked him. But afterwards I learned. . .'

I didn't hurry her.

'He was the first of them,' she said. 'Just as you. . .you were the last. When I realized what was happening, I hated him; reacted to him far more strongly than – well, this goes without saying, I hope – than I would have reacted to him now.'

'When *did* you realize?'

'Oh, practically at once. It was sometime in the week which followed Christmas.'

And it had changed her, I knew. An end to frothy hats and silly poses; an end to springtime in November and skylarks which sang when I saw you. You put your shoulders back from then on and faced the world with wariness. Or aggresssion. Or defiance. You zealously protected the one person who had provided you with your real reason for living. . .and in the process you became hard.

'Yet you stuck his picture in the album,' I observed.

'It was a happy Christmas,' she answered. 'Perhaps the last *really* happy Christmas until. . .'

'Until?'

I asked it hopefully; and she responded to my hope.

'Yes,' she said. 'Until the Christmas before last.'

But then she shuddered.

'Though as for this one gone by. . .!'

'Please don't,' I said.

But then I went on swiftly, before I could receive any tart rejoinder to do with just deserts or easy sentiment.

'How long had Oliver known him?'

'A month? Possibly two. He was stationed at the aerodrome Oliver got posted to. Bomber Command. He had some leave – no family to spend it with – Oliver invited him down here. It was the end of everything.'

Or maybe a beginning.

For some.

'A short time later he was dead.' I was glad she said that with a perceptible note of bitterness.

Edmund Marshall burned to death in his Spitfire, screaming, the radio still on.

Dear God. Dear God.

And what were *you* doing, God, all the while he screamed? Pressing your hands to your ears?

Or turning up the volume?

I know that you were smiling.

'It was he,' she said, 'who gave Oliver that St Christopher. I don't mean he bought it for him – it was his own. He gave it to Oliver the night before he died. I'm not sure why. If one were superstitious one might even say. . .' But then she shook her head. 'Do you wear it now?' She must have known the answer.

'Always,' I said.

Edmund Marshall – Oliver – then me.

I drew it out but didn't take it off. She touched it for a second.

'Do you want it back?' I asked.

'Why?'

'Perhaps I should never have made you part with it.'

'It would simply have sat there in my jewellery case – just as it was doing the last time that you came.'

I was relieved to note she didn't give a shudder.

'Anyway,' she repeated, 'after he died, things were never the same. Something in Oliver died with him. Until he met you, that is. And then that something returned to life.'

I heard the tick of the carriage clock on her mantel.

'And you've no idea,' she said, 'how very much I hoped. . .!'

At which point her voice broke. But an instant later it was back under control.

'Yet it's been pleasant sitting here like this; I can't deny it. In other circumstances I think we could have been fond of one another, you and I. Quite fond,' she added, sadly. It was a virtual repetition of what she'd said before.

I asked timidly: 'What will happen to this album when. . .?'

'When I die?'

'Yes.'

'You mean, the photographs of Oliver?'

'Not only them. Those of you. And even that one of Edmund Marshall. He was important in your lives. And – as you said – he had no family.'

'My dear Mr Wilmot,' she replied. 'What usually happens to old photographs when you've had the misfortune to outlive your children and you have neither grandchildren nor anybody else to call your own?'

'But have you no nephews? Nieces?' She had pointed out an older brother in the first few pages. Also an older sister.

'Yes, a few – although they neither come to visit, nor invite me to their homes. In justice, however, I do have to say they live a long way off, and always send me Christmas cards, inscribed with flowery messages.'

She added: 'And, of course, it's highly probable that they'll now grow a little more attentive – once it's sunk in, I mean, that Merriot Park is mine. Well, no doubt that's already sunk in but they don't like to seem too hasty.'

It sounded bleak; so bleak. Perhaps I hadn't wholly realized – not until I heard her say that – *quite* how much I had damaged her life. Possibly ruined it even more than I had ruined my own.

Which was maybe the hardest thing I should ever have to admit.

'So I repeat,' she said. 'What usually *does* become of old photographs which nobody wants? At best, they get shoved into the corner of some attic.'

Was that at best? It was difficult to say. I'd often seen discarded photographs in junk shops, along with the cracked china and the tinny cutlery. Young men in army uniform; wedding day pictures; poses like 'First grownup dance. Partnered by Oswald. May 1909.' Even when I was a child it had always struck me as pathetic. Fascinated, I had once asked my father, 'Haven't they any mummies, then, to love them?'

'I don't suppose you'd consider,' I said, slowly, 'leaving this album to me? I promise you I'd value it.'

She answered tersely. 'Oh, at this stage I can't be thinking about anything like that!'

And shortly afterwards I drove away. Before I went she gave me tea – relations had manifestly improved. But on this occasion I looked about me with a melancholy I hadn't experienced the last time. Or not so fully. The reason was laughable. This had been Oliver's home; he had been born here. 'One of these days,' I'd said to Elizabeth, 'possibly we could buy it.' But I doubted now that such a thing would ever happen and I felt a heaviness in my heart which owned a deep mistrust of the future.

36

By nightfall my melancholy had turned into another crippling depression. I spent the whole of the next day in bed. I returned to work on Tuesday feeling only slightly less apathetic – and this was a state which lasted, allowing for minor gradations of light and shade, all through the next ten weeks. I did everything I had to;

I even smiled at times, and laughed; I went to the pictures; but just a hair's breadth beneath the surface lay only emptiness and self-pity.

During a rare bout of activity halfway through February I wrote to Elizabeth saying I must have a clear-cut decision. Apart from a Christmas card, I had heard from her only once since November – and that, most non-committally. She now answered that she had made up her mind to stay on in America and that I should therefore start divorce proceedings. She hoped we should 'always remain dear friends'. I thought I'd been prepared for this: had believed that I didn't much care. But her letter was still a shock. Its finality made me recall qualities I hadn't really thought about since her departure. It was always the same. Apparently I only began to value things as I was losing them.

My awareness of this made me write and nearly post a mawkish sort of screed begging her to reconsider. Yet in its place I eventually dashed off a deliberately short note saying, 'As you like. But is that really your final word? It seems we had a lot going for us, and still could have. I was never in love with you – of course you know that – but we were always fond of one another. I believe we could work something out: contentment if not happiness. And I promise you – in regard to mentioning Oliver – I'd do my very best to be careful. Think about it. Johnny.' Which appeared a truthful statement of the facts. . .and left me in precisely the same position. Though not for long. Her answer came speedily. 'I *have* thought, Johnny, believe me I have. And it honestly seems better for both of us that I should stick by my decision. There's a man here who is anxious to marry me. By your standards, a not very exciting person, but he will make me a good and thoroughly dependable husband and I believe I shall be able to make him a good wife. He clearly worships me – it's a nice feeling! He's a widower with a young child, a little girl who's perfectly sweet and now refers to me as Lizzykins!

Also my parents do approve – I must admit that counts. . .' And she reminded me about the instructions contained in her previous letter for sending on the few things she still wanted.

So that was that. I remembered her saying I love that man, I love that man so much it hurts, I shall love him till the day I die – and I wrote a card telling *her* to start the divorce proceedings because, if she must know, *I* didn't have the energy. Again, my predominant feeling was one of waste. What had I done – what had I *done* – what in the end had any of it amounted to? The lunacy! The sheer lunacy! For a short time I'd had everything a person could have wanted. . .could possibly have wanted. . .and what had I now?

Nothing. I had already slipped back into my (currently) more normal state of apathy.

On March 24th I took the day off. Legitimately. It was a Thursday. Fittingly cold and damp and dismal. I awoke early, despite the aspirins I'd swallowed the night before – and the quantities of Scotch. (More and more of my money, these days, went on drink.) I knew it was said to be dangerous to mix aspirin with alcohol but I had done it deliberately and defiantly; almost hopefully. At any rate, I thought, *that* would have been one solution. Perhaps the best. Life was a mess. But I'd awoken in fact with nothing worse than a headache and the conviction that even if I stayed in bed all morning I shouldn't be able to get to sleep again. The rain beat down against my window.

I got up and had breakfast: another whisky – a large one, out of last night's glass – and a handful of ginger nuts. The ginger nuts were soft.

It was nearly half past eight. This time last year I'd been sitting over orange juice and eggs and bacon, triangles of toast and strong black coffee. Oliver had commented on my lack of appetite – although he himself very seldom took breakfast. (He usually came in, however, just to be sociable. 'I'd hate to think of you as missing me,' he'd once said, 'and feeling all unhappy and alone!')

I said: 'I ate too much last night.'

'In the pub? What nonsense! You hardly ate a thing. I'll march you off to the doctor if you don't watch out.'

'Stop fussing.' I managed to get through one of the eggs.

'What's on your programme for today?'

'This morning I mean to write some letters.'

'Will you model for me again next week?'

'Of course.' I could scarcely get the words out.

'And this time, I swear to it, you'll be recognizable!'

'Okay.'

'Perhaps one day I'll attempt a portrait. How would you like that?'

I nodded.

Oliver looked at me inquiringly. But he didn't express the inquiry in words. He threw down his napkin, got up and came to stand behind me. Put his arms about my shoulders and his cheek next to mine. Finished by giving me a quick kiss on the temple. 'See you then. By the way, I shan't be here for lunch. Happy letter-writing!'

He came back and stuck his head round the door. 'And drink up that orange juice, please! Have to look after yourself! You're precious.'

Well, I'd done that all right. At least. . .such had been my intention.

But would I ever be precious to anyone again? In that same way.

I doubted it.

Nor did I even want it.

A soft thud on the doormat informed me that the post had arrived. I felt glad of the distraction. But it was only the electricity bill; and a letter from Folkestone, which – dear God – was precisely what I needed. The usual inquiries about work and did I yet know when Elizabeth was coming back – surely her mother must be on the mend by now? My eye skimmed through to the closing sentences: 'Write soon and give us all your news. I do hope you're eating properly while she's away. You *must* look after yourself.' Sweet Jesus Christ!

I decided I had to get out. I needed fresh air. I needed to walk. Blindly. Fast. Anywhere. I grabbed my raincoat and some money and slammed the door behind me. It was only after I'd done so I realized that I'd forgotten my keys. Well, what the hell? I could worry about that later.

I put my head down against the rain and made for Regent's Park. By the time I reached it my hair was drenched and there were trickles running down my neck. I didn't mind: the rain was cold and stingingly insistent and had a numbing effect even on my thoughts. Also it seemed to make my headache better – headache, hangover? Somehow I negotiated traffic – umbrellas – puddles; the first meant as little to me as the second or the third. I found myself on Primrose Hill – in Fitzjohn's Avenue – at length on Hampstead Heath. Carried on to Highgate. At Highgate, soaked, I had a coffee. Misguided. Memory set up again.

Back to the road. Archway? Seven Sisters? I no longer knew the names. I was jostled by the lunchtime crowds. They were grumbling, single-minded, aggressive. . .better, though, than laughing. Strips of neon lighting spilled their brightness onto pavements. Mud splashed up from underneath the wheels of cars. Still I went on.

I arrived back in Baker Street by five. The rain had stopped but I felt chilled and shivery. I went into the Moo Cow Snack Bar and ordered soup – followed by spaghetti on toast. The soup was lukewarm and I made a fuss. Yet when I found the toast rubbery I couldn't be bothered. Not again. I wasn't hungry.

I thought about a long soak in steamy water. But I baulked at the idea of going home; of inactivity. Outdoors, at least, there were people to watch. I supposed I could go to a cinema.

An option I dismissed: the cinema would be useless.

And, besides that, it would be wrong. Totally wrong.

I could walk down to the West End. Mingle with the crowds. Pass the evening in a pub or two.

If I stayed on my own I'd go crazy.

The clock in the snack bar said a quarter to six.

At this time, of course, I had been in the car with Elizabeth.

'Mr Wilmot drives north. Did you ever see,' I asked, 'a film called 'Mr Denning Drives North'?'

'You and your films!' She had laughed.

'I can't remember it exactly. I believe he had a body in the boot.'

'In the trunk? Well, at least there isn't one in ours. That makes life a *bit* less complicated!' She paused. 'Why did Oliver want to come to warn my parents? Honey, why did you tell him in the first place? Did you have a row?'

I shook my head. 'He's just slightly old-fashioned in some ways. Outmoded sense of duty. I don't know why I told him.'

My throat hurt. It really did hurt.

'But that was a good film,' I said. 'This journey reminded me of it.'

I battled on determinedly.

'John Mills and Phyllis Calvert. Sam Wanamaker.'

'Who's Phyllis Calvert?'

Yes, Elizabeth and I. . .we had been in the car.

Where had Oliver been?

I stayed on in the snack bar. I had spent the whole day fighting it off. I was tired of fighting it off.

After the rings, what then?

Incredibly, I had never thought about this. What *had* Oliver done? After he'd left Gloucester Place, had he gone to the Savoy? No, the Sheldons would have said so. Then why hadn't he; what had prevented him? Had he been overtaken by the Englishman's traditional sense of fair play – or, more like it, by his own innate unselfishness?

Or had he suddenly recognized what he must have seen as the utter futility of trying to stop us. . .and then descended into lethargy?

In any case, what had he done during that nine or ten-hour gap which separated all his known movements? I wished there was some way I could find out; short, that is, of asking James.

An hour later I left the snack bar. I began to walk again. But this time my destination was more specific.

If I'd been Oliver I'd have gone and got drunk. Or, rather, if it had been Oliver who'd taken off and I'd felt about Oliver then as I felt about him now (yet I think I had; I think I almost had), I would have gone and got drunk And perhaps even more depressed as I did so.

In Victoria I stopped at a pub and drank two double whiskies, fairly fast.

While I was there, a young Salvation Army officer came in with a collecting box. She reminded me of 'Guys and Dolls'. But unfortunately it was nothing from 'Guys and Dolls' which her colleagues were playing on the pavement. Memories of endless school assemblies merged with those of Damon Runyon and Frank Loesser.

> 'Time like an ever-rolling stream
> Bears all its sons away;
> They fly forgotten as a dream
> Fades at the opening day. . .'

I could no longer agree with the last half – indeed, it seemed especially ironic tonight – but I gave the officer a half-crown, because it was all I had in my pocket apart from a ten shilling note and a few coppers, and because something in her manner reminded me of Elizabeth. Besides, I thought drily, soon *I* might be joining the ranks of the down-and-outs; one of these days *I* might be glad of some hot soup and a warm blanket. I didn't know how long I could face going on at Selfridge's.

Anyhow, Selfridge's mightn't be too happy about having its customers served by a dipsomaniac.

'God bless you,' said the girl.

'And God bless *you!*' I riposted, in some way believing this to be witty. I was already half drunk. That meal in the Moo Cow hadn't provided much absorbent.

Soon after she had left I followed her example. I hardly thought Oliver would have gone to a pub. I thought he'd have done all his drinking at home. I pictured him sprawling in one of those armchairs by the fireplace, with the lights out, mechanically raising the glass to his lips, an uncapped bottle near the foot of the chair.

I walked to the Embankment. It was dark, of course, but at least I had no difficulty in pinpointing the window of the sitting room. Right there at the top.

The rain had started up again.

Yet I stayed walking up and down opposite the flats for over an hour, sometimes stopping for as long as a minute to stare up at that unlit window and try to imagine the feelings which – behind it, at this very moment a year ago – might already have been whispering, seductively, of suicide. Indeed, it wasn't all that hard to imagine; definitely it was easier than it would have been some twelve or thirteen months earlier. Now I could empathize in a way that I could never have done then.

But a little after ten I received a shock. I had supposed – illogically, after so long a period – that the flat remained empty.

Yet suddenly a light went on.

I shied away.

Shied away, before I'd see some stranger cross to draw the curtains. I'd fleetingly believed it was Oliver whose hand had flicked the switch.

Now I went on believing it – whilst knowing very well that I didn't believe it at all.

I pictured him standing at the desk in the other room, deliberating on whether or not to write a note. Dismissing it as pointless; a dissipater of impetus. (Where ran the line between apathy and impetus? What culminating thought had goaded him to cross it?)

Now he saw the paperweights: those fat bronze Buddhas: gloating, smug. He picked one up, weighed it in his hand. He would need to wear his overcoat.

I pictured the closing of the front door, the rapid descent of those many flights of stairs. (Where had James been, where on earth had James been?) Were the weights already in his pockets, or did he hold one in each hand? What a grim and pointless exercise: this endeavour to relive the final moments of a desperate man. Yet I couldn't stop. I was obsessed. I stared at the glass doors which formed the entrance to the block. I practically *saw* Oliver come striding through them. Head up, expressionless; a resolute, unfaltering stride. Practically *saw* him cross the road.

Cross the road. Mount the pavement. *This* pavement!

In fact, he came so close to me we almost touched. Made off towards the bridge.

His footsteps echoing sharply in the cold quiet crispness of the night, as I too move off along the pavement.

This year, the night is neither cold nor crisp. The lamps gleam softly through the drizzle; the intermittent benches are deserted – green paintwork glistens. Yet still I keep that other man in sight, on that clearer, finer evening. I hear the chill, dank splash of the river. No craft that I can see. On the opposite bank, lights emanate – dully – from an office building: cleaners getting ready for tomorrow?

The bridge comes into view. I pass two lovers leaning against the wall of the Embankment – the woman's hands twined around the man's waist. They're elated; joking; warm with love. I put my hands inside my pockets and make them into fists. For some reason (it hasn't re-entered my mind all day) I remember I'm without my keys. A trivial recollection – pitiably so at a time like this – but suddenly the knowledge overwhelms me. It's grown to be too much. I feel so tired. I can't stand the thought of having to disturb some neighbour. I can't stand the thought of having to engage in piffling conversation.

A wind has sprung up. Or possibly I'm only more aware of it, now that I'm on the bridge. So far as I can make out in the shadowy pools of lamplight I appear to have the entire structure to myself. When I'm halfway along it I stop and wonder. Was it here? Was it *here?*

I don't even know from which side Oliver jumped. But automatically *I've* turned towards Wandsworth. Why – because I'm right-handed? Well, Oliver was also right-handed. I assume he did the same.

The wind seems even stronger. I can hear it whistling round the struts. It tugs at the bottom of my raincoat – *come to look down here, my fair laddie! Come to look down here!* Only once had Oliver called me that.

I accept its invitation. The parapet seems low. The river is a black mass.

Perhaps, a year ago, there was moonlight. Perhaps, a year ago, you could make out the swirl of the current. I gaze down. I try to become dizzy. 'I don't like heights,' I tell myself, 'I do *not* like heights!' *Wuthering* heights! The spirit of the dead calling out to the spirit of the living! A reunion to coincide, joyously, with one's final breath, one's final heartbeat. Oh, Oliver. Oliver. If only I could believe that. . . If only I could honestly believe. . . I continue to gaze into the abyss.

Anyway, there's a complication.

I don't have any weights!

Nothing. No ugly brass Buddhas. Nothing. There might be a rock or two somewhere, caught up in the mud along the water's edge, but not here, not in the middle of the bridge. And for the moment. . .that walk all the way down to the shoreline. . .and then that walk all the way back. . .no, I'm sorry, I simply don't possess the energy.

Yet, on the other hand, I've never swum in jumper, trousers, raincoat, shoes. And I feel so drained, so utterly drained – shouldn't *that* make a difference? And I wouldn't try to fight it. . .at least, not so far as I can tell, I wouldn't. I've nothing to hang on for. I don't even know how I'm going to get back into my flat.

This way, of course, I wouldn't have to.

And they say that as you drown you relive things. In a good way. I remember reading about a woman who'd been saved at the last moment and hadn't even wanted it; resentful of an intrusion which had dragged her back from a womblike state of comfort.

Had it become comfortable – comforting – for Oliver?

And if it had. . .

Well, a minute of panic maybe, of fighting frantically for breath, but then. . . A minute isn't long. (Oh, yes, it *is*! Oh, yes, it can be!) Yet after that – an end to suffering. After that – tranquillity.

Release.

Oblivion.

And life will go on without me; life will go on. (Do I truly find *that* a source of reassurance? How *can* it just go on?) Tomorrow night, people will still queue outside the Classic, chatting, laughing, looking forward to the film. Quite as much as if none of this were happening now – as if I'd merely gone back to Gloucester Place as I had earlier supposed I should. The programme will continue to change every Sunday and Thursday. Nothing will be different. People will enjoy themselves.

Yet at some point Mrs Cambourne is almost bound to hear. Hear not only of my death but about the manner of it.

Then how will she react?

Will her forgiveness reach out a little further? Will she perhaps forgive me altogether? Will she understand I tried to repay a debt which – despite its being so far beyond repayment – at least I did my very best to honour?

I wonder what will happen to the photographs.

My thoughts are growing confused.

Did yours become confused – this time a year ago? Did any of your actions – even the smallest, least considered of them – did any of your actions parallel my own?

Did you, as well, cling to the parapet and feel the roughness of the stone beneath your palms? Did you, as well, turn up the collar of your overcoat, senselessly seeking protection from the harshness of the wind?

Oh, Oliver.

They say it's instinctive we should cling.

But surely we're not *obliged* to.

So then, my darling. . . Please look after me, just like you always did. Help me to do what I have to do.

Want to do.

But it isn't so easy in a coat, is it? Not even in a thin mackintosh, with nothing in its pockets. I can't imagine what it must have been like in your heavy old Crombie, with those two damned Buddhas further weighing you down, further obstructing you. . .!

And you were so alone. You were so horribly alone.

Oh, God! How desperately I wish you hadn't been!

(I realize that's nonsensical. Nonsensical. Delirious.)

Truthfully, it's higher than it looks, this parapet.

But you did it. I can do it, too.

Right. Now the other leg. Bring that one over.

Good. Well done. We're there.

Arms braced behind us.
All set.
No need to think about it.
The work of an instant.
Why hesitate?
Nothing to stay on for.
Now!

Part Three

37

But I couldn't do it.

I turned and swung my legs back onto solid ground; stumbling, feeling ashamed, feeling guilty.

Hating myself.

Yet it hadn't been my fault. Not altogether. Such an act would have needed the courage of a really deafening desperation. Twelve months ago I would have had that; but now the pain had grown supportable. More or less. I'd learned to live with it.

Or, anyhow, exist with it.

And, unlike Oliver, no one had betrayed *me*.

Now I had simply the quiet kind of desperation they said so many of us had.

I returned along the bridge feeling flat, feeling doubly treacherous (*I* had betrayed *me*) but also feeling, in some way, purged. A little remote from everything; on the outside of things; curiously calm.

I caught a bus part of the way back.

I was alive. It was a weird sensation. Tomorrow evening, if I wanted, I could go to join that queue outside the Classic.

Maybe I would. One thing I'd learned. It was time to turn my back on any thoughts of an afterlife, self-deluding, sentimental, cheap. There was only one life and I had to start living it again – now. It was time to turn my back on any thoughts of what might have been. Forget the past year. Forget the past eighteen months. Exorcise. Exorcise.

Perhaps the worst was over.

Perhaps it was. What I considered an excellent augury was the way I re-entered my flat. The main door was always locked after five-thirty but a woman to whom I had once or twice said good morning was now standing on the threshold, searching in her handbag, and she heard my shout as I came running down the street.

She then lent me a strong chisel which I was able – whilst standing on an upturned pail in the yard – to slide beneath my kitchen window. Also, she not only supplied me with a powerful torch but came and directed its beam. After which, the window was so easy to open that from the moment I'd arrived on the doorstep to the moment I had wished her a grateful goodnight, barely ten minutes had elapsed.

It was all so remarkably simple.

So simple that I determined the time had now come to take a long overdue precaution. I had no wish to be burgled. On the following day I must definitely visit an ironmonger's.

Except that, on the following day, something happened which thrust window bolts entirely from my head. I received a note from Mrs Cambourne.

With it were two enclosures. The first was a cheque for five thousand pounds.

'I'm not sure why – recently I've had you much in mind. I still feel it will be best if we never meet again. Put not your trust in princes, etc – especially when you know it's for the second time! But I want you to accept this money gracefully, and without argument. Don't even thank me. It's a small amount compared to what you might have had.

'But please don't think it arises from any pricking of my conscience. It's more a feeling that Oliver has been prompting me to send it. In any case, I *want* you to have it. Leave it at that.

'I'm also sending something else, which I think requires no explanation. I do not do this lightly but have been feeling more and more of late that I ought to let you see it. I don't ask to have it back. It's yours. I know that you will treasure it.'

And for a long time I did absolutely nothing but stand there in my hallway and gaze at this second enclosure.

It was a letter from Oliver.

*

In the handwriting which was so achingly familiar, and in the Royal Blue ink he'd favoured even then, it was dated December 29th 1939 – and was addressed from an RAF station in Suffolk.

'My darling Maman,

'Thank you for our leave. It was superb. I know that Edmund's also dropping you a line – odd fellow, for some reason he seemed quite to like you. But seriously, I was awfully glad the two of you hit it off.

'Yet this didn't stop me from being in a slight quandary at the time – a quandary, as it happened, that was only resolved in London on our way back to camp.

'You see, I'd been thinking over Christmas how I ought to make my will. Even at twenty, 'when the blast of war blows in our ears', a man should have the comfort of knowing that his affairs are all in order.

'As it stands, of course, everything would come to you. But I should also like to leave a largish sum to Edmund. I thought something of the order of twenty thousand pounds. Naturally I shall get this seen to as quickly as I can, but in the meantime – and for obvious reasons – I wanted you to know.

'I hope the strength of my feeling for him won't cause you any hurt. For otherwise I can in no way regret it –

indeed the contrary – I feel proud. Well, you saw the fine type of person he is, need I say more? I love him, love him second only to yourself. And were it possible to make another kind of bequest I should then want to leave him what I consider quite the best gift imaginable: a place alongside my own in the affections of a truly remarkable woman. For if anything *did* happen to me I'd like to feel the two of you still had each other. That would be my dearest wish.

'I want you to know I have never been happier in my life. The only thing I need to complete a happiness as nearly perfect as I feel conceivable in wartime would be some sign of *your* understanding of it.

'However, after all you've just read, you may be surprised to hear that Edmund isn't the only reason for this present euphoria!

'On our way back through London yesterday we had an hour between trains. We were wandering around in search of a pub when we came to a small church – surprisingly it wasn't locked – and Edmund suggested we go in for a short time. Well, as you know, this is probably the last thing which would have occurred to *me* but E seemed quite eager about it and therefore it was what I wanted too.

'The church was absolutely empty. We sat at the back and didn't talk and I can't think at all why it happened (I should have said I was the least likely candidate you could possibly imagine) or what I started off with in my mind, but I was suddenly aware of a great stillness, which had nothing to do with the outer stillness which existed in the church – and then I found myself at Calvary, wrapped about in that same stillness, sitting at the foot of the cross. And *he* was looking down at me. But it wasn't your usual white-skinned Jesus, fine-featured, frail – oh, no. This was a strong broad-shouldered Arab type with the sweat pouring down his face, and his beard all matted, and every line of his body expressing the agony he had been sentenced to endure. But his eyes were what held me. Those eyes that seemed to be gazing straight down into mine with a look which if I live to be ancient I shall never forget, and which I'm not even going to attempt to describe, beyond saying it was utterly all-seeing and utterly all-forgiving. 'Be still, and know that I am God.' (Mr Hanbury's favourite text – I'm afraid it never meant a whole lot to me in the past!) And I did know. Suddenly I did.

'I'm not sure how long it lasted. Only a minute, perhaps. Yet when it finished, one of the convictions which gradually settled on me – amongst so many others! – was of my need to be in every way straightforward. With everyone... but especially with yourself. Hence – the dramatic resolving of a dilemma.

'But why should it have happened to *me*? Why should *I* have been singled out for such a blessing? E says that probably more people have visions than you'd expect, yet feel chary about revealing them. Would that be *your* opinion? Already, from time to time, Satan sneaks in to make me wonder if it might not have been imagination – 'a brief moment of sleep in conducive surroundings,' he'll slyly whisper. But mostly it seems so real and is still so vivid I can laugh at him and say, 'Hop it! Scram! Vamoose!' And now I have a little mantra. *Beat the Devil*!

'Anyway – enough. All that remains is to say once more how much I love you and how greatly we enjoyed the leave you did so much to make an incredibly special one. I wish you the very happiest New Year Herr Hitler will allow. And give big hugs to Tommy and Rita – tell them we'll have more 'spooky hauntings' and treasure hunts etc, just as soon as I (and E?) come home again. Write soon. God bless.

'Oliver.'

*

Oh God, I thought. Oh God!
Oh, fuck you, Oliver Cambourne!

38

That same day I reached the decision to quit Selfridge's again. With money in the bank I could perhaps spend the summer trying my hand at some further writing – working title: 'On Leaving Drury Lane' – or, if that didn't succeed, at least looking round for a better paid and more demanding form of employment.

Frustratingly, though, my timing in one respect couldn't have been worse: I'd arranged to go down to Folkestone on the same Friday evening my notice expired and I remembered with foreboding my mother's views on leaving even the most menial of jobs before you'd been accepted for your next. Inherited of course from my father, they were virtually the same as Mr Sheldon's.

When my train pulled in she was standing at the ticket barrier. I was surprised: she hadn't met my train in ages. Clearly she had a hot line to Mr Chauncey.

She kissed me, almost perfunctorily.

'What a crowd! Did you get a seat?'

But she didn't even wait for my answer.

'I wanted to warn you. Clara's behaving very oddly. She keeps thinking we employ a maid – Violet, she calls her. I believe there used to be a maid called Violet when your father was a child. She gets so cross with me for doing all the work. 'Violet will do it!' she keeps saying. 'Violet will do it!' This morning she lectured me on not forfeiting the respect of the servants! She did the same thing yesterday – *and* the day before that – I think it all began on Tuesday.'

'What did you say to her? What *do* you say to her?'

'At first I said she was mistaken. People didn't often have maids any more. But she grew so annoyed with me – and, anyhow, it didn't seem to register – that I've taken to telling her it's the maid's day off. That's easier.'

'Have you seen Dr Hall about it?'

'Not yet. I don't suppose there's much that he can do.'

I hesitated. 'He may suggest a home.'

'Clara can't afford a home. And all the council ones have astronomic waiting lists. Besides, I don't think she'd be happy in a council home. No, I don't know what we're meant to do. It's driving me crazy.'

'We can't have the pair of you going crazy.'

In no way did she acknowledge I had tried to make a joke.

'I'm even reluctant to go to work these days, for fear of what she may do.'

'What she may do?'

'Set the house on fire. Something like that.'

'God! Then you really do see it as being *that* dangerous? Leaving her.'

'Oh, perhaps I'm exaggerating. But I'm so worried. Do you know what she was doing last night? She was counting up all the Christmas and birthday presents she had given you over the years – almost from the time that you were born; calculating how much it had cost her.'

'Poor old soul. . . It all seems rather sudden, doesn't it?'

'It may seem sudden to you. I can assure you that it doesn't seem sudden to me. Do you realize it's been over three months since you were here?'

'Yes, I know. I'm sorry.'

'It would have helped to have had you home occasionally.'

'But if only you'd given me some inkling. . .'

'Besides, nowadays you hardly ever write, or telephone.' By this time we had nearly reached the house. 'And sometimes I wonder if you even bother to read the letters which *I* write.'

'Of course I do,' I returned. Uncomfortably.

'Anyway, I was glad when you rang last Sunday.'

'To tell you the truth I've been feeling a bit depressed since Christmas.'

'And that's another thing I wanted to say. I think Elizabeth's behaving very strangely. Is she ever coming back to you?'

'No – she's not.'

I hadn't meant to deliver it so baldly. But, even so, it was a relief finally to have made the admission.

'I thought as much. No girl spends months away from her husband just because her mother's ill.'

She clearly thought it necessary to raise a warning finger.

'Don't mention it to Clara, though. We'll talk about it later.'

I'd been alarmed by what I'd heard but – as it turned out – my aunt seemed no different to usual. Not to begin with. She greeted me effusively; said how handsome I was looking and asked how many fresh hearts I had broken in the past few weeks. 'When the cat's away. . .,' she smiled. 'Yes, I know all about it, my dear! Mice were never to be trusted!'

We sat down to supper and she inquired, tongue-in-cheek, if I intended to swim the following day.

'Of course I do. As long as you'll swim with me.'

'April fooling,' my mother reminded us, 'finished at midday!' Her pretence at sternness mightn't have been entirely a pretence but at least she was more relaxed now. *Much* more relaxed.

Aunt Clara chuckled. 'The last time I went swimming I took in a mouthful of water – spluttered – and let out a mouthful of false teeth! You remember that, don't you, Norma?'

'Shall I ever forget?' To my infinite pleasure my mother laughed too. She turned to me and said, 'At the next low tide we all became beachcombers! Clara, myself, your father and you. Oh – and the Baedeckers from next door!'

'Yes,' I said, 'I think I remember.'

'Well, you'd have been about nine. And the rubbish we found! Old boots, bottles, tins. But no false teeth.'

'It wouldn't have mattered whose!' cried Aunt Clara. 'I was desperate!'

'Yes,' I exclaimed, 'you couldn't have been the first it had happened to – not by a long chalk! Old men who looked like Popeye and old women who –'

'No, stop it, you two! You're putting me off my soup.'

'Oh, really, Norma, you *are* fussy! They'd all have been well washed! Only wait, my girl, till one day it happens to you!'

It was one of those occasions which – if you'd been recounting it – would hardly have seemed funny at all, but which at the time had a sort of hysterical appeal to it.

'Whatever became of the Baedeckers?' asked Aunt Clara at last. She was having to wipe her eyes.

'They went to live in Devon and we lost touch.' My mother collected up the soup bowls. 'We'll starve for the rest of the weekend but tonight we have the fatted calf. Roast mutton.'

The kitchen adjoined the dining room. I called out: 'Can I help?'

'Oh, she won't let you,' said Aunt Clara. 'Norma isn't happy unless *she's* the one who's doing everything. Working all day long, then coming home to cook a meal like this!'

'But it's a celebration meal!' cried out my mother. 'Darling, do tell us about life in London. I'm just coming in. How's Selfridge's?'

'Selfridge's?' I hesitated. This time I had intended not to lie.

'*Violet* ought to be the one who's doing everything. The cooking and the serving *and* the washing up!'

'Oh, Clara, did I forget to mention it? This is her evening off.'

'Actually,' I said, 'there *is* something I've been wanting to tell you, about Selfridge's.'

'Something special?' My mother had now returned and was setting down the plates and the vegetable dishes.

'But wasn't it her evening off yesterday?'

'No. Today. That's not important, though. Let's hear what John has to tell us.'

'I've left Selfridge's,' I said.

'You've what!' exclaimed my mother.

'Servants so easily get out of hand. Even the very best of them!'

'Be quiet, Clara! Oh, for heaven's sake, be quiet! John, did you say you'd left?'

Two minutes later both the women were in tears and had hurried, separately, out of the room. I alone remained at table, not eating, watching the joint grow cold on the carving dish and the gravy form a skin in the sauceboat.

*

Next morning I sat at the old desk in my bedroom with both elbows resting on the deeply scored lid and my face propped heavily between my hands. My window overlooked a small park where I could see a foursome playing tennis. The house was very quiet. I'd gone downstairs late, after my mother had left for work, and had made a cup of instant coffee to take back to my room. (I'd found a burnt pie dish soaking in the sink; what had been in it had been scraped into the bin.) My aunt, I imagined, was still in bed. Normally we'd have been sitting together in a café at about this time, or strolling along the Leas, and I remembered I had been looking forward to this first day of my renewed freedom. Ironic.

And it was part of the same irony that ever since the arrival of Mrs Cambourne's letter – and despite my initial reaction to much that had been in Oliver's – I'd been feeling what was for me these days a rare sense of wellbeing; and that something else I'd been looking forward to was making myself a far better companion than I knew I had been for well over a year. My mother and aunt had always seemed so touchingly pleased to see me and I'd invariably come away feeling I'd shortchanged them. (Elizabeth, though, had usually been particularly cheerful while at Folkestone.) Now, this weekend, meaning to move forward on my endless trip of penance, all I'd accomplished was to reduce them both to tears. Life was certainly a comedy.

But to hold such a point of view was unhelpful and I had recently made a vow – something no doubt engendered by that atypical period of wellbeing: vowed that henceforth I would tell only the truth, honour my commitments, become in every way as decent a person as I could. In short I had experienced a renewal of that sense of purpose which had visited me by Oliver's graveside, instantly withered, but flowered again more productively in July. No further lies, laziness, negativity. So far as possible I knew I had to grow to be worthy of him.

Yet now. . .*this!* From my window I saw my aunt picking her way unsurely along the road which bordered the park; I hadn't even registered the closing of the front door. It was unheard of for Aunt Clara to go walking on her own when she knew that I was home. But today she must have been deliberately avoiding me; had probably, come to think of it, made her way out through the kitchen. What a bloody mess it all was. If only I could have waved a wand. . . I felt so completely worthless. . .

So completely helpless.

*

But then, suddenly, the thought arrived.

*

Arrived, yes, without any warning.

No sort of preamble.

No preparation.

And in its entirety. There didn't even need to be any pause before I could start to express it.

'Okay,' I said; I said it aloud. 'Okay! A challenge! I want proof. If you really are there, if you really do exist – you, with your utterly all-seeing gaze and your utterly all-forgiving heart – then cure my aunt! Go on, do it! Take away her illusions about the maid. Don't let her grow senile. Make her happy. Make my mother happy. And give me a sign – *please,* by the time I leave here, give me a sign! And if you do this – if you do this – then I'll believe. A sacred pact. I promise! I'm aware it's arrogant to hope to strike a bargain with you, but in this instance I can't think of any other way. I can't. Your sign for my belief.'

I remembered, rather shiftily, that I had said something pretty similar before – on that fateful day of the telegram – but then, when I had thought my aunt to be out of danger, had conveniently forgotten.

Yet this time I swore that I honestly would keep to my side of the bargain. I continued watching her until she'd rounded a bend in the road, out of sight behind the tennis courts. Then I repeated – still utterly saddened, utterly incapable, unmistakably aggressive – 'All right, *heal* her. Show that you can! Heal her, heal her. . .and I'll believe!'

*

I was given my answer the following afternoon. The whole Sunday I'd been tense, even nervous, feeling an undercurrent of excitement. After lunch, which had passed uneventfully but under the same strained atmosphere that had permeated the entire weekend – and was strongly reminiscent of the winter of the previous year – Aunt Clara went off to rest, as was her habit. When the washing up was finished my mother sat down with a pile of my mending and said, 'Now tell me about Elizabeth.' She bit off a length of cotton. 'Sweet heaven, what a weekend it's been. Elizabeth – your job – Clara. I really don't feel I could take one more thing.'

'Shall I come down again on Saturday? We'll all go out to dinner and the theatre – my treat. We'll forget about this. What are they doing here next week?'

Upstairs in my suitcase there were two presents which I'd bought in London on Friday, but the right moment for giving them hadn't arisen. Definitely hadn't arisen. I now thought I would save them until the following weekend, turn it into a bit of an event.

But my mother, tying a knot in her thread, totally ignored both my suggestion and its allied inquiry. 'What happened with Elizabeth?' she asked.

'Things went wrong between us. That's all.'

'Yet she seemed such a nice girl. And so very much in love with you.'

'Please, Mum. I'd rather not talk about it.'

'But is there no chance of your making up?'

'None at all. There's someone else she's going to marry. She's started divorce proceedings.'

'Someone else? Already? Oh, I see. So that's why she left you. Well, I must say, John, I'm surprised. She didn't strike me as that type, not in the least. But I imagine she's been spoilt. . .all that money in the family! And these days people seem to take their marriage vows so lightly –'

'Oh, for Christ's sake! It wasn't like that at all. You know nothing about it. She wasn't a bit spoilt. You go on and on and on, and it's just plain stupid. Stop it!'

After this outburst we sat in silence. At last I said: 'I'm sorry. I shouldn't have spoken that way. But it simply wasn't like that.'

'What *was* it like?'

'Do we really have to go into it?'

'I suppose not.' Her voice was expressionless. 'But I'd like you to tell me just *one* thing. Was it because of another man?'

'No. I think she only met this fellow well after she'd left me.'

A few seconds elapsed. 'That wasn't what I meant.'

'What, then?'

'Did *you* have another man?'

'No, I did not! Oh, for fuck's sake! What do you take me for?'

'I don't know. I really don't know. You tell me.'

'Bloody hell! This *is* a fine weekend. I haven't enjoyed such a fine weekend in years!'

I saw the tears well up in her eyes. I remembered my resolutions. After a moment I went and stood beside her. I laid my hand on her shoulder.

'Come on, love. It really isn't as bad as all that.'

'Go away,' she said. 'Leave me alone.'

She had begun to cry in earnest. She reminded me of Marnie Stark. Good God, I thought – Aunt Clara was right – everywhere I went I left a trail of broken hearts. Practically everyone I touched lived to regret it, was damaged by the contact. I felt like a murderer.

Which, to some degree, I was. A murderer. This wasn't the first time I'd confronted it.

I stood looking down at my mother.

'Shall I make some tea?'

There was no indication she had heard, but I went to put the kettle on. While it heated I stood at the kitchen window and listlessly observed the garden. The contrast between the brightness in the garden and the gloom in the house was pitiable. Once, I'd have been out there building up a light tan; now a light tan could scarcely have mattered less. Dimly I heard some movements overhead, the sound of running water. Then the kettle began to boil and I made the tea. Had I been standing on the bridge right now I thought I'd have experienced little hesitation.

This was patently untrue. But all the same I felt it.

I went back into the living room. My mother had stopped crying and was staring into the fireplace, a handkerchief crumpled in her hand. I set her tea on the floor beside her chair.

'There you are, lady! Nice and hot. Do you good, that will!'

She said nothing.

I reverted to my normal voice. 'Like some sugar in it? Just this once?'

No response. Not a flicker.

'Why don't you take it upstairs, lie down for a bit?'

I wasn't sure what to do. I sat down again. It would have seemed heartless merely to leave her.

'Go away!' she said. Slowly and emphatically. 'Go away!'

'Is there nothing I can do?'

'Yes,' she answered. 'For all I care, you can leave this house immediately and never come back to it.'

I trod wearily upstairs. On reaching the landing I heard the quiet but unmistakable sounds of sobbing. Could all of this be happening? It was surreal; I had the feeling I was caught up in some awful dream. I would open my bedroom door and the room would be filled with all the people I had ever met – or perhaps had yet to meet – weeping before me in helpless accusation.

But this sound was coming from the bathroom and it was not the weeping of all the people I had ever met. It was the weeping of my aunt. Yet the nightmare quality persisted. It intensified. Feeling hugely apprehensive I knocked on the door.

'Who is it?'

It was a startled – almost a frightened – whimper.

'It's me. Are you all right in there? May I come in?'

'Oh, John. I don't know what to do. Is Violet in the house?'

'No, I'm afraid she isn't. Is something wrong? Maybe *I* can help?'

After a moment there came a shuffling. I heard the key turn. My aunt was in her dressing gown. Her face was pale and tear-stained. Her hair was straggling in a way I'd never seen it; I realized for the first time how sparse it had become. She clutched me by the wrist and I saw that the sleeves of her dressing gown were wet.

'Oh, John, I'm so glad it's you. I've had an accident.'

'What sort of accident?'

'It could happen to anyone.'

I walked past her and saw the bath half-filled and a candlewick bedspread partially submerged. She had clearly been using the hand soap to wash both the coverlet and some of her underthings.

'I don't want your mother to know,' she said, coming up beside me and again taking hold of my wrist. 'You won't tell her, will you? I am not, I am *not*, going to get incontinent!'

She released me in order to seize the back brush out of the scummy water and give a couple of darting prods at the heavy pink bedspread.

'And if you can only help me wring it out and hang it on the line,' she entreated, 'it will soon dry in all this sunshine. I know it will.'

Wordlessly I looked at her. She seemed so frail, so very insubstantial. I took her in my arms. The tears ran down my face.

'Please help us,' I thought. 'We can't cope. We're useless. We truly can't manage any longer. Oh, God – please help.'

39

I decided to spend the week in Folkestone. On the Tuesday morning I rang *The Copper Kettle* to inform Mrs Watson my mother was unwell. Mrs Watson was extremely sympathetic. 'Well, now,' I thought, as I came away from the telephone, 'who'd ever have believed it?' Not a profound reflection but a salutary one.

Mum stayed in bed for the first part of the week, coming downstairs only for a short time in the evenings, to have her supper and a game of cards. Aunt Clara and I shared the shopping, the housework and the cooking. . . .and, in a quiet way, we enjoyed ourselves. My mother mainly read, or listened to the radio, or slept. The rest transparently did her good. No one could have said she was the essence of jollity for the remainder of the week, but at least she seemed content to be pottering round the town with the two of us: having coffee and a pastry, browsing through antique shops, strolling down to the beach. On the Thursday we went to the pictures. On the Friday we went into Canterbury.

It was while we were sitting over lunch in Canterbury that Aunt Clara – supposed to be studying the menu for a dessert – nervously cleared her throat.

'Norma, dear, I've been thinking about something. I believe I may shortly go to live at *The Elms*. . .that is, if it's all right with you, naturally? You know I have a friend there, a Mrs Maxton? She says they sometimes get a vacancy and that it's really very nice. Besides – living there – I could hardly be closer to home, could I?'

'But Clara. These things cost money.'

'Yes, I know, dear, but I do have a small amount put by. . .even if at times I have been living just a fraction beyond my means. In my day, you see, we were always encouraged to save. So I'm positive I can manage – especially if I share a room. Mrs Maxton has mentioned, indeed, that she'd be more than happy to share with me.'

'But that won't be necessary,' I intervened. 'I've a bit of money. I can help you. Five thousand pounds,' I added, quietly.

And as I spoke I was thinking: This must be right. Please make it right.

'Five thousand pounds?' repeated my mother, staring at me.

'A legacy,' I said. 'From Oliver Cambourne. The painter. The fellow I told you about. He died last year.'

My mother touched my hand. The gesture was so quick it might have been an accident. Almost, she might just have been brushing away a crumb.

'He must have been very kind,' she said. 'He must have been a good man.'

'Like you, John,' said Aunt Clara. 'Like you!' It was doubtful, though, how much of that last brief exchange she had actually understood – her mind was too full of *The Elms* and of Mrs Maxton. 'But did you say you'd be able to lend me money? I could never allow you to do that, you know.'

Yet I was confident something could easily be arranged. With either the matron or the management. My aunt need never know.

Nor my mother, come to that.

The following day, as I'd suggested, I took them to the local rep. The play was 'Private Lives', which we'd all seen before, but that didn't mean we didn't enjoy it. Far from it. From time to time I would glance at their faces in the dark and there was never a time when they were not smiling.

We had our meal at a Chinese restaurant and it was after midnight when we arrived home. But I gave them their presents then: a pair of Dresden figures for my mother; a Copeland cup and saucer for my aunt. And the next morning, while my mother stayed behind to prepare the dinner, Aunt Clara and I went off to church.

'It's such a pity Norma couldn't come,' she said to me, following the service. 'I believe she'd have enjoyed it.'

I waited for the inevitable reference to Violet.

'Of course, it was always so much easier in my time, when every household had its own parlourmaid and cook. But these days – well, I ask you! – who can afford *that* type of luxury? Oh, the Grosvenors, maybe, the Duke and Duchess of Westminster

– do you think we should drop them a line to find out? – but remarkably few of the rest of us.'

We both shook hands with the vicar. Yet even this didn't long distract her.

'And talking of luxury, my dear, let's go and have some coffee! Do you think you could manage a doughnut – without mentioning it to your mother? Or letting it spoil your lunch?'

*

In the train that evening I reread Oliver's letter. . .despite now knowing it practically by heart.

The previous night I'd had another vivid dream about him, the first since that sun-splashed idyll with the harsh awakening. Yet this time its effect wasn't depressing; the more oddly, since it involved the night of his suicide – in it I actually saw him jump. But the bridge he jumped from was no longer across the Thames. It was the little bridge at Biarritz leading from the beach to the big rock on which the Virgin Mary stood. And in my dream the statue had come to life and had leant over, lovingly, to scoop him out of the water.

There had been a time when he believed.

Couldn't a remnant of that belief somehow have survived? A dim, far-off memory of a hypnotic pair of eyes that was utterly all-seeing, utterly all-forgiving. . .?

And if it hadn't survived (though I remembered the bitterness he'd shown, when stating the Lord had hardened the heart of the Home Secretary, in the case of Derek Bentley) – well, if it hadn't survived. . .did that matter?

I put the letter away. I had kept it on me, in one pocket or another, ever since receiving it.

'Oh, Lord, I believe. And if it *does* matter – then can't I believe enough for the two of us?'

At first I must have frowned with the sheer effort of concentration.

'Make it all right for Oliver!'

There was another point, though.

Suicide…

Regarded as the one cardinal sin. The one human act bound to sever its perpetrator from God. Eternal and inescapable separation.

But I couldn't – wouldn't – believe in a God who hadn't infinite understanding; infinite mercy; who wasn't prepared to make untold allowances for…for the balance of the mind being temporarily disturbed. I didn't mean to set conditions. It was simply that all else would have made nonsense.

Heaven, in fact, wasn't a place I should want anything to do with, if that kind of ordinance prevailed.

And yet in my heart I knew it couldn't. (Oh, yes, *talk* about arrogant!) In any case, the real sin had been mine, not his. So if anybody had to pay…

'Make it all right for Oliver.'

Even if you find – the question came to me abruptly, and was majorly disconcerting, but at least the thought had finally been acknowledged – *even if you find that you'd have to share him with Edmund?*

Yes! Even if I find that I'd have to share him with Edmund.

Or even if Edmund should have him entirely to himself?

Yes! Yes! Just so long as Oliver is there…

Then suddenly I smiled; caught sight of my reflection in the window but immediately turned away from it.

'You've always known that one day I'd be asking you. *Imploring* you… And I shall go on imploring you; I shall drive you mad with my persistence. You'll say in the end, 'Oh, no – that Wilmot! I never knew how quiet it was until *he* decided to start on me…'

'Make it all right for Oliver!'

*

I *had* written to Mrs Cambourne, naturally. But a few days after I returned from Folkestone I resolved to pay her another visit. And this time, following a hunch, I again threw some basics into my pigskin suitcase.

On the way into Surrey, halting at a traffic light, I happened to glance at my watch.

Well, how many times in the course of a day does the average person glance at his watch? Possibly a dozen? But now, for some reason, that glance took me right back to my nineteenth birthday. Oddly, not to the moment when the watch had been given, but to one much later, well after midnight. We had been to see *West Side Story*. Oliver had booked for it as soon as we had returned from France but hadn't told me until that morning. It was only the fourth night of its London run and I grew wild with astonishment and delight, three times hurrying back to hug him, when rightfully – frightened that I'd be late in meeting my mother and aunt at Charing Cross – I should have been back at Gloucester Place by then. . .back with the wine and the salmon and the list of things I meant to pick up from my local grocer. Anyhow, at the theatre, there was a five-minute standing ovation and at least ten curtain calls. As we slowly emerged into the Haymarket, amid a glowingly intoxicated crowd, Oliver touched my elbow with a look of grave concern. 'Respectful adaptation, would you say?'

'Oh, yes, very! Shakespeare is well satisfied.'

'Songs grew spontaneously out of the action?'

'Absolutely! *Absolutely!* Although I could have done with a lyric saying it's mean of you to mock.'

He laughed. 'Yes, I bet you could! But I'm awfully glad that you can take it.'

We went to Stone's (me with my carrier bag!), where we had a light but excellent meal; and finally got home shortly after one. The customary nightcap – or two – and then to bed, roughly an hour later.

'Thank you again and again for this,' I said, admiringly holding up my wrist as we undressed.

'Oh, don't mention it. You've already done so a good deal more than enough.'

'And for the message and the pun. Actually I rather *like* that pun. It's so awful it's cute. It's endearing. For all time,' I teased him. 'For *all* time.'

But he refused to be shamed.

'Yes, for all time,' he answered evenly. 'For all time and beyond.'

'*And* beyond? Then vot can vun do with a man like that? Such a sweet *shepsel*! So vithout shame!'

'Well, I don't know what the Chief Rabbi might advise,' he replied, taking a purposeful step towards me, 'but at least – in the meanwhile – let *me* come up with a suggestion.'

For all time. . .and beyond. Suddenly, whilst I sat waiting at those traffic lights, it seemed – incontestably – a message of corroboration.

And that message remained at the forefront of my mind – probably always would (well, if not right at the forefront, certainly somewhere near it) – when an hour or so later I turned into the drive of Merriot Park: a returning prince who, with God's help, would this time show himself much worthier of trust.

I drew up outside the front door, stood in the sunshine, and gazed about me. Unhurriedly.

It felt like coming home.